WARNING SIGNS

Marc Dean's first hint of what awaited him on his Corsican caper was a smash on the jaw that nearly removed his head.

The next bad vibes came when the ex-wife he was trying to woo back walked out on him—and left him with a female daredevil as dangerously explosive as she was sensually exciting.

His final warning was when he discovered that the police, the army, the government, and the press had all been stacked against him by a man called Nessim, the supreme satanic ruler of an empire of death girdling the globe.

Dean knew what he was getting into. But he didn't know how he'd get out alive. . . .

SCHOOL FOR
SLAUGHTER

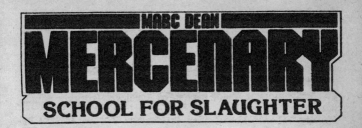

MARC DEAN
MERCENARY
SCHOOL FOR SLAUGHTER

#5

PETER BUCK

A SIGNET BOOK
NEW AMERICAN LIBRARY
TIMES MIRROR
PUBLISHED BY
THE NEW AMERICAN LIBRARY
OF CANADA LIMITED

PUBLISHER'S NOTE

This novel is a work of fiction. Names, characters, places, and incidents are either the product of the author's imagination or are used fictitiously, and any resemblance to actual persons, living or dead, events, or locales is entirely coincidental.

NAL BOOKS ARE AVAILABLE AT QUANTITY DISCOUNTS WHEN USED TO PROMOTE PRODUCTS OR SERVICES. FOR INFORMATION PLEASE WRITE TO PREMIUM MARKETING DIVISION, THE NEW AMERICAN LIBRARY, INC., 1633 BROADWAY, NEW YORK, NEW YORK 10019.

The first chapter of this book appeared in *Operation Icicle*, the fourth volume of this series.

First Printing, April, 1982

    2   3   4   5   6   7   8   9

 SIGNET TRADEMARK REG. U.S. PAT. OFF. AND FOREIGN COUNTRIES
REGISTERED TRADEMARK - MARCA REGISTRADA
HECHO EN WINNIPEG, CANADA

SIGNET, SIGNET CLASSICS, MENTOR, PLUME, MERIDIAN and NAL BOOKS are published in Canada by The New American Library of Canada, Limited, Scarborough, Ontario

PRINTED IN CANADA
COVER PRINTED IN U.S.A.

Terrorists, urban guerrillas, anarchists, freedom brigades—what are they but mercenaries paid in the false currency of ideals?

—Meyrick Johnston, *Behind Closed Doors*

In one sense, a mercenary is nothing more than a terrorist deriving his satisfaction from money rather than ideas.

—Kent Delaney, *Fire in the Blood*

CLASSIFICATION: CONFIDENTIAL
SIGMA SIX

NAME: DEAN, Marcus Matthew.

DATE OF BIRTH: 06/06/44, Johnstown NY,
USA.

CATEGORY AND NATIONALITY: White Anglo-
Saxon Protestant. American.

PARENTS: Elmer Roland, MD, former
aviator. Decd. Mary Elizabeth
(née Ballantyne), social worker.
Decd.

FAMILY: Older brother (George Alick) (m)
and sister (Hester Ellen) (m).

EDUCATION: Graduate of Wilmington,
Delaware, high-school; Bachelor's
Degree (Yale) languages; Master's
Degree (USC) political science.

PERSONAL HISTORY: Divorced. Former wife
Samantha (née Hurok) daughter of
USAF Colonel.
Grounds for divorce: Incompati-
bility; Mental Cruelty.
Children of marriage: 1 son,
Patrick, b.1975.

No prison record. No smuggling or
drug offenses. Womanizer. Moderate
drinker.

OFFICIAL HISTORY: ROTC (Yale) 1963-66;
Lt. (infantry) Vietnam 1966-68;
secretariat member, Senatorial

Committee on International Relations 1969; Peace Corps executive in Biafra, Uganda, Central African Republic 1970-71; AID pacification specialist, Vietnam 1972-73; program evaluator for Eastern Electronics (Orleans, Mass.) 1974; subsequently arms salesman for FN, Omnipol, Vickers, etc. Territory: Africa, Middle East. Became mercenary adviser, leader 1979.

MERCENARY ACTION: (While working as arms salesman) trained volunteers to fight against Soviet and Cuban rebels, ANGOLA (1975); with French mercenaries fighting for Emperor Bokassa, CENTRAL AFRICAN REPUBLIC (1976-77); hired by President Mobutu to defeat Katanga secessionists, ZAIRE (1978).

(As fulltime combat leader) aided Israeli govt. in raid on Palestinian camp, SYRIA; advised Christians in LEBANON; trained and led commando-style raids WEST AFRICA, HAITI and (with secret CIA approval) BRAZIL.

KNOWN ADDRESSES: Apt. 6c, 132 Rue Cavalotti, Paris 18, France. 117 bis, Avenue Yannick Bruynoghe, Brussels 2, Belgium.

MISCELLANEOUS: General surveillance at request of member states. Report unusual activity (SEE ALSO: INTER/INT/6092/USA).

Gorilla

Of all the signs in the twelve-year Asiatic lunar cycle, that of the Monkey produces people with the most extraordinary nature. Those born in the Year of the Monkey (1944, 1956, 1968, 1980, 1992 *et seq.*) can overcome any difficulties, succeed in anything—provided they are permitted to follow their chosen vocation. Monkeys born under the zodiacal sun sign of Gemini are especially adept at extricating themselves from "irretrievable" situations.

—Ancient Chinese Horoscope Manual.

1

Jason Mettner

It was one of the toughest fistfights I've ever seen, and on the crime desk you get to see some. It was also one of the shortest. It took place in the lobby of a two-bit hotel in a hick town west of Sudbury, just over the Canadian border on the shores of Lake Huron. One of the guys was a tall, rangy character with blue eyes and sandy hair—rugged enough but lean with it. The other was a gorilla from the backwoods, around eight feet tall and almost as wide, weighing not a lot more than a Greyhound bus, with about the same expression. I couldn't see the color of his eyes: they were hidden behind the hair on his chest. The battle was on account of a broad, of course.

She was a honey-blond. Sage-green corduroy pantsuit, tan Cuban-heel boots, black-and-tan foulard by Dior or whoever. Her hair was gathered at the neck with a wide black bow and she had one of those mouths that said "Yes," and "Please," and "Don't you dare!" all at the same time.

Did somebody ask did this dame have class? You could say that.

She and the lean character, they were the kind of folks would never have been there only some smart-ass promoter was staging a retro routine to beat them all—a 1920's-style barnstormer air circus, complete with period planes, would you believe it!

I wouldn't have been there myself if it hadn't been unusually quiet on the crime front that week. The mug-and-rape figures weren't even into three figures. Not that *Worldwide* would normally waste a half-inch squib among the body-

3

building ads on page 87 or an antique air meet in Canada, but in this case there were extenuating circumstances. Number one, it tied in with a series of have-we-*really*-progressed articles we were running because one of the big computer houses had canceled their advertizing. Number two, the guys masterminding this show happened to be Brits and the proprietor—maybe because the President was on an anti-European kick right then—the proprietor was plugging the Old Country kith-and-kin line for all the publication was worth. And as far as news magazines go, it was worth about the same as *Time* or *Newsweek.* So there was the Windy City's ace crime-feature man all set to turn in a color piece for the leisure supplement, byline Jason Mettner II, Our Special Correspondent in Joinville Falls, Ontario.

There was plenty of color, all right, and all of it was gray. It had been raining for a week, and the lake was gray, the sky was gray, the macadam of the wet parking lot shone gray where automobiles and their owners had stayed away in thousands. The locals should have made the effort at that: they'd have been able to hear the selection of tasteful evergreens played by the Joinville Falls Brass Ensemble not twice, as usual, but three times—one coming out of the horns, a second time through the PA speakers around the field, and a third time echoing off the rows of empty seats in the grandstand.

Oh, sure, there was a grandstand. Right in front of the clapboard clubhouse, beneath the control tower where red neon letters spelled out the legend "Joinville Flying Club," or most of it. It had been run up out of steel scaffolding tubes and raw planking, and it didn't look strong enough to hold up any more than the hundred stalwarts huddled on it against the drizzle drifting in from the lake. Maybe the Ontarians were right not to share my editor's enthusiasm for the mechanical marvels of yesterday. I wouldn't know. But certainly the backward look was pulling them in okay in the U.S. You couldn't write "Go Home Reagan" on a wall without you defaced a poster inviting you to a vintage-automobile rally, a Victorian toy fair, a sale of clothes from the rock-'n'-roll era, or a jamboree with Victrola music by Glenn Miller on 78-rpm disks. Some of them even had pictures of Elvis Presley. Seeing it the way Granddad saw it was getting to be quite a popular entertainment. Except, it seemed, in Joinville Falls, Ontario.

But about that fight. It happened after the first performance in the three-day season. They'd done the wing-walking, the sky-writing, the delayed parachute drop, and the simulated dogfight, and now the aviators, the production team, and some of the hangers-on were sinking their sundowners in the lobby of this Hall's Hotel, which was the nearest thing in town to a regular bar. I was chatting up one of the jumpers, asking didn't he feel safer outside one of these disinterred museum pieces than in it—even at five thousand feet—when I heard voices raised on the far side of the room. "Raised" is an understatement: the lumberjack was yelling his fucking head off.

I couldn't make too much of the intellectual content of his argument, but what it boiled down to was that the lean guy should piss off . . . or else. From a careful study of the faces of those concerned, I formed the opinion that the storyboard stacked up as follows. The blond girl was with the lean guy. While he was trying to blackmail the bartender into giving them a drink, the gorilla sees the chick, thinks he could do with a piece of tail just that shape and size, and tries to horn in. The lean guy returns and remonstrates, only to be invited to vacate the premises. Now read on.

"Are you goin' to fuck off outta here, punk, or do I have to smear your son-of-a-bitch face all over that wall?" the big one inquires.

"I don't think you'll do that," says the lean man, kind of quiet.

"Oh, no?" snarls the apes' Don Juan. "We'll see about that!" And he hauls off and pastes him one smack in the center of the chest. The guy must weigh all of 240 pounds and he puts everything he's got into the punch. The lean guy sails clear over the back of a chair, slams full-tilt into the wall, and slides to the floor. But wait! Maybe he rides the blow. I don't know. All I know is that he's up like a rubber ball, over the chair, and cracking one against ape-man's jaw that sounds like one of those old newsreel soundtracks of the Babe hitting a home run. Ape-man staggers back, shakes his head, and then comes in to deliver a second haymaker exactly like the first.

At least, that's what he meant to do. But someplace in between the launching pad and the target, the latter goes out of orbit and the hairy missile sails into space. Now your man steps up to bat. He swings one in, very short, very straight, right to the solar plexus. I guess there's about 120 pounds behind it, but, brother, it goes in right up to the elbow! *Zap!*

AM looks surprised, almost hurt; he ain't used to this kind of routine. So he brings one looping up from the floor . . . and he moves fast too, very fast for a man his size. It's slightly off-center, but the lean guy isn't quite quick enough and it catches him on the shoulder, spinning him around. The gorilla grins and moves in for the kill. Then—I don't quite know how it happened; I still can't figure it out—somehow the lean guy completes the turn and with it he throws a *colossal* punch that homes on the jaw just where it meets the ear. The gorilla's head comes down as he folds forward. The lean guy's knee comes up and connects with it. The edge of his hand chops down hard as a plank of teak on the back of the ape-man's neck. There's a noise like the aftermath of the San Francisco earthquake, and the man mountain's facedown on the floor, with no further interest in the proceedings.

But you know what that girl said? She looked up, kind of cool, and she said, "Matt, why *do* you have to keep on fighting?"

Women!

Even so, I wouldn't really have paid the incident any mind if it hadn't been for one thing. A half-hour before it happened, I'd seen a fistful of bills change hands, and I'd heard a guy who looked like a mafioso out of Central Casting tell our gorilla, "Pick a fight over the broad or something—but make sure you do it good. And make sure you lay him out good and cold, too."

One thing a crime reporter learns over the years is that real hoods always *look* like hoods (how else would those *Washington Post* guys have gotten onto Nixon so quick?). So here, right in this backwoodsman's paradise, some underworld characters wished to have the boot put in so that the lean guy would be out of commission for a while. Why? Not on account of the chick, for sure. She was Vassar material if ever I saw any, and the torpedo category don't go so strong on female brain. It makes them nervous. A kidnap routine, then? I didn't think so. I ran a check with the office back in Chicago. She was a divorcée, name of Samantha Hurok, daughter of a retired Air Force colonel, deceased, comfortable but not rolling. The gallant aviator had been on the board of Eastern Electronics, but he hadn't left all that much loot behind him when he took off for the last time.

6

So the lady was out. Why else would anyone want her squire out of the way? Some kind of contraband operation across the lakes? It didn't seem likely: there were easier ways. I slipped a fin to the night clerk and checked out the man himself. Marcus Matthew Dean. Nationality: American. Residence: Paris, France. Profession: Military adviser.

There were French guys among the Brits running the air circus. There was an indirect aviation connection through the girl's father. But, shit, would a half-assed operation like this bring an *adviser* with them all the way from Europe? Uh-uh. Not at current rates. In any case, I don't think the guy even knew the circus people: I never saw him talking to any of them. Allowing that they *had* brought him, the sixty-four-dollar question remained: why should members of the bent fraternity be embarrassed because an expatriate American, WASP all the way, happened to show up in Joinville Falls, Ontario? Why should they want him out of the way?

It was a good question. I couldn't answer it. So I decided to tag along awhile and see what broke. A news sense is something you learn, not a gift you're born with, and after all these years in the business, mine told me there was a story here someplace if only I could nose it out.

So there I was the following morning, playing private eye in among the grandstand clients. There was a much bigger crowd because the rain had stopped. The attendance figures were up to 103. The first item on the program was this 1920's-style air race around a ten-mile circuit marked by pylons on the airfield and on two islands out on the lake. There were a couple of single-seat racers from that era in the circus' stable—spiky supercharged crates with 375-cubic-inch motors that looked like outsize mosquitoes—and the organizers challenged any private fliers with pre-World War II machines to compete against these in a series of fifty-mile dashes rewarded with a five-thousand-dollar purse donated by local advertisers.

I guess there's a certain spectator thrill, watching four or five ships carve each other up making vertical banks around steel posts when they're flying at 150 mph about eight feet off the ground. If there is, the blond girl sure shared it. She and this guy Dean were sitting next to me . . . about a hundred feet away along the planking seat. And she couldn't take her eyes off the vintage machinery. But Dean seemed more interested in an ancient Ford Tri-motor parked on the apron below the control tower. Pretty soon I could see why.

The final race was still on, and the next act was billed as an exhibition of wing-walking by someone with the name of Laurence Chateauroux. A French Canadian, I thought, idly looking the way Dean was orienting himself. I went right on looking. They had begun wheeling the Tri-motor toward the runway, and the performer was walking beside it. Not only was Laurence a girl—she was a Creole and she was stacked. Was she stacked? I'll say she was! She was about the sexiest thing I'd seen since the third grade. She was tall and big-breasted, and she walked like a cat. She had dark hair and dark eyes and a shine on her lower lip you could have seen from over the horizon. I thought, if it's color you're after, Mettner, why look any farther? The next thing I thought was that I didn't want to see that chick doing gymnastics on an airplane wing five hundred feet up in the air; I wanted to see her without any clothes on, doing quite another kind of gymnastics about five inches below me. And I didn't want any crowd around, either, even a crowd as small as the one at Joinville Falls.

The announcer was doing his nut over the intercoms. *"Just take a look at that!"* he said breathlessly. *"Mueller took him on the inside at the home pylon! Now the Grumann has the speed, but can the local boy make up the lost ground before they reach the first island? No. . . . But wait, folks! Wait a minute there! . . . Mueller's trying to outpace Harbison: he gained a hundred yards on the leader around that lake pylon; he's turning closer on the pylons, folks, because he knows he don't have a chance on the straightaways. . . . There's two more laps to go. Can he make it? Oh-oh: watch now—he's gonna try and take Harbison on the home pylon, unless he pulls the wings off of the ship. There! . . . There! Did you see that, folks? Oh, man—just watch the av-i-a-tor fly!"*

The folks didn't see. They weren't watching. They were staring like me and Dean at Laurence Chateauroux as she walked beside her mobile gymnasium. She was wearing a tan leather windbreaker, a skating skirt, and short white boots. In between the skirt and the boots there was room for a lot of leg. The legs were sensational.

It was odd, just the same, Dean showing such an interest in the girl. I mean, with a blond like that right beside him. And it didn't look as though he knew her or anything: the way I read him, his expression was more curiosity than lechery.

Very strange. After the wing-walking act—and that was

pretty sensational too, when you think of the risks—Dean said something to the blond and hightailed it for the clubhouse bar. She shrugged and settled down to take in the simulated World War I dogfight.

I followed Dean, ordered a Bloody Mary, and interviewed what seemed to be a glass of paregoric, wood alcohol, and reputed tomato juice in private behind a potted palm. Dean took a soda and poured his own liquor from a hip flask. I said there was intelligence in back of that rugged face.

He was sitting beside a low table in one of those clubhouse chairs—chromed frame, imitation black leather, and a sigh of resignation when you lower your weight onto the seat. There was a copy of the *International Herald Tribune,* folded back to an inside page, spread out on his knee. From where I stood, I could see that one of the classified ads had been neatly framed in red marker.

So there was another question. Why in the world would an American domiciled in Paris come to Canada with a newspaper that was printed in Switzerland and distributed only in Europe, and then sit in a crummy club bar with one of its ads displayed on his knee? Even if he was a "military adviser," whatever that means. Answer that one, Mettner.

As it happened, I could. Pretty soon Miss Laurence Chateauroux rippled into the bar. She had changed into a loose-fitting turtleneck sweater in turquoise blue, and a pair of skintight maroon ski pants. Now I knew that her ass was shapely too.

There were about twice as many folks in the bar as there were on the grandstand. All of them looked her way when she came in. It was obvious if you were watching closely. She stared this way and that—like she was searching for a friend. And the moment she lamped that paper on Dean's knee, she undulated right over and sat down next to him.

It was equally evident that they'd never set eyes on each other before—at least, not at close quarters. Don't ask me how I knew. The way he stood up? The expressions on their faces? You just knew, that's all.

So the *Tribune* must have been a recognition signal, something to identify Dean to her. And that meant they didn't want to meet openly in the hotel or anyplace else. A secret rendezvous, then, in the smartest place: a crowded bar. But for what?

If I was to find out, the first thing I had to do was try to read that ad. To do that, I had to pass Dean's table. And the only valid reason for doing that would be to go back to the bar and order another drink. I gritted my teeth and strolled over.

I ordered another Bloody Mary. The bartender mixed it and I took a sip. "Do they still have Prohibition in Canada?" I asked.

"Come again, friend?" said the barkeep.

"Let it go," I replied. I set a course by the stars and steered my way back to the potted palm. If you've been in the newspaper business as long as I have—and if your old man was a reporter in Chicago in the Roaring Twenties, as mine was—you'll have worked in a printshop on the stone, correcting late news flashes they didn't have time to pull as proofs. And that means you'll have been familiar with copy set up by hand or on linotype machines when it was still in lead. Which means in turn that you'll have the facility of reading print upside down. I glanced casually at the paper as I passed Dean's table for the second time. The ringed ad read:

EX-OFFICER WITH COMBAT EXPERIENCE required to train and lead a small expeditionary force for one-time foreign operation. Strictest confidence. Generous fees. Apply to Box KL/010756.

This begins, I said to myself, to look interesting. There wasn't too much difference between a military adviser and an ex-officer with combat experience. At least not in my book. The way I read it, then, Dean was answering—or had answered—the ad. And he'd been instructed to come to Joinville Falls, at which metropolitan paradise he would be contacted and maybe given his orders.

Clearly the lush Miss Laurence was the contact.

That alone would have given me the urge to follow up the story. But a one-time foreign operation? An *expeditionary* force? That sounded like big-time stuff to me. Dean had to be some kind of mercenary leader. But what was he being asked to do? And why come to Canada to make the briefing? A French connection yet! Were they planning to sequester Quebec province and return it to France? Another helicopter attack on Tehran without the Pentagon to foul up the operation?

I had to find out. The hell with the color piece on circuses, old or new. This could be some story I'd stumbled on!

I told you my old man was a reporter. My old lady was Princey Hartz. You may have read about her in the showbiz histories. She was a nightclub singer, but she'd also worked in vaudeville—and one of the acts she worked with included a lip-reading routine. When I was a kid, just for kicks she taught me the trick. And how to separate the rise and fall of voices *musically*, so you could marry up one with the other and eavesdrop even in a crowd. I was going to use that knowledge now. I edged closer to Dean's table. This is what I learned.

"Just give me that again?" Dean was saying. "In *Corsica*, you said?"

"In Corsica," the girl repeated. She had a cute French accent but she spoke English pretty good. "You know what happened with the Arabs ever since oil prices exploded back in the seventies. They have so much money they don't know what to do with it. There's nothing they can't buy, if they set their mind on it. So some of them are spending it on—how would you say?—on buying *events* rather than things."

"Buying events?"

"Playing the power game. Underwriting politics. Subsidizing organizations or groups whose aims they support."

Dean didn't reply. He just sat staring at the girl, waiting for what she was going to say next. His eyes were a very bright blue.

"This man Nessim," Laurence said. "The Sheikh Abd el Mansour Nessim. He has a percentage on every barrel of crude that passes through the straits. He's about four times as rich as Howard Hughes, Paul Getty, Aristotle Onassis, and Nubar Gulbenkian rolled into one. And he hates the West because he's only been getting that percentage the last ten years instead of the last thirty."

Dean said with a straight face, "You mean he wants to be twelve times as rich as those four guys?"

She stared at him, frowning, and then went on. "Also he's a fanatical Muslim, so he hates the East too because they're antireligious."

"How does he feel about Israel?"

"Do you need to ask?" the girl said. "He would like to see the whole structure of European-American society destroyed. He would like to see anarchy and chaos throughout the industrialized world. He would like to say—how do they put it?—the Third World rules, okay?"

"And he's actually started a school—?" I lost the rest of Dean's sentence because there was a burst of laughter from some redneck group behind me and a posse of newcomers walked up to the bar and cut off my view of the couple at the table.

When I was able to get a line on them again, the girl was saying, "So he bought this huge tract of land in the wildest part of Corsica and he's spent millions, hundreds of millions of dollars, making the place virtually impregnable, a fortress."

"And inside the fortress?"

"It's a school for terrorists. Just that. Battle courses, weapon training, classes in sabotage, assassination, hijacking, the fabrication and placing of bombs. They even built a replica of a city street so they can train urban guerrillas."

Dean looked as interested as I felt. "Who are the pupils?" he asked.

"People like Italy's Red Brigade, the Polisario, the Baader-Meinhof group, the IRA, the Tupomaro, the more extremist members of the PLO. Anyone who wants to destroy for the sake of destruction." She shook her head. "Frankfurt, Entebbe, Lod airport, the railroad station in Milan—all of them were masterminded by people trained by Nessim. So were most of the political murders and kidnaps during the past five years. Carlos is a graduate."

"And you're asking me . . . ?"

"We want you to make a reconnaissance, to form and train an assault group, and then—how is it said?—to take the place out."

The chair sighed and then creaked as Dean leaned forward. "Just two questions," he said. "Who exactly is 'we'? And if this school—which is obviously illegal by any standards—is on French territory, why the hell don't the French authorities move in the Legion and take the place out themselves?"

Laurence answered the second question first. "Corsica is a special case," she said. "From the point of view of administration, it is considered to be part of metropolitan France. Like Alaska and the U.S. It used to be a single *département*, now it is two. But there is a very strong nationalist movement; many of the people believe in a Corsican nation and wish for complete autonomy, just like in Algeria. If the French army or the Foreign Legion moved in, the Nationalists would make capital out of it. They would say it was an excuse, an invasion. There would be riots—perhaps a civil war. Just the kind of thing Nessim wants. So it is considered more . . . prudent . . . to have an anonymous, outside force." She paused a moment, and then added, "Also, there is a very strong lobby in Paris that would discourage any intervention. Nessim has a great deal of money available."

"Got it," said Dean. "He spreads it around in the right quarters—for the right to be left alone. But if there's oil involved—I wouldn't want a part of anything that could boomerang on the U.S. I mean, I wouldn't want to find myself fighting against the legal French authorities if they decided they wanted to throw us off the island . . . to find myself held up as an American invader, a mercenary aggressor or anything like that."

"There would be no question of that. Oil is not involved—except insofar as it happens to be Nessim's source of income. Oil *supplies* to your country could in no way be affected: he has no allies among the other sheikhs. So far as the French are concerned—well, part of your job will be to make the assault efficient, thorough, and above all, brief. If you succeed in that . . ." Laurence shrugged.

"You mean people will be kind of looking the other way? Okay—but you didn't answer my first question," Dean reminded her. "I assume my employers would be . . . that you're working as an undercover agent for the French government themselves?"

She smiled. How could a broad with a smile like that be anything to do with any government? "Let us just say interested parties, Mr. Dean," she said. "The suppression of international terrorism is not only the concern of the French. What is important is that *none* of the parties should be seen to be connected in any way with you or your mission. Thus this . . . rather theatrical method of meeting."

"Okay. Now, there's one other thing—" Dean began.

But the girl had gotten suddenly to her feet. "Any other questions," she said, "you must leave until the meeting tomorrow. You know where and when. I will see you there." She blinded him with another smile and left the bar.

I followed her out and ran for a phone. A school for terrorists off the coast of France; a private army hired to mount

13

an attack on NATO territory—I had to get my editor's okay to follow this up, but fast!

Great, I thought as I waited for the connection, I already knew what it was all about, and why and who. I even knew more than at least two of the characters involved: I knew the gorilla Dean had floored had been hired to pick that fight. Whatever the girl said about none of the parties being connected with the deal, this had to mean that someone had been tuned in to the Corsican job—and wanted to stop Dean making the contact and getting it—before the guy himself knew it existed.

But like Dean, I still had a couple of questions that wanted answering.

Minor: how come a supposed agent working for the French intelligence service came to be doing handsprings on an ancient airplane wing in Canada? Like my ma on the vaudeville stage, was she just making a change from singing in a nightclub? Major: where the *hell* did the other chick fit in—the classy blond Dean had left alone on the grandstand?

2

Marc Dean

"The blond one? Sure, it's the fella's wife, isn't it?" said the little man with the nutcracker face. "Leastways, his ex, if you want to be accurate."

"Marc Dean's wife?" Jason Mettner frowned. "Samantha . . . Hurok? She went back to using her unmarried name?"

"Certainly." The little man's Ulster accent was strong. He grinned. A fissure in the walnut face. "There's a kid, see. And Mom don't want junior tied in too closely with his old man—not when the guy's in the battle, murder, and sudden-death business. She figured it was a bad atmosphere for the nipper to grow up in."

"She divorced Dean because he was a mercenary?"

"You could say that. It's not what the judge said, but. I guess they call it mental cruelty."

"But, according to the morgue, her father was an Air Force colonel?"

"That's right. But *he* pressed the trigger because it was his duty, see; Marc does it for the lolly."

"Didn't the gallant aviator draw his pay?" Mettner asked.

The little man shrugged. He couldn't have been more than five feet, four inches tall, he had a stiff leg and he limped heavily, but he looked tough as hell. He said, "You wouldn't be after askin' me to explain the workin' of a broad's mind, would you?"

"Uh-uh. But they seem kind of friendly, Dean and his old lady?"

"Sure they are." The Ulsterman's name was Sean Hammer. He had known Dean—and worked with him—a long time.

"The way I see it, they still, you know, carry the torch for each other. Only, each time they look like they're gonna get back into the sack again, something comes up in the way of Marc's business an' she quits once more. On account of the boy."

Mettner nodded, remembering the words he had overheard when Dean was attacked by the pug. *Matt, why do you have to keep on fighting?* "Maybe that's why he keeps that knockout French brunette as a spare?" he suggested.

"Come again?"

"Forget it." Raring to find out more, the newspaperman was nevertheless unwilling at this stage to reveal what he knew already. "Would you be in the fighting business yourself, Mr. Hammer?" he said carefully.

"Fightin'?" Hammer unwrapped a stick of gum and fed it into his mouth. "Haven't I just come back from the ould country? There's a cousin of me brother's in Belfast owes me a few bucks he dropped on an animal in the Kentucky Derby. Since I already paid out the bookie, I figured I better reimburse meself before the creature gets himself blowed up or something. That's a right mess they're in over there, I'm tellin' you, boyo. Petrol bombs, shootin', fellas puttin' in the boot every which way. They'll not be the better of it till there's a few heads knocked together."

"It doesn't sound too different from what your friend Dean does."

"Away outta that! Not a-tall! Your man's a professional." Chewing, Hammer contrived to look outraged. "There's all the difference inna world between a well-planned action, with proper logistics, and the kind of nonsense yon cornerboys are up to in the North."

"Who do you think is to blame for the situation there?"

"The both of them's as bad as each other," Hammer said.

The professional himself, meanwhile, was watching the two men with a certain amount of curiosity from the far side of the Hall's Hotel bar. They were an oddly assorted pair. Mettner was tall, thin, slightly hollow-cheeked. He had large hands, and the jacket of his seersucker suit hung from his shoulders as if it had been made for a broader man. Dean had yet to see him without a cigarette in his mouth. Beside him, Sean Hammer's chunky, muscular form appeared almost ludicrously short.

Half-hidden, in his turn, by a potted palm, separated from

16

them by several groups of drinkers, Dean speculated idly on the subject of their conversation as he watched. Hammer, still chewing furiously, was becoming animated. His arms wind-milled and his bullet head bobbed up and down as he spoke. Mettner held his head on one side, one eye half-closed against the smoke spiraling up from the cigarette slanted from a corner of his mouth. He seemed mainly to be listening, moving his lips only occasionally to pose a question.

"The guy you were talking to in the bar," Dean said later, when he and Hammer were waiting for Samantha to come down to dinner. "Isn't he a newspaperman?"

Hammer nodded. "He is that."

"What was he carrying on about? You were certainly making with the words!"

"Ah, nothin' in particular. Just chewin' the fat. The troubles back home, the troubles in the Middle East, the troubles in bloody Africa. You know."

"He didn't try to pump you? He didn't say anything about our . . . about this Corsican deal?"

"How would he know?" Hammer asked.

"Good question. But suppose he did . . . just suppose. Could anything he asked you have had a bearing on it? Even indirectly?"

"Don't see how," Hammer said. He scratched his head. "I mean, well, okay, he asked if I was a fightin' man like yourself, if that's the kind of thing you mean. But—"

"He knew I was a combat leader?"

"Isn't it down in the hotel register, for God's sake?"

"Sure it is, but it's not everyone checks out the register."

"Maybe it's kind of a routine. For a newspaperman, I mean," Hammer offered.

"Maybe." Dean's rugged features creased into a frown. He remembered seeing Mettner among the crowd at the airfield, and again at the clubhouse bar when he was contacted by Laurence Chateauroux. The guy didn't look like a small-town hack, somehow. What would he be doing in a dump like this? "Just the same," Dean said slowly, "I wonder . . ."

Before Hammer could answer, Samantha emerged from the hotel's one elevator and joined them. The honey-blond hair had been swept upward, and she was wearing a flowered dress in filmy voile with huge sleeves gathered at the wrist. Hammer thought that she looked as if she had stepped straight out of an ad in the front part of one of the glossies.

The steak was tough, the French fries were limp, and the vegetables, although brightly colored, tasted of nothing. Attendances on the third and last day of the meet, moreover, had been as disappointing as the other two. The atmosphere in the dusty dining room was therefore somewhat funereal. Sir Daniel De'Ath, the veteran British aviator who directed the circus, sat in glum silence with his two French partners. Pilots and specialty acts filled one long table, mechanics and riggers another. But there were enough gaps in the conversation for the drumming of rain on the windows to become noticeable. Only in the corner by the swing doors leading to the kitchens, where Laurence Chateauroux was installed with the two senior racer pilots, was there any laughter.

"Is that right, Marc," Hammer asked in a low voice, "the name of thon fella? It's not a cod—I mean, he really is called Death?"

"It's a real name," Dean confirmed, smiling. "Quite a well-known family in England. But nobody likes to be called that, so they began to write it differently and made it two syllables—dee-ath."

"You can't get away from it, can you?" said Samantha.

Dean ignored the barb. He glanced across at the Britisher—bulging blue eyes, an aggressive mustache, orange-peel cheeks webbed with tiny red veins. De'Ath was still wearing a leather flying jacket with a fur collar. For most of the three days he had also sported a thin leather helmet with unbuttoned ear flaps and goggles pushed up above the forehead—presumably, as Samantha had said unkindly, to make sure that he was not mistaken for an automobile salesman. The two Frenchmen, who were assumed to have put up the money for the project, were much less flamboyant—meaty individuals with hooded eyes, blue-gray suits, and jowls to match.

One of them—his name was Maurice Duclos—Dean knew better than he was prepared to admit. The man had a French passport, but he could have been Lebanese, Armenian, Greek, or even Egyptian. It had been with him and the girl Laurence that Dean's secret meeting in connection with the Corsican project had taken place. It was the second day of the circus . . . and the conference had been organized in the cabin of the Ford Tri-motor, while the ship was airborne, before and after Laurence's wing-walking act. "You may think it theatrical, monsieur," Duclos had said. "Perhaps even a trifle vulgar. But I assure you that, given Nessim's limitless funds and the sophistication of modern surveillance techniques, the stratagem is necessary. I can think of few places *totally* immune from electronic eavesdropping—beneath a running shower perhaps, amid the snows of Kilimanjaro—but we thought you would find the cabin of a piston-engined aircraft in flight more comfortable." He favored the combat leader with a wintry smile.

"It is not simply that," Laurence had added. "The secret operator today does not advertise either his trade or his allegiances. He will be a gray man, unnoticeable among the crowd."

"How do you know I'm not one of your gray men myself?" Dean shouted over the racket of the motors. "Sent in reply to your ad, to worm out the secrets of your plan and pass them on to Nessim?"

"Believe me, Monsieur Dean," said Duclos, "your dossier has been most carefully and minutely examined. You yourself have been . . . investigated . . . over many months. If there was the least doubt about your probity, your loyalties, or your—shall we say?—reliability, you would not be here today, I assure you."

"Yeah, but that *Tribune* ad—"

"Was placed to attract you, and you alone. It was felt that this was the wisest course. In case our people were being watched. Or you yourself were being watched for some reason. In which case a direct contact might have been significant. Any other applicants who answered the advertisement were told the post had been filled."

"You sure take precautions," Dean admired. "You said 'our people.' Just who are your people, exactly?"

"Those who will be paying you to remain discreet," Duclos replied. "I will now outline the terms on which you will be employed. Provided they meet with your approval, I will then talk about the operation itself."

The two subjects were separated by Laurence's wing-walking specialty. Looking through the oval ports of the cabin, catching sight of a flash of brown legs against the leaden rain clouds over the lake, Dean reflected that it was a tough way to earn a living. Especially, he thought, glancing below at the scatter of cars in the parking lot, the thin sprinkling of spectators on the makeshift grandstand, when there was no public to appreciate it. But did she make a living cartwheeling five hundred feet above ground? Or was it just a crazy cover for her contact activities? If so . . . surely she could have chosen something easier! But maybe she always had been a circus act, and it was the undercover work that was a way of earning extra money? Perhaps he would get the chance to ask her.

She was back in the cabin, panting a little, and the pilot was taking them up to five thousand feet to leave space for some other kind of aerobatics. "Corsica," Duclos was saying, "is shaped like the back view of one of those pointing hands you see on notice boards. The left hand. The finger, indicating due north, is Cap Corse. The tip of the thumb is Bastia, the knuckle of the little finger is Calvi. And on the other side of Cap Corse from Bastia—between the middle finger and the forefinger, you might say—there's a fishing port called St. Florent." The Frenchman paused, staring out at the wisps of cloud streaming past the Tri-motor's wingtips. "Picturesque little place," he observed finally. "At the inner end of a deep gulf. Surrounded by mountains. But between those mountains and Calvi there's an extraordinary stretch of country known as the Desert of Agriates."

"And it's there," Dean queried, "that this man Nessim . . . ?"

"Partly. Hundreds of years ago, the desert was rich pastureland, but it's been eroded by wind and sun, eaten away by sea salt, until now there's no topsoil and no vegetation—just a wilderness of granite more than ten miles wide, stretching five miles inland from a rocky shore."

"It's completely desolate," Laurence said. "There's no road, no trail, scarcely even a sheep track."

"No houses or farms?"

She shook her head. "A couple of shepherd's huts, over an area of forty thousand acres, more than sixty square miles, and that's all."

Duclos said, "Nessim has bought half the area. He uses it for training exercises. But he's also bought an enormous tract of land on the landward side of the desert, bordering the highway from Calvi to St. Florent. It's heavily wooded, hilly, and there's a fortified château at the highest point, surrounded by an abandoned village that he's remodeled into living quarters for his terrorists."

Dean said to Laurence, "I think you told me he's spent millions of dollars making this fortress impregnable?"

"Hundreds of millions. Not just the fortress: the whole

place. It's called the Domaine de Murenzana. He's got radar, sonar, sensor-actuated, computer-controlled rocket batteries, machine-gunners, on twenty-four-hour watch, killer dogs patrolling between electrified wire fences. There isn't an inch of that property that isn't surveyed night and day by closed-circuit infrared TV cameras."

"I thought that was illegal—electrified fences and that kind of thing?" Dean said mildly.

"They're twenty or thirty yards inside the property boundary," Duclos said. "Well beyond the high wall, past the 'Private' signs and the 'Danger—Keep out!' notices. Nobody can touch them by mistake from outside. You have to be a trespasser to get electrocuted. Also, he spent a lot more millions in Paris and Ajaccio, buying himself official immunity from the law."

"And you want this place neutralized, destroyed? And all the guys running it, including the boss man, eliminated?"

"We want," Duclos said, choosing his words with care, "to ensure that no school for terrorists exists in Corsica. And that there remain no . . . uh . . . possibilities of a similar institution being established once the existing one has been . . . ah . . . closed down."

"Got it," said Dean. "You don't wish to give a specific order for the . . . liquidation . . . of this guy Nessim, right?"

"It would be an impertinence, Monsieur Dean," Duclos said politely, "to instruct a man of your experience precisely how to obtain a desired effect."

Dean grinned. "Okay, so I go there, make a recce, work out the best way of . . . obtaining the desired effect. Then I come back to you and we talk about the hardware, the number of men required, and all that jazz. That correct?"

"That is correct."

"And however many men you need," Laurence added, "don't let it worry you: there will be no difficulty finding the right amount of money."

Dean nodded. "Talking of men, I know there's no French army base on the island, but isn't there a Foreign Legion depot?"

"After Algeria became independent," said Duclos, "the Legion headquarters were moved from Sidi-bel-Abbès to Aubagne, near Marseilles. But there has, as you rightly suggest, been a Legion presence in Corsica ever since World War II.

The most important camp is at Corte, the ancient capital, in the center of the island."

"You don't think they'd play rough if a company of airborne infantry dropped and there was a minor amphibious landing by foreigners in the north?"

"It is likely that your own action would coincide with a Legion exercise in the south," Duclos said suavely.

He still looked suave, Dean thought, regarding him covertly the following evening over dinner, when he was part of the air-circus entourage. But this was the kind of bland and expressionless smoothness that went with the punter awaiting a return on his money. Or was it a return on something else? Was the circus just a cover for him too? There certainly seemed to be plenty of money around: Dean had been staggered when he was told the amount available.

He looked at Sir Daniel De'Ath. The Englishman's braying voice rose above the subdued murmur of conversation. "Oh, I say! Look here, this piece of meat's tough as old boots, what!" Was it possible that this flying fool was in some way allied to Laurence Chateauroux and Duclos? With the other Frenchman, whose name was Ancarani, they sure formed a bizarre quartet! And whether De'Ath was in on the deal or not, the barnstormers act was a lulu: who in God's name would expect such a group to be an antiterrorist executive?

Dean was aware that Hammer was claiming his attention. The little man knew that Dean's ex-wife liked him as a person but deplored his professional relationship with the father of her child. Military matters were therefore a taboo subject when the three of them were together—which at times left Hammer in the middle of an awkward silence, wondering what in hell he could dredge up next as a subject of conversation. Dean came to his rescue now with a ribald appreciation of De'Ath's chances of success at the circus' next date, at Des Plaines, near Chicago.

"All the same," Samantha said later, when she and her ex-husband were sipping coffee and Tia Maria in the bar, "I cannot for the life of me think why *we* should be here, however few people there are at Des Plaines. I mean, sure, it's good to get away for a few days and leave Patrick with your sister in New York. But . . . Niagara Falls? And now here? Why on earth did you want to come to Canada? For the food?"

"You know I'm crazy for vintage machinery," Dean parried.

"Do I? I know you had a period when you were besotted with ancient cars—Bentleys and Bugattis and Maxwells and such. But I didn't know you still had it . . . or that it had broadened to include period airplanes."

"I have my pilot's license," Dean reminded her.

"So you do. But I can't imagine you ever wanting to fly one of these. So what are we doing, Matt, in Joinville Falls? Did you come specially to chat up that rather common dark girl who shows off her legs up in the air?"

"As an ex," Dean told her, "you are not supposed to indulge in the sin of jealousy. You are supposed, in a sisterly way, to say: How nice for you; I hope you'll have a lot of fun together. But as it happens, that's not why I came; I'd never heard of her and I'd no idea she'd be here. Anyway, if that was the play, I wouldn't have asked you to come along, would I?"

"Why *did* you ask me to come here, Matt?"

"I came here for . . . business reasons. You wouldn't want to hear about them."

"And you brought me with you?"

"Because I want to fuck you more than anything else in the world," Dean said roughly.

She flashed him a look from under her long lashes, breathing suddenly rather fast. "Matt! Don't let's start . . . Please!"

"The mechanics are simple," Dean said. "I was in Paris. I had to come Stateside. I wanted like hell to see you . . ."

"And Patrick."

"Yeah, and Patrick, of course. My legal right of access. But this time it was you, just you."

"Cue for a song?" Samantha said lightly.

"If you want. Night and day, you are the one—it's corny, but the words do fit. I figured it would be good for the boy, spending a week with Hester." Dean's elder sister was a New York socialite.

"And you carried me off to romantic Joinville Falls, Ontario, determined to win back the love of your life?"

"Oh come on, honey." Dean flushed. "Be fair. Niagara was just a whistle stop on the way west. A joke. It wasn't my fault that they . . . that I was contacted the day we were there and asked to come on over to this dump. It's a drag, okay. But it would have been crazy to have left you out there, or sent you home and come on my own. When we get so damned little time together."

"We *are* divorced, Matt," she reminded him. "And one of the main reasons for the divorce was also the reason why we have—had—so little time together. Your . . . profession."

"Okay," Dean said again. "Okay, let's not go into that now. Let's talk about today. We *are* together. And I want you like hell."

She studied him over the rim of her glass. He had been born on June 6, 1944, the day of the biggest combined operation in history. His old man had been a buddy of her own father's, in the Air Corps and later in the USAF. He'd been drafted to Vietnam. Maybe it wasn't so strange after all that he'd gotten stuck on the military life, that he'd turned his back on the cultivated existence that his intelligence deserved, quit the safe job with her father's electronics corporation, and chosen to be a soldier of fortune. It certainly hadn't spoiled his looks. At thirty-eight he was still all man. Life and vitality pulsed beneath the lightly tanned skin of his face, and the pale hair was crisp and curly as a college boy's. His deep-set blue eyes were steady and clear. The mouth—Samantha saw with a pang—the mouth that could switch so suddenly from cruelty to tenderness was as firm and determined as ever.

And (running her own eyes swiftly down the hard, muscular length of his body) it was clearly, evidently true that he desired her. She set down her glass abruptly and rose to her feet. "I think I'll go upstairs," she announced, "to bed."

Dean glanced around him. Two of the older pilots were hunched over tall steins of beer at the bar. Hammer was talking to the journalist, Mettner, at a table in the far corner. The bartender had disappeared in back, to the stillroom. Otherwise the place was empty. "I'll see you to your room," Dean said. He got up, held the door open for her, and accompanied her to the lobby and the elevator.

"I'll be absolutely straight with you, Mr. Hammer," Mettner said, putting one card face upward on the table and holding the rest close to his chest. "I'm a newspaperman. This air-circus story is a dead fucking duck. I figure there may be something cooking with your friend Dean—but of course I've no idea what it is. Yet there's this screwball scenario: a guy looks like a syndicate hood hands out a fistful of dollars to a

24

gorilla and tells him go pick a fight with Dean. Now, why in hell would he do that?"

The Ulsterman shrugged. "Search me. How would I know?"

"I heard the dialogue," Mettner pursued. "The instructions were to lay Dean out, but good. So he should stay out for some time. In my book, that only means one thing: somebody wanted to stop him doing something or going someplace. Do you have any idea what?"

Hammer shook his head. He wasn't showing any of his cards. "The big guy was pissed and he wanted the broad?" he suggested.

"I could have bought that if it had just been the big guy on his own. Not when he was like paid to do it."

"I give up, then. You tell me."

Mettner fished a crumpled pack of Camels from the breast pocket of his jacket. He extracted a cigarette and put it between his lips. He was determined not to let on that he knew Dean was being hired to eliminate a terrorist-training center in Corsica. But if he wanted to follow up the story, he had to know something about times and dates and places. He had, in some way or other, to get himself on the inside . . . without revealing that he knew what it was all about. Because in that case everybody would clam up and he'd lose the whole goddamn thing. It seemed to him, therefore, that this tough little man—who had to be a fighting associate of Dean's: he had appeared so conveniently after that first meeting in the clubhouse—it seemed that Hammer would be his best lead, that through him he could get close to the combat leader in a way he could never make on his own. He struck a match and held the flame to the limp tip of his cigarette. He inhaled and blew a long plume of smoke toward the yellowed ceiling of the bar. "I'm hoping that you'll be able to help me, Mr. Hammer," he said.

"Oh, yeah? What's your problem?"

Mettner shook out the match and dropped it into an overflowing ashtray. "I want your advice, that's all. It sticks out a mile to the trained eye"—the newspaperman plucked another card from his hand and laid it on the table—"that your buddy Dean is brewing up some military broth, that he's involved in some deal. Why else would such a guy be in a place like this?" He held up one hand. "I don't know what it is," he lied. "I wouldn't want to know. I wouldn't want to in-

25

trude. But the problem is simply this: without bugging the guy, do you think I should wise him up? Should I tell him about that gorilla being paid to beat him up? I mean, you know, whoever it is—they might decide to try again."

Hammer rose to his feet and clapped the journalist on the shoulder. "Don't worry," he said. "I'll look after it. I'll tell him myself, mister. Obliged to you for lettin' us know. See you around, huh?" He nodded and walked briskly out of the room.

Mettner leaned back in his chair and took a long pull at his cigarette. He was pleased with the way he'd handled the situation. Dean would be sure to contact him, once Hammer had passed on the warning; he would want to question Mettner himself and find out the details. He'd need exact descriptions, Mettner's recollection of the words he'd overheard. And that way, with the mercenary leader obligated to him, Mettner would have a genuine acquaintanceship he could use.

Unfortunately, the warning, when it was given, was a little late.

Upstairs, in the dimly lit second-floor hallway, Dean stood with Samantha outside the door of her room. She had put the key in the lock but she hadn't turned it yet. Dean reached out his arms and grasped her just above the elbows. He could feel her flesh cool through the thin, flowered stuff of the sleeves. "I don't think—" she began hesitantly.

"Right," he cut in. "Don't think. Act. Feel."

For an instant his fingers clenched on her arms; then he let go of her, turned the key in the lock, opened the door, and pushed her through.

The bedroom drapes had not been drawn and a faint radiance from the streetlamp at the corner below illuminated an armchair, the boudoir table, a wide divan with the covers folded back. She stood facing him by the window. In this curious light, the voile was almost transparent: he could see the outline of the brassiere that held and separated her breasts. Her eyes were shadowed but there was a gleam of white in among the darkness beneath her brows.

"Sam!" he said hoarsely.

"Matt?"

Her face was upturned. Her lower lip shone moistly. He placed a hand on either side of her pliant waist. Now the flesh seemed to burn against his palms. He pulled her gently toward him, until he could feel the soft swell of her breasts against his chest. Their two mouths approached, touched, clung together. There was a sudden thrusting and a curl of hot, wet tongues. Dean pulled away, breathing hard. "Sam!" he whispered. "Oh, Sam! Oh, my darling . . ."

She collapsed backward and sat down heavily on the bed. She kicked off her high-heeled pumps, one after the other. "My shoes are giving me hell!" she said shakily.

Outside in the night, a car hissed past along the wet street.

"Sam, darling. There's never been anyone but you. We—"

"You know damned well that isn't true," she interrupted. "I know it, and you know that I know it." She gave a small, breathless laugh. "But somehow . . . tonight . . . it doesn't really seem . . ."

He leaned over her, standing beside the bed, his fingers searching for the fastenings at the back of her dress. She reached up and touched him, drew in her breath sharply. Her pulse was racing. "Oh, what the hell!" she murmured. She lay back suddenly and he heard the crisp swish of silk or nylon sliding over skin.

"Come here, you sexy bastard!" Samantha said fiercely— and she pulled him down onto the divan.

Glass from the window exploded inward and shattered on the pine floor. As he fell forward, Dean felt the wind of the huge steel-jacketed .500 Magnum bullet that had just missed him fan the back of his neck. The echoes of the gunshot— fired from a room on the far side of the street by a Mauser Express rifle equipped with an infrared night sight—were still reverberating in his ears when water from the night-table carafe smashed by the slug started splashing to the floor.

3

Sean Hammer

The second attempt on Dean's life—and the third attack he had suffered in seventy-two hours—took place on the following day. Before it happened there were various minor dramas scheduled. Sean Hammer's room was next to his leader's. He had been waiting patiently for Dean to return so that he could pass on the information he had been given by Mettner, when the shot that so narrowly missed Dean was fired.

Hammer knew the sounds of heavy-caliber ammunition leaving a weapon and arriving on target. He also knew—it was a normal part of his backup routine—where Samantha's room was. He was down the corridor and through the unlocked door before the water from the smashed carafe had stopped dripping.

Dean was already on hands and knees beneath the low sill of the window, reaching up at one side for the acorn that terminated the cord operating the blind. Samantha was still on the bed, the top of the voile dress held across her breasts, her mouth compressed into a thin, angry line. Not until the blind was rolled down did Dean signal Hammer to switch on the lights. "What the *hell* . . . ?" Hammer said.

"Unexpected," said Dean. "Fired from across the street, I guess. I'd sure like to know why."

"Don't know why, Marc," Hammer replied. "But not altogether unexpected."

"What do you mean?"

Hammer summarized the conversation he had had with the newspaperman and added, "Will we try to find out what they aimed to get you with this time?"

It wasn't too difficult. They pried the flattened slug from the far end of a three-inch tunnel drilled into the plaster wall beyond the pulverized water carafe. "Christ!" Hammer exclaimed. "They must've been shootin' at you with a bloody elephant gun!"

Dean nodded. "Probably a Mannlicher or a Mauser Express." He turned the deformed bullet over in his hand. "Four-seven-six or .500 caliber, I should say. Not as accurate as a modern high-velocity rifle firing 5.56mm ammunition, but kind of lethal when it's just from one side of a street to the other. Punch a hole in your chest as big as a barn door. They must have been using an NSP-2 or a Trilux night sight: the drapes were drawn but there was no light on in here."

"How come they missed you, then?" Hammer asked.

Dean coughed. "I . . . uh . . . I happened to bend down, to lean forward at the critical moment." He avoided looking at Samantha.

Hammer stared at the slug. "Boy, were you lucky!" He said.

Someone was knocking at the door. Dean crunched across broken glass and opened it. There were people in the passageway outside: the night clerk, one or two startled guests, a man in pajamas who said he was the house detective. "It's all right," Dean told them. "Kids playing with fireworks, I guess. No harm done. We'll pay for the window and the water jug. Send me the bill for fixing the damage to the wall."

But the house dick was not to be cheated of his hour of glory. He insisted on calling the police. Ten minutes later two RCMP troopers arrived outside the hotel in a white Mercury with a flashing rooflight and warbling siren. Then the whole story had to be dragged out—or at least that part of it relating to the shot. Nobody mentioned the fistfight three days before. But there were questions to be asked, depositions to be taken, investigations to be made.

The weapon had been fired from the second floor of a rooming house on the other side of the street. The barrel had been supported on a bipod: the legs had scratched distinctive marks on the soft sandstone of the windowsill. There was of course no sign of the gunman or his rifle. "Must of used the fire exit," commented the landlady—a creased blond with a faded kimono and hair that had gone dark at the roots. She relit the cigarette stuck to her lower lip. He had arrived that afternoon and paid in advance, she said. A foreign-looking man with a weekend case and one of those long canvas sports grips; the kind of things tennis players used, although the man didn't look as if he played much tennis. No, he hadn't signed the register; yes, of course she knew the regulations, but in these days you had to take what you could get, and she was sure they could understand that a girl in her position . . .

The troopers sighed and snapped shut their notebooks. Finally, when Dean had blandly assured them for the fourth time that he had no idea, no idea at all, why a foreign-looking man would want to fire an elephant gun at him in the middle of the night in Joinville Falls, Ontario, they climbed into their car and drove away. It was after 3 A.M., and nobody had thought to ask whether or not the lights in the room had been switched on.

Hammer, playing the startled guest, had not mentioned his association with Dean and had said very little. Jason Mettner had arrived on the scene after the police. But, the little man remarked, he had taken no notes and asked no questions of anyone. Which was odd, when you came to think of it, for a journalist on the inside of an attempted-murder case. Samantha had replied coldly to the questions put to her and said nothing more.

"There's one thing here sticks out a bloody mile, Marc," Hammer said when the glass had been swept up and Samantha's room restored to order.

"Yeah? What's that?" Dean had fetched the carafe from his own room and was filling it from the cold tap in the bathroom.

"The fact that the bastard knew where to fire."

"What do you mean?" Dean came back into the room and stood mopping the drops of water from the outside of the carafe with a hand towel.

"Your room's farther along the corridor. Nobody could know or guess when you'd be in it—or likely to be in this one—especially with the lights out, except they saw you and Samantha leave that bar. Or were tipped off that you'd left it."

Dean frowned. "Okay, I'm with you. Go on."

"There wasn't time for anyone in the bar to quit the hotel, cross the street, and set up the gun. So it must have been a tipoff." Hammer paused. He said slowly, "The only folks in the bar when you two left were the two aviators, meself, and the newspaper guy, Mettner."

"And the bartender."

"And the bartender, that's right."

"Though, come to think of it," Dean said. "I don't believe the bartender was there when we got up to go."

"You're right! He was in back, in the stillroom. So either he'd sussed out that you were about to leave and was on the phone to his sniper buddy, or one of the aviators tipped the guy off. Meself, I don't figure Mettner for that kind of guy."

"I guess not. I never met him." But at the back of his mind, Dean suddenly heard the voice of the girl Laurence. *The secret operator today does not advertise either his trade or his allegiances. He will be a gray man, unnoticeable among the crowd.* For the second time he thought: What would a guy like that be doing in a place like this at a time like today?

Before he could voice his doubts, Samantha, who had been sitting on the bed, rose suddenly to her feet. She had slipped a white wool cardigan over the voile dress and she was hugging it close to her. There were red patches on her cheeks and her eyes were angry. "Stop it! Stop it! Stop it!" she shouted. "Get out of here and leave me alone; I can't stand any more; I won't!"

The two men stared at her in astonishment.

"You're as bad as each other!" she stormed. "You . . . you discuss this thing as if it were a . . . a chess problem or a crossword. For God's sake, Matt, somebody tried to *kill* you! They shot at you with a gun. You could have been murdered across my bed."

"Honey, I'm awfully sorry. It was thoughtless of me." Dean put the carafe down on the night table and moved to her side, a solicitous arm around her shoulders. "Of course it was terrible for you. I understand. Christ, a traumatic experience! But it's all over now, I promise. You've nothing to be afraid of."

She pushed him roughly away. "You don't understand a damned thing, do you?"

Dean fell back a pace, bewildered by the venom in her voice.

"It's your beastly, filthy, murderous trade," Samantha cried. "Ordinary people don't get shot at with elephant guns in hotel rooms in hick towns. Ordinary people may have bad dreams, but the dreams don't come true. Ordinarily, decent people don't make a living out of killing other people. That's why nobody shoots them at night."

"Sam," Dean pleaded, "be fair. It's not my fault if—"

"It's all your fault. It always has been. You and your dirty profession. It's ruined our marriage and nearly corrupted our child and . . . and . . . it rubs off on everything you touch. Sometimes I feel tainted, Matt, just being near you."

"Honey . . ."

"Don't try to sweet-talk me. I can't stop you seeing Patrick—but don't expect ever to see me again. Not ever again, Matt."

Hammer stole to the door, opened it, and slipped outside. He could hear Samantha's near-hysterical voice all the way down the passageway to his own room.

Things seemed little better the following morning. Before eight o'clock, he saw her loading her baggage into the trunk of a taxi outside the hotel entrance. It was raining again. Dean stood by the cab's passenger door. He was gesticulating. "No, no, no, and again no!" Samantha's angry voice carried clearly to the window of Hammer's room. "I refuse to have any part of your life in Europe, Matt. I don't want to be within a mile of your despicable activities."

"But, honey, it's not . . ." The rest of Dean's reply was too low-pitched to carry as far as the second floor.

"I don't care what you say: I tell you I don't want any part of it," Samantha said. "There's a train leaves here for Toronto at eight-thirty-five, and I intend to be on it. From there I shall fly to Boston and then I shall go home." Dean's ex-wife lived in a village near Orleans, on Cape Cod.

"Sam, look . . ." Dean tried again.

Samantha jerked open the door of the cab and got inside. She leaned out and said, "I can't stop you seeing Patrick. But the next time you're due for a visit—if you last that long— you can make the arrangements through my lawyer. I won't be home."

The door slammed. Dean made a helpless gesture, standing bareheaded in the downpour as the cab pulled away from the curb. It checked briefly at the lights and then turned right and headed for the railroad station, spraying wide fans of water from its wheels.

"What was all that about, then?" Hammer asked fifteen

minutes later when the two of them were sitting alone over limp waffles and gray breakfast coffee.

"What was all what about?" Dean looked morose.

"The spat with herself. If you don't mind a fella askin'."

"Of course not. Most of the neighborhood must have heard it anyway." Half-smiling in spite of himself, Dean added, "I asked if she'd maybe care to spend a week with me on the sunny isle of Corsica. We were supposed to be on a ten-day reconciliation trip anyway." He cleared his throat. "She . . . didn't favor the idea."

"Gee, Marc, I'm sorry." Hammer was genuinely sympathetic.

Dean shrugged. "It's happened before. I guess it will again. It would have been good for her, too. And regular. My first visit's on the level—to see how the place shapes up as an invasion target. I'll be making like a tourist, and the best way to do that's with a dame. Nicer, too." He sighed. "Too bad. Never mind, I'll take someone else."

"Any ideas?"

About to shake his head, the combat leader stiffened. His eyes brightened. "Yeah," he said slowly. "Yeah, I guess I have, at that!"

Hammer said, "You don't think *two* couples would make the cover more convincing?"

Dean laughed. "You're not old enough to be a dirty old man. But I want you there, Sean. Not with me. On your jack. Best if we have no contact at all. But you can work on the logistics while I check out the strengths and weaknesses of this guy Nessim's hideaway. Okay?"

"Sure. How exactly d'you aim to play this, Marc?"

"I'll tell you on the way to the airfield."

"Airfield?"

"The party's over. They're packing up this morning, readying the ships for the flight to Des Plaines. There's a couple of things I want to check with my contacts before they take off."

The little Irishman chuckled. "I think I smell a rat!" he said. "A rat with long brown legs, skipping rope on the wing of an airplane."

The town of Joinville Falls lies on top of a bluff. Beyond the cliff-face cascades that give the place its name, the road loops down to the flatlands beside the lake, where the airfield had been laid out. Dean drove the rented Volvo across the suspension bridge spanning the river just above the falls and took the long, straight downgrade leading to the first of the hairpin curves.

"Right, then," Hammer said. "We know we're bein' hired to take out this terrorist-trainin' school on Crosica and zap the head man. We been told it's one hell of a tough job. This much you let go when I showed up in answer to your cable. Now, how about fillin' me in on some of the details—who the boss man is, what you know of his defenses, the strength of the local law, an' all that?"

"Sure. The guy beyond the school is called Nessim. Abd el Mansour Nessim, if I remember right. He's an oil sheikh, rich as . . ." Dean stopped in mid-sentence, a puzzled look on his face.

"What is it, Marc?" Hammer asked.

"I don't know. I . . ." Dean was pumping the brake pedal. The heavy Volvo was cruising fast, arrowing down the wet roadway toward the first hairpin. The needle on the dial indicated 55 mph. He pumped harder, but there was no appreciable retardation. "Goddamn brakes!" he said. "The hydraulics . . . these son-of-a-bitch rented cars!" His knee jerked furiously up and down, but the car continued to gain speed.

"Try the handbrake," Hammer said anxiously.

Dean hauled on the lever. It shot upward. There was no resistance to his pull. "Okay," he said tightly. "The cable's been cut. The hydraulics are sabotaged. Tighten your belt: this may be rugged."

The white needle hovered on the 70 mark. In fourth gear, on a downgrade, even with the foot lifted off, the motor had virtually no breaking effect. Hammer swallowed. He knew there was only one thing Dean could do if he was to slow the runaway car: shift down, and if possible shift again.

The Volvo had a stick shift. Dean grabbed the lever, trod on the clutch pedal, and slammed the knob forward. There was a scream of tortured metal. The lever jerked from his grasp. He tried a second time, and a third, with the same result. He shook his head. "If I shove any harder, I'll strip the damned thing; the gear wheels'll come up through the floor," he rasped. "Somehow I've got to reduce speed enough to get her into third."

Hammer swallowed again. The hairpin was rushing toward them; the needle was on 75; and the curve was cut through solid rock. The drone of the motor was almost drowned by the sucking hiss of tires on the wet macadam. His right hand flew up in protest and he gave an involuntary cry of alarm.

Dean had swung the wheel hard over, yards before they reached the hairpin.

For an instant the car answered to the helm and slewed toward the bank. Then the tires lost their grip and aquaplaned. The Volvo spun completely around, still hurtling toward the corner. But as a result of Dean's maneuver, it was the rear quarter and not the front that smashed against the rock wall.

A rending, tearing jangle of metal. The two men rocketed against their safety harness under the impact. Every window in the car shattered. The windshield went opaque. Dean put his fist through it, fighting with the wheel while the car cannoned off the rock, shot across the roadway to hit the opposite bank, and then swerved drunkenly onto the crown of the road as they came out of the turn at the top of the next straightaway.

They were still traveling at more than 60 mph. A tanker pulling a trailer was climbing the grade toward them; three hundred yards ahead, a Volkswagen Beetle crawled in the direction of the next hairpin. Dean allowed the tanker to pass and then began deliberately swinging the Volvo from side to side, skidding first into the nearside and then the offside bank as the tail swung wide.

"God save us all!" Hammer exclaimed. "What are you tryin' to do?"

"Smash the rear fenders in so that they'll touch the wheels and act as a brake."

"You'll be killin' the both of us first," Hammer said.

Dean leaned on the horn button, waving frantically through the gap in the windshield. The VW was going too slowly: it wouldn't be around the corner before they hit it. Through the little car's rear window they could see the driver adjust his mirror and then make don't-bug-me signs. Dean cursed, wrenching the wheel over so that the Volvo approached the corner on the left-hand side of the road.

Hammer felt the sweat start on his brow. If there should be something entering the hairpin on the way up . . .

The sideswiping had reduced their speed some. Once more Dean de-clutched, stamped on the accelerator, and shoved the lever with all his strength. This time it went in. The gearbox screeched. The engine roared and the tachometer needle raced around the dial. The whole car shuddered as their speed dropped below 50 mph.

But the corner was almost on them. No rock wall on this one; just an embankment covered in rough grass that sloped steeply down from the roadway. Dean ran off the road for ten yards as the bank fell away, clipping a final outcrop with the offside rear fender. It was a jackpot move. The battered metal was staved in enough to foul the wheel.

It was staved in so much that a sharp edge rubbed against the tire, filling the Volvo with blue smoke and the odor of burning rubber.

The needle dropped back to 40 mph and the tire exploded as they made the apex of the curve. The car staggered as though it had been hit by a giant fist. Parts of the ripped tread streamed away behind them like black snakes. The wheel rim and then the brake disk bit into the blacktop, swiveling the Volvo to the left. The offside front wheel ran over the lip of the embankment . . . and then the whole car tipped over and rolled, once, twice, three times, before it came to rest on its roof forty yards below the road, at the foot of the slope.

Sean Hammer received a kaleidoscope of visual impressions as they quit the highway—the astonished face of the VW driver whisked away behind them; rain clouds wheeling across the hole of the windshield; a grassy slope above his head; the agonized expression of a truck driver entering the hairpin on the upgrade. "It was like the fuckin' titles on *The Thomas Crown Affair*," he said later.

It seemed a long time afterward that he realized he was unhurt. He was hanging upside down in his harness, but he was unhurt. There was a stink of gasoline and overheated metal added to the burned rubber now. Somewhere behind him, liquid splashed.

Christ! he thought. Gasoline . . . hot metal . . .

He released the clip on the belt, slumped to the crumpled roof, and crawled out through the shattered window. Fragments of glass tinkled from the frame as he rocked the car getting out.

Dean was on his feet on the other side of the wreck, picking granules of the smashed windshield from his hair. Beside him, one of the front wheels was still slowly revolving.

"Well, then," Hammer said heavily, "so we made it."

Dean nodded. "Thanks be!"

There were cars and trucks parked at the edge of the road along the top of the embankment. People were running down the slope toward the overturned Volvo. Rain falling on the hot muffler hissed an accompaniment to the ticking of contracting metal as the engine cooled. "It's all right," Dean called. "Nobody hurt . . . thank you very much . . . very kind . . . Yes, a brake failure: lucky it wasn't worse."

The failure, they saw as they waited for the cab that the Volkswagen driver had promised to send out from the airfield, had been very carefully engineered. The handbrake cable had simply been cut through, and the severed ends attached to the chassis with Scotch tape. But the hydraulics had been tampered with in a more sophisticated way. A hole had been drilled in the master cylinder, and then sealed with wax in such a way that mild braking at the beginning of a journey would not affect it. But the fluid pressure under heavy braking—or heat from the engine when the car had been running some time—would dislodge or melt the plug and all the brake fluid would be lost.

"Neat," Hammer said. "Could happen anytime, anywhere—especially on a long downgrade in the rain. And everyone has a cast-iron alibi of course. Who wants to stop you taking on this Corsican job, Marc?"

Dean shrugged. The shoulders of his jacket were dark with moisture. "Search me. Nessim's men, if they knew about it—but I don't see how they could. Also I'd expect something a little more adventurous from them—a poisoned needle, a bomb wired to the ignition, a submachine gun at least. I mean like they'd make sure." He shook his head. "But a barroom brawl, sabotaged brakes, an old-fashioned big-game weapon? I don't buy that."

Another car had stopped at the top of the embankment. A lanky figure, trench coat flapping, belt buckled in back, was hurrying down toward them between the clumps of wet grass. It was Jason Mettner.

"Holy Christ!" he called, snatching an unlit cigarette from his mouth. "Are you guys all right? What happened?" And then, when he had reached them, breathlessly: "What in God's name happened?"

Dean looked him in the eye. "Don't you know?" he said levelly.

4

Laurence Chateauroux

"Lot of damn nonsense, if you ask me," Sir Daniel De'Ath grumbled. "Airworthiness certificates, homologation details, bills of lading, *customs* clearance, for heaven's sake! Didn't have to mess with all this rubbish in the good old days, when these crates were flying. Just had your rigger twirl the bally prop . . . contact, contact! . . . and you were away." His angry blue eyes roved the hangar, past the crated gear to the ancient machines waiting on the apron outside the open doors—the Tri-motor, a Bristol Fighter, an SE5-A, a Grumman Martlet, a replica Fokker Triplane, and several others. "Red tape an' all that hogwash," he said. "Don't know what my guv'nor would've said. Turn in his bloody grave! Left to me, I'd give the signal now and we'd take off PDQ."

"You have to wait for Maurice to get back," Laurence pointed out. "Until he files the papers with the control tower here, Toronto won't accept your flight plan, and you won't be allowed to overfly the frontier."

The baronet grunted. "Never worried about bloody frontiers before the war. London to Australia nonstop. Who are those chaps?"

She followed the direction of his glance and saw Dean and Sean Hammer emerge from a glassed-in office at the rear of the hangar. "The tall one is a man I know," she said evasively. "I think the little one with the limp must be a business associate."

"Looks a bit of a bounder, if you ask me. One of those lumberjack things with suede shoes! Hah!" Sir Daniel buttoned the chin strap of his flying helmet and moved away.

Laurence made the gray day look brighter. Her cinnamon-colored skin glowed with health. Her eyes were bright and her glossy hair shone. She was wearing a coral-colored trouser suit with a silk shirt in slate blue. The suit jacket was fastened with a single button, but the revers gaped above it where the shirt was thrust out by her formidable bust. The nipped-in waist was nicely judged to balance this with the gentle swell of her hips.

The two men were talking animatedly as they approached her. She heard the shorter one say, "I don't buy that, Marc. Why in hell would the guy want to tip you off that the fight was rigged if he was in some way behind the attempts?"

"I don't know," Dean replied. "But for my money he shows up just a little too damned often at the scene of the crime."

"He's a journalist, but."

"So he says. That doesn't stop him being my number-one suspect." Dean stopped as they came up to the girl, smiled, and said, "Good morning. May I present my associate, Mr. Hammer. Sean, this is Mademoiselle Laurence Chateauroux."

Laurence held out her hand. "I didn't expect to see you here today," she said to Dean.

"I didn't expect to be here." He looked around him. Apart from a group of De'Ath's mechanics standing by the rolled-back doors, they were alone in the huge hangar. "Unfortunately, however," he said in a low voice, "somebody seems to be onto us."

"Onto us?"

"Aware of our plans—and determined to wreck them."

She frowned. "But that's impossible! How could they possibly know? How could anyone? I don't believe it."

"Unfortunately it's true. Somebody at any rate is trying quite hard to stop me carrying out my part of the bargain—or anything else." Briefly he told her about the two attempts on his life and the faked-up fight in the hotel on the first day of the circus. "I wouldn't have paid the fight any mind," he added, "if we hadn't been told that the man had been paid to stage it. What complicates things is that the guy who tipped us off to that is himself a suspect."

"But this is . . . it's crazy," Laurence said. "The first day? You realize what that means?"

He nodded. "Sure. It means they knew about the offer before I did. Our rendezvous was for the second day. The fight was meant to stop me keeping it. Once they knew I'd seen you —and they'd guessed I would accept the offer—they weren't content just to put me out of action: they tried to kill me."

"Somebody sure hates the idea of that school closing down," said Hammer.

"It doesn't make sense," Laurence said. "Our security is a hundred percent. I cannot see how *anyone* could . . . I mean, not before . . ." She broke off and shook her head in astonishment.

"It's just another hazard," Dean said. "Something else that has to be watched. You know. That's what we're paid for, after all."

"Yes. But it must be attended to. I will pass the information on to . . . our principals . . . at once. There must be a leak. They will find it and take action. What shall you do in the meantime?"

"Carry on as planned," said Dean.

"Is there anything else I can do for you?"

He grinned. "As it happens, there is. May I ask an indiscreet question? Do you by any chance come from Martinique?"

"Guadaloupe."

"Ah. A French island, just the same."

She stared at him, puzzled. "Yes. But why . . . ?"

"Don't you find you miss the exotic island atmosphere sometimes? The freedom? The summer sea under blue skies?"

"I suppose. Sometimes. I still don't quite see . . . ?"

"I was just wondering," Dean said innocently, "if you would care to spend a few days on another French island? On Corsica, to be exact."

"A few days . . . ?"

"I have to make a reconnaissance in depth. The best cover on a vacation island is to be a vacationer. Preferably one of a couple."

She hesitated. And then suddenly the wide mouth—she was wearing very dark lipstick—the wide mouth smiled. Her eyes sparkled. "Why not?" she exclaimed. "After all, it's my mission too! One condition, though: the couple must have separate rooms."

"What modern couple doesn't?" said Dean.

5

Sean Hammer

Sometime before Marcus Dean read the advertisement in the *Herald Tribune*, he had been involved, together with Sean Hammer and a number of other mercenaries, in a skirmish with Soviet security forces in the Baltic. The defecting scientist they had been hired to spirit away to Sweden was safely removed from Russia—but Dean's trusted lieutenant had left a leg behind after a direct hit on the power boat they were using for their getaway.

It was two months now since Hammer had begun to walk on his artificial leg, but the pronounced limp he still displayed was not so much due to the difficulties of equilibrium and reeducation (the amputation had been above the knee) as to the weight of the false limb itself. It was Hammer's own idea: it had come to him in a Stockholm hospital, watching a television replay of *The Day of the Jackal*. In that movie the gunman had passed through stringent police checks disguised as a one-legged army veteran, using the barrel of a specially made collapsible rifle as a supposed pegleg. In fact, Hammer knew, it was impossible to strap the lower part of a leg up tightly enough behind you to fool anything but a film camera or the reader of a novel. However loose the clothing, the telltale bulge of a foot would show behind or from the side. But for a man who no longer *had* the lower part of one leg, it occurred to him, there should be distinct possibilities.

Once out of hospital, he had arranged a conference between an orthopedic surgeon, himself, and Gaston Jammot, the Belgian arms specialist who supplied Dean with the hardware for most of his operations. As a result of this meeting, and several subsequent encounters for tryouts and modifications, Hammer's lightweight artificial leg became heavier by several pounds because of certain components inside the aluminum casing. These included a tiny cylindrical, transistorized radio transmitter/receiver; a plastic grenade; a Dural-framed burp gun firing .22-caliber high-velocity rounds on the principle of the Armalite AR-5 survival rifle; and several other more sophisticated devices that it would be useful for a man in his profession to hide. For long-range work, the calf part of the leg could be detached from ankle and knee joints and screwed to the gun frame as a shoulder stock.

In the middle of the afternoon, on the day that Dean's brakes had been sabotaged, he went back to Hall's Hotel and prepared to check out. Dean had flown off to Chicago with Laurence and the man Maurice Duclos, to finalize the business side of the Corsican project.

The hotel was gloomier than ever. Now that the circus folks had left, it was practically deserted. The people of Joinville Falls were still busy in their shops and offices. If the police were investigating a midnight murder attempt by a mysterious foreign-looking stranger, they were keeping their inquiries within the station house. Perhaps, Hammer thought, they didn't relish the idea of getting those dude uniforms wet: the rain, pelting ceaselessly down, was bouncing high off the empty sidewalks.

In the hotel bar, two salesmen were exchanging whispered telephone numbers over their beer. The only other customer was Jason Mettner, staring pensively at a bourbon on the rocks. He looked up as Hammer limped in. "Hi! No aftereffects from the smashup, I hope? Visitor Cheats Death in Mystery Wreck. Rented Car Runs Amok on Heartbreak Hill. Sit down. What'll be it? You can help me celebrate."

Hammer lowered himself into a chair. "Thanks. A rye-and-dry, I guess. What are we celebrating?"

"Thursday," Mettner said lugubriously. "Like the hippopotamus in the story."

"How's that?"

"Forget it," the newspaperman murmured. "The story dates from my old man's epoch. 'I grow old, I grow old. I shall wear the bottoms of my trousers rolled.'"

Hammer stared at him.

Mettner swung around in his chair and called to the bartender, "Set 'em up, Joe. The same again, and a rye-and-dry."

For a few minutes they talked about the circus, and about the driving skill Dean had displayed in averting a fatal crash. Then Mettner looked straight at Hammer and said, "It was sabotage, of course?"

"Marc thinks you should know," Hammer said.

"What!" For once Mettner's rather weary voice was explosive.

"Tell you what," said Hammer, "I missed out on lunch . . ."

"Me too, as it happens. But what—?"

". . . so why don't we finish these and go swallow a sandwich someplace? Maybe even here they could—"

"Kitchen's closed, sir," the barkeep's voice said behind them. "Dining room opens again at seven-thirty P.M."

"That's what I thought." Hammer said. He laid a hand on the journalist's arm, jerked his head toward the door. "What say we get outta here? There's some kind of a diner right across the street, beside the rooming house where—"

"That's okay by me," Mettner said. "But just tell me—"

"Later." Hammer pushed himself upright and headed for the door.

The diner was almost empty too, but there were shaded red lights on the wall, and in comparison with the hotel, even the rose-colored reflections in the puddles beneath the brass rail at the foot of the counter looked inviting. They ate scrambled eggs and bacon, with kidneys and mushrooms, washed down with tall glasses of beer. "All right," Mettner said when their order had been served, "suppose you tell me what the hell you meant by that remark."

"Dean figures you showed up too often for coincidence during the past three days. He's seen your face at the scene of both murder attempts, at the rigged fight—and it seems you were standing near him at the airfield clubhouse during a certain conversation."

"Do you believe that tags me a guilty man?"

"Would I be sittin' here talkin' to you if I did?"

"I guess not."

"The point is, himself does. Or at least half does. To make things easier all round, is there anythin' you could tell me . . . any way you could explain these coincidences? Any way you could convince your man? Sure it's a hard thing, askin' a fella to prove his innocence, but . . ."

Mettner sighed. "If I want to get any farther with my own

job, I better come clean. I'm going to trust you, Mr. Hammer, and take you into my confidence."

Hammer swallowed a mouthful of beer. "Fire away, son."

"The fact is, those were *not* coincidences. Your friend's right, at least in part: there was a reason for me to be in those places, at those times—though not the reason Dean supposes."

"All right," Hammer said. "Lay it on me."

Mettner said, "The truth is that I . . . overheard . . . Dean's discussion with the colored French chick. I know she was acting as a front for some organization that wants Dean to liquidate some kind of terrorist-training college on Corsica."

"Jaysus! But you're not . . . ?"

"I am a newspaperman, Mr. Hammer. But I like to think I'm a responsible newspaperman. And the news review I work for is responsible too. You're afraid that I'll blow the story and fuck up the whole deal, aren't you?"

"It had crossed my mind," Hammer said dryly.

"You already had one offer in the past three days," Mettner said. "Here's another. I've been hanging in, sticking to you two guys like a leech, trying to figure out from the evidence who could be aiming to stop you—who apart from the terrorists themselves, that is, because these attempts don't smell to me like a terrorist M.O. So far, I haven't come up with anything. I haven't written anything, either."

Mettner paused to light a cigarette. "Smoke?"

Hammer shook his head, reaching into his pocket for a stick of gum.

"Let me make this clear," Mettner said. "There's a good story in this so far. But not a great story. Also—here's where you stand by for the responsible number—I'm against the spread of this urban-guerrilla, down-with-democracy, terrorist routine. I think it's a great idea, smashing this school, if it exists. I'd hate to write anything that could foul up that operation."

"But?"

"But like I said, I'm a newspaperman."

Hammer was chewing. "You mentioned an offer," he said conversationally.

"Okay. I'll continue to file no story—provided you give me your word that as soon as the job's done I'll get a world exclusive: the full inside story, with interviews, quotes, every-

44

thing. And that you'll keep in touch and tip me off when that time arrives."

"Marc Dean don't like any kind of publicity," Hammer said.

"I don't have to use his real name. Commander X." Mettner leaned against the back of the booth and blew smoke into the air.

Hammer sucked his teeth. "I'd have to check with him," he said, "but I think you got yourself a deal. You wouldn't be expectin' us to kick in with an itinerary and a battle plan as well, would you?"

"I would not. So long as you accept the fact that I might decide to take a Corsican vacation in the near future."

"I guess we can't stop you," Hammer said.

"Swell. Let me know as soon as you get Dean's okay, and I'll stay clammed up until the end of the story. Oh . . . and if I happen upon something of interest myself, of course I'll pass it along."

Hammer nodded. "What do you aim to do right now?"

"Now? I was figuring on a short visit to police headquarters and an informal chat with the boss man. He doesn't need to know that I'm not going to publish anything in the immediate future—and it'll all be good background color when the full story gets written later."

"You hope," Hammer said with a crooked smile. He got to his feet and held out his hand. "If you're on the paper's time, working up a story, you can pick up the check and charge it to expenses!"

He limped back through the downpour to the hotel. Now that he knew Mettner would be safely out of the way for some time, he could play out the final act of the personal investigation he had decided to make that day.

After a visit to the men's room involving the temporary removal of his aluminum leg, he went back to the bar. The place, as he had expected, was empty. The bartender was polishing glasses behind the counter. He was a big man, with black curling hair and a low forehead. "Bar's closed until six," he said briefly.

"Hotel resident," Hammer said. "You can serve me anytime, day or night."

The man gave a theatrical sigh. "What do you want?"

"Tequila and lime," Hammer said, having noted already

that neither of those drinks was on display among the bottles racked behind the bar.

"Jesus! I don't even know . . . I'll have to go take a look."

"I ain't in a hurry," Hammer said genially.

With a long-suffering air, the barman turned and went into the stillroom. Hammer was right behind him. He kicked the door shut. In his left hand he held a small blue bottle stoppered with a rubber cap. His right hand was fisted over a flat bar of metal, from which a long, thin, needle-sharp spike protruded between the knuckles of his forefinger and middle finger.

The barman swung around, scowling. "What the fuck d'you think you're doin', Mac? Get outta here before I bust you one—"

"What do you think this is?" Hammer interrupted. He plunged the spike through the rubber diaphragm and withdrew it, glistening with fluid. "Hydrocyanic acid. Plain cyanide, if you like. One scratch from this needle, a single drop in your bloodstream, and you're a dead man within seconds."

"Christ!" the barman said. There was strong smell of almonds in the air. He backed away. "Are you crazy or somethin'? You wanna be careful—"

"Very careful indeed," Hammer snarled. He moved forward, feinting toward the barman's hand with the wet needle. "You can't knock it out of my hand because it's attached to this bar; you dare not try to hit me, because I could still scratch you, however hard you hit."

The man had snatched his hand away. He was backed up against a counter supporting kegs of beer and sherry and port. Hammer leaned toward him and advanced the spike until it touched the skin of his neck, just below the chin. The bartender's eyes opened wide. A rash of sweat dewed his low forehead. He swallowed, trying desperately not to move his lower jaw. "What . . . you want?" he croaked through clenched teeth. "Till . . . behind bar."

"I don't want money, I want information." Hammer pressed very lightly, so that the needle point pricked the quivering skin. "All right," he said as the bartender froze, "who did you call last night when Marc Dean and his wife left the bar? And who told you to tip them off?"

"Don't know . . . what you mean," the bartender groaned.

Hammer increased the pressure until the top layer of skin

46

broke. *"No!"* the man screamed. "Don't . . . I . . . they'll kill me."

"Who?"

Hammer pricked harder. The bartender was at the point of collapse. "It's . . . Frankie Klein," he choked. "Frankie said there'd be . . . century in it for me if I . . . phoned across . . . road."

"Who's Frankie Klein?" Hammer released the pressure fractionally to allow the man to speak. "Who was across the road?"

"Frankie's a Syndicate collector. For the numbers. The . . . I don't know the other guy's name, honest. He's . . . an enforcer, a contract man . . . from Montreal, Frankie said."

"What's his name?" An infinitesimal increase in pressure.

"I don't *know!*" the man shouted. "Oh, Christ! Leave me *alone!*"

"Very well. And if you breathe a single word of this to Frankie—or anyone else—I'll be back."

"No, no, no! No. Honest to God. I promise. They'd kill me."

Hammer nodded, satisfied. He backed slowly away, hooked his artificial foot around the door, opened it, and retreated into the bar. The bartender fell to his knees and vomited into a bucket beneath one of the kegs.

Back in the washroom, Hammer replaced the spike knuckle-duster inside his hollow leg and flushed the almond oil from the bottle down one of the handbasins. He tossed the blue bottle in the bin along with the used paper towels and then checked out of the hotel.

Before he left his room, he rolled down his sock and twisted a small knob that appeared to be part of the aluminum ankle articulation but was in reality an on-off switch for the tiny wire recorder that worked with the radio in the magic leg.

He just had time to make the post office before he caught the train for Toronto. The cable he sent to Dean read:

METTNER CLEARED BARKEEP GUILTY SYNDICATE CONTRACT JOB CONTRACTOR UNKNOWN STOP EVIDENCE IN HAND STOP HAMMER

II

Scorpion

It may take a little time to get into your stride, but later happenings make up for an earlier setback or difficulty. Your plans go forward and will bring surprises, useful contacts, and probably an unexpected gain.

—Leon Petulengro, astrologer

6

Marc Dean

Tourists, Dean reasoned, as a rule concentrated on pleasure beaches, marinas, panoramic beauty spots, and sites which were of either historic or aesthetic interest. If he was going believably to spend any time in what was accepted to be the least picturesque part of the island, therefore, he would need to pose as something more than the typical gaping vacationer. The obvious thing, it seemed to him, was to pretend a passion for geology. Most of the region he wanted to prospect, after all, was bare rock. Yet a glance at a specialized map showed him the improbability of this: the Desert of Agriates was unrelieved granite; in other parts of the island there were schists and gneiss and porphyries and ancient sedimentary rocks—enough variety to absorb the most blasé geologist; but some extra interest was needed to validate a concentration on this barren northern zone. Mineralogy was the answer, he thought. Accordingly there were rock specimens, bottles of different reagents, slides, and one or two illustrated textbooks along with the geological hammer in the stout burlap knapsack that he carried. His hair had been darkened, straightened, and brushed forward. He had grown a mustache. He wore large shell-rim spectacles with plain glass lenses—and to complete the picture of an unworldly, unmodern academic, he was dressed in brown corduroy pants, a checkered shirt, and open-toed sandals with oatmeal-colored wool socks.

Laurence, not without reason, was proud of the persona she had invented to complement this scientific nonentity. Her hair was center-parted and hung down on either side of her face, which was innocent of makeup. Her eyes were hidden behind jumbo-size sunglasses. Above a mauve dirndl skirt that was unfashionably long, she wore a printed Indian top hung about with so many necklaces and beads and chains and medallions it was impossible to see that her splendid breasts were unsupported.

"There's only one thing I regret," she told Dean, lacing the black string of her espadrilles while they waited at Nice for their flight to Calvi to be called. "I didn't have enough time to let the hair on my legs grow."

"I'll try to survive," Dean said.

From 29,000 feet, jade green across the wrinkled blue sheet of the Mediterranean, Corsica could almost be one of the Pacific isles, or a more civilized member of the East Indian archipelago—crescents of white-fringed sand backed by conical tree-covered hills rising to ridge after ridge of blue mountains in the interior. Even planing down to the single 2,500-yard runway of Ste. Cathérine airfield, Dean felt that stir of excitement at the approach of the exotic experienced by travelers arriving in Tahiti, Papua, or Samoa. It was only when the minibus ferrying them to the center passed through the outskirts that it became evident this could be nothing but European.

Calvi lay at the western extremity of a 2½-mile curve of pleasure beaches, its outer ring of modern buildings and tall, shallow-roofed apartment houses clustered around a rocky spur topped by the towering thirteenth-century citadel. The huge stone bastions of this complex, rising more than one hundred feet from the water on the seaward side, sheltered a small domed cathedral, a military barracks garrisoned by a company of Foreign Legion parachutists, and the narrow, steep, shadowed lanes of the original medieval city. On the far side of the bay, beyond rows of pines bordering the sandy shore, a long, low granite spit only partly covered with scrub thrust into the Mediterranean. And inland the 7,000-foot summits of Mts. Grosso, Corona, and Cinto heaved themselves into a cloudless sky.

Dean and Laurence sat at a sidewalk café waiting for the package-tour coach that was to take them to St. Florent. It was late afternoon and there were long shadows across the square at the end of the street. Although they were more than halfway through September, it was still very warm.

The girl stared at the pleasure boats ranged on the ink-blue surface of the sea and then up at the frowning fortress walls. "When Maurice says this place of Nessim's is impregnable," she mused, "I hope for your sake he doesn't have anything like that in mind!"

Dean smiled and shook his head. The mustache, glasses, and brushed-forward hair made him look almost benign. "Those walls were built to keep out centuries of seaborne attacks by Saracens, Moors, Genoese, the French, the British, bands of roving pirates. That's why the place couldn't be anything but European: you don't get that kind of sophisticated fortification against heavy, organized assault in tropical countries where there's no history of invasion and conquest, or wars of religion and succession. Nessim's defenses are more sophisticated still—but it's a matter of electronic alerts rather than unscalable walls. At least, that's what Duclos says. I sure hope so: you can get around computerized gadgetry with the right kind of hardware; but I wouldn't have a hope in hell, with the limited punch I can command, of storming a citadel like that. Not without a regiment of artillery or missles with air support!"

"Thank you, Professor," Laurence said. "I think that's our coach on the far side of the square."

They had booked on a tourist package because that seemed the most anonymous way of going where they wanted to go without arousing suspicion. Dean had, however, arranged with the travel agency in Nice that they could stop off at St. Florent ("There is a quantity of fascinating felspars, pegmatites—chalcedony and jasper too—in the region") and rejoin another party organized by the same company two days later. Their companions appeared to be mainly Dutch, German, and northern French—most of whom were complimenting themselves on the money they had saved by waiting until after the high season. The conversation in the coach revolved at first entirely around the cost of living and was not at all connected with the physical qualities of the region eulogized by the uniformed blond preaching into her microphone as she stood in the aisle behind the driver.

From Calvi they took the national Route 197, which turned inland through the orchards and olive groves of the undulating coastal region known as the Balagna. Sometimes, below and to their left, they caught glimpses of the astounding blue of the sea—though most of the creeks and inlets were disfigured by campsites, trailer parks, and "vacation villages" whose cheap-jack chalets had proliferated like fungi among the scrub. Only Algajola—a web of arcaded streets beneath a small fort—had retained its dignity as a holiday resort.

After the curiously named Ile Rousse ("Red because of the rocks, ladies and gentlemen," the guide intoned, "but not really an island, it was founded in 1758 by Pascal Paoli to rival Calvi, which was too Genoese for his taste"), the railroad which had been running beside them all the way veered toward the interior, the road narrowed, and soon they were winding northeastward between the ocean and a range of low hills covered in scrub. Almond trees, fig trees, vines, and properties farming citrus fruits were left behind; there were no more houses. "Here," the blond girl told them, pointing to lines of breakers creaming into a sandy bay, "is Peraiola Beach—the last time we look at the sea before we reach the Gulf of St. Florent."

"But, miss, there's the whole of the northern coast!" one of the Dutch tourists protested. "Is there no way—?"

"There is no road," she said firmly. "In any case, there is nothing to look at: the area is a desert."

"Nothing to look at?" Dean said to Laurence in a low voice. "That's all she knows!"

The Domaine de Murenzana, they had been told, lay between two hamlets named Salone and San Pancraziu, no more than five miles from St. Florent. What they hadn't been told, first, was that although a great deal of the Desert of Agriates was naked rock, there were also large tracts covered by stunted trees; second, that the Murenzana property was adjacent to a Foreign Legion artillery range.

The first they knew of this was when they felt, rather than heard, a shattering concussion, followed by a second and then two more. The coach lurched slightly and the big wraparound panoramic window in back vibrated in its frame.

"Surely there cannot be a thunderstorm?" one of the Germans inquired, craning his head to look up into the clear sky above the mountains in the center of the island.

"No, no," the guide said. "It is just the guns."

"The guns?"

"*Le champ de tir de Casta*. A restricted military area. They try out new weapons—and improve their aim with the old ones. At least that is the theory. There is a range on either

54

side of the road: about two miles long between here and the sea cliffs; five or six in the direction of the interior."

The German stared out the window. Now they could see the high fence and the red-and-white warning notices surmounted by a skull-and-crossbones on either side of the road. "I hope their aim does not require too much improvement!" he said as another explosion shook the vehicle.

"Pretty smart of Nessim," Dean commented to the girl. "To buy up land next to forbidden military ground. Any firing his students do will be put down to the Legion boys. I was wondering how they explained away the noise."

It was also pretty smart—he discovered when they returned to the place on the following day—from the point of view of privacy. From the road to the cliff edge, the eastern side of the wedge-shaped Nessim tract was bounded by the artillery range. The long northern boundary was the sea. That left would-be intruders the choice of a narrow frontage bordering the road or a five-mile ridge of weathered granite that rose to a height of more than 1,200 feet and was known in the region as Mt. Genova.

Because it was the most difficult, Dean chose to prospect the ridge forming the western flank of the property first. They had been unable to rent an automobile in St. Florent: the most the local *garagiste* could offer was a pair of bicycles. Climbing slowly up into the foothills along departmental Route 81 was therefore a slow business: half the time, the grades were steep enough to force them to push their machines. But by midmorning they had passed the artillery-range warning signs and approached San Pancraziu—a collection of tumbledown houses, half of them abandoned and the rest patched up with their roof tiles held down by football-sized rocks. Dean persuaded an old man in faded blue coveralls to serve them a glass of wine on a bench outside one of the cabins. "One says," he observed conversationally, "that an Arab gentleman has bought land and constructed an imposing property not far from here?"

"Gentleman?" the old man echoed. "He doesn't even buy any of his supplies from St. Florent: he has everything delivered by the big shops in Bastia. Work is scarce around here, yet he imported foreign laborers for almost everything." He spit into the dusty road. "Such people would not have been permitted in the days of my father. Mule tracks and footpaths across the desert—trails we have been using all our lives—are now closed to us. There are wire fences and men with guns. Like all of the very rich, I think this Arab must be a very frightened man."

"That must be most distressing for you," Dean sympathized. "And most unfair. After all, what harm could it do . . . ?"

"There is the sound of shooting," the old man said. "Some say they are making a motion picture; others that the shots are fired by *légionnaires*. But how could the *képis-blancs* continue to operate weapons down here when they have been taken back to their barracks in trucks, tell me that?"

"I believe the entrance is between here and Salone?"

"Nearer to Salone. Much nearer. The men of Salone worked on the stonework of the gates," the old man said, as if that explained every infamy that Nessim had committed.

"There's your actual backwoods peasant mentality," Dean said as they pedaled away. "No wonder this was the country that invented the vendetta. You know how far away that unknown enemy territory of Salone is? Less than two miles!"

"But the vendetta thing no longer exists, surely?"

"Only as a legend to give pleasurable shivers to the tourists. The vendetta today is against France and the French officials who make laws and prevent the Corsican's running their own country."

"Then if this man Nessim had any sense, he would get the country people on his side, rather than make them angry— pretend his school would in some way help them in their struggle for independence."

"Who knows how many Corsican separatists there may not be on his class list?" Dean said grimly.

Murenzana was up an unpaved cart track that twisted away from the road between the shoulders of two steep hills. The valley was densely wooded, with holm oaks and pines and neglected olive trees. There was a large notice warning the public in French, Italian, and German that the property was private and patrolled, and that trespassers ventured farther at their own risk. But from the road it was not possible to see any stone gates—or indeed any sign of habitation at all. Beyond the hamlet of Salone, which was smaller and even more dilapidated that San Pancraziu, the road turned south and from the corner they could see the bleached granite ridge stretching away northward toward the sea.

It was a perfect natural barrier, a continuous row of near-vertical escarpments, broken only occasionally by steep-sided gullies zigzagging down the bare rock faces. Along the foot of the cliffs a narrow torrent frothed between stony banks.

"Christ!" Dean said, braking the bicycle to a halt and resting one foot on the road. "I wouldn't like to storm that baby with a squadron of armored cars!"

They dismounted and leaned their machines against a drystone wall. The road was deserted in each direction. Dean was unarmed, but he carried a powerful pair of Zeiss field glasses. Leaning his eblows on top of the wall, he scanned the barren, scrub-covered wilderness between them and the ridge. The electrified fence emerged from a ragged wood half a mile away and climbed toward the summit. "The son of a bitch has been smart enough to buy the right amount of land," he observed, adjusting the focus wheel with his middle finger. "That fence runs along the downslope, twenty yards on *this* side of the crest—so there isn't a hope in hell of checking out what goes on the far side."

"You could see from a helicopter," Laurence said.

"Oh, sure. You got any friends around here that keep a chopper in their backyard?"

"Yes, I have," she said coolly. "Not right here, but not too far away. The trouble is, it would take several days to organize—at least in a way that wouldn't risk a lot of gossip in the wrong places."

He stared at her. "I'm sorry," he said. "Truly. I should have known. Can you lay one on, then? Please?"

Laurence smiled. "As soon as we get to a phone. There seems to be some sort of a track heading for the riverbed. Do you want to play geologist awhile?"

He shrugged. "We're not going to find out a damned thing east or west. Until your chopper's available, the valley entrance at night—or maybe the sea by day—is our only chance of learning anything." He squinted his eyes against the sun and looked up at the ridge. "Still . . . we better keep up the cover roles, stay here the two days as planned—and, yes, maybe wander into the desert some and chip a few rocks. Even if we can't see anything, it'll give us a chance of finding out how much *they* can see."

It took longer than they thought to reach the riverbed. The weathered granite outliers were crumbly and rotten, sometimes powdering away into crystals at their feet. And between the rocks there were fissures full of thorn brush and spiky, dried herbs. In half an hour they were both panting and drenched in sweat. And Dean had seen—twice, from different positions along the ridge—the telltale flash of sunlight on the lenses of binoculars.

"They have the whole damned perimeter outposted, by the look of it," he said. "There may be electronic surveillance nearer the fortress, but right here the guards are human, and I'd lay money on the fact that I saw the light gleaming on something pretty tough—a bazooka or an antitank gun or something like that—last time I had the glasses on them."

"Will these men stay on guard all night, do you think?"

"Or will they be replaced by infrared scanners? We shall see," Dean said. He took out the geological hammer—it was shaped like a coal hammer, with one blunt and one chisel end to the head—and made a pretense of chipping away rock specimens in several places. Then they returned to the bicycles and rode back toward the cart track that led to the entrance.

The gates were around a curve in the valley—massive fifteen-foot wrought-iron barriers hung from solid masonry posts, with a stone wall running away in either direction. Evidently the men of Salone had worked well. Ten yards inside the wall, bristling once more with warning notices, was the chain fence. Beyond it, a paved driveway curved out of sight between the trees—and there was still no sign of any buildings.

Dean dismounted neatly beside the gates. On the far side of the iron bars a swarthy man of about forty stood cradling a Uzi submachine gun. "Good morning," Dean said. "I am a subscribing member of the Washington-Arab Association, and I wondered if perhaps—"

"Piss off!" said the guard. His voice was not friendly.

Dean raised his eyebrows. "If I might be permitted to view the rock formations on your side of the Mt. Genova ridge," he pursued. "There are some interesting igneous extrusions that might—"

"We don't like snoopers here. On your way, buster." The guard was heavily mustached and his eyes were hard. "Can't you read?" he added. "This is private property."

"In the cause of science, most owners of private property ... In any case, I am not *on* your property."

"You're on our property as soon as you leave the road. Now, will you—?"

"My good man," Dean interrupted in what he hoped was

an autocratic, professorial voice. "I am not in the habit of bandying words with employees. Be off and fetch the owner at once: I will make my request to him directly. A person named Nessim, if I am not mistaken."

The guard compressed his lips. He snapped his fingers twice. Two Doberman pinschers loped into view from somewhere behind the wall, and stood beside him with fangs bared. "If you're not out of sight around that bend in a quarter of a minute, I'm going to open the gates and set the dogs on you," he threatened.

Dean tutted in feigned anger and turned to Laurence. "Come, Judith," he said. "I can see we shall get no further here. I shall contact Herr Nessim by other means."

The guard unslung his gun and moved toward the gate. Dean remounted hastily and shepherded the girl back toward the road. Just before they rode around the curve, he said in a loud voice, "Ignorant fellow! I suppose you can't expect any better from these Arabs."

Laurence looked at him curiously as they pedaled up the rise in the direction of San Pancraziu. "Judith!" she said. "You could have spared me that!" And then: "Did you have to make that last remark? Even if the man was rude? You're not usually racist, are you?"

"Only when I'm mad," Dean said.

But his ill humor was not entirely due to the guard's insolence or to the fact that they been able to discover nothing of value concerning the details of Nessim's defenses. It had started the previous evening, after they arrived at St. Florent.

It was almost dark when the coach deposited them on the small square in front of the harbor. St. Florent was a small town—like many of the Corsican coastal resorts, it boasted fewer than 1,500 inhabitants—and it lay at the head of a five-mile gulf separating Cap Corse from the Desert of Agriates. In such a sheltered position, the rose-colored, white, and ocher houses, with their gray and red roofs, were able to rise straight out of the water, even on the seaward side of the L-shaped mole. On the landward side, St. Florent had been built at the confluence of two rivers, in a natural amphitheater of mountains—the granite boss that rose to the artillery range on the west, and the 4,000-foot ridge that ran the length of Cap Corse to the east. Southward, the great bulk of the Nebbio massif rose into the darkening sky.

Half the members of the tour had been lodged in a tall,

shuttered *pension* in the old town at one side of the square. Laurence and Dean, together with a dozen more Belgian and Dutch tourists, found themselves in a more modern building a little way inland, below a circular fifteenth-century Genoese fortress.

Sipping an aperitif beneath the white concrete arches of the terrace, they watched the surrounding hills darken from violet to purple. Out in the calm waters of the gulf, shrimp boats and crabbers with orange sails moved slowly toward the port. "It seems a long way from the Red Brigades and terrorist schools, doesn't it?" Laurence said.

"Not so far," Dean replied. "Not for this island. It's not like the Caribbean islands where you were born. There's a history of slavery there, and the occasional pirate stronghold; but these people have been fighting guerrilla warfare ever since the Phoenicians, the Greeks, the Romans. The Saracens and the Genoese are latecomers here. That's why the Corsicans are not really sailors or fishing folk: they've always turned away inland, hiding in the mountains to escape the plunderers who came from the ocean." And later, strolling in the warm dark after dinner, he looked up at the single-story fortress with its 360-degree embrasures, the smaller circular *lanterna* that surmounted it, and the round tower that housed the spiral staircase at one side, adding, "This place here—all the hundreds of watchtowers built around the coastline by the Genoese—they made them circular because they were designed to warn the conquerors against attacks from the interior as much as assaults from the sea."

As they turned to retrace their steps, Dean blocked her path and put his hands on her shoulders. The sky was clear and the stars exceptionally bright. In the reflected light from streetlamps illuminating the port below, the lines of her face were blurred and mysterious. Only the twin highlights of her eyes as she looked up at him betrayed the wariness of her expression. "What system do *you* use to warn against attacks from the outside?" he asked softly.

She reached up and pushed his hands away. "I make a treaty," she said. "Separate rooms, remember?"

"We have separate rooms."

"Yes—but that doesn't mean one has to stay unoccupied."

He sighed. "Baby, you're the most fabulous thing since—"

"Since your honey-blond ex-wife walked out on you, is that it?" Her voice was sharp. "I'm not a second-fiddle girl."

"There's no fiddle involved. You're beautiful. You're splendid. You can't expect me to . . . I just want you. It's that simple."

"Look, Marc: our relationship's strictly business. I thought we'd agreed to that. I don't play understudy to anyone, especially in bed."

"It's nothing to do with Sam," Dean said angrily. "I want you because—"

"You want me because it's a warm, romantic night, and you're horny, and I've got big tits," Laurence said. She pushed past him and ran down the path toward the hotel.

It was not until after their abortive bicycle trip the following day that Dean's fury abated—not because he was mad at her for refusing him; his ire was directed exclusively inward, at his own gaucheness in contriving both to offend her and to frustrate himself.

He apologized fairly handsomely over a late lunch. Afterward, they played tourist awhile and then he hired a small outboard dinghy and two sets of scuba-diving equipment. They were going, he told the boatman, to examine some of the underwater rock formations farther along the coast. It was the cliffs below the desert, rather than the strata plunging into the sea along the length of Cap Corse, that interested them—but he had heard that the new owner of the land beyond the artillery range was . . . difficult. Did the boatman think they would run into any trouble landing on any of the beaches below his property?

The Corsican laughed. "No trouble at all," he said. "Because there isn't a single place you can land anyway. There isn't a beach between Fornali, at the end of the gulf here, and the Marina di Peraldu—a creek with a lagoon behind it, just beyond Nessim's land."

"Nessim? He is the owner of the new development?"

The boatman spit into the dust. He nodded. "An Arab. Oil. They say he's rich as Croesus. But I don't know about any development: it seems he's spent several fortunes just the same. Who knows what on? You can't see a thing from outside. Even deliveries have to be left at the gates." An eloquent shrug. "Sometimes there is shooting after the range is closed. Perhaps he has installed wild animals in there."

After the coach had carried away the rest of the tourists, Dean returned the bicycles to the garage where he had rented them. Before he left, he bought one of the specialized aerosol cans, fitted with a valved tube, designed to reinflate automobile tires in case of a puncture. Laurence raised her eyebrows but said nothing. She helped him load the scuba equipment and several other packages into the boat, and he started the motor and headed out into the gulf.

The sea was calm, the air was clear, and there was a very slight breeze blowing from the west. Before they turned toward the setting sun, they stared with tourist delight themselves at the medieval fortress village of Nonza, six or seven miles away on the vertiginous coast road that circled the *cap*. Below tiny terraced gardens bright with flowers and green with the foliage of lemon trees, the houses rose straight from a black rock face that dived five hundred feet into the blue water. The cliffs below Nessim's land were lower, sometimes no more than fifty or sixty feet high, but they were equally sheer and just as unscalable. The sun had set when Dean left the tiller and busied himself with the packages lying on top of the scuba gear.

"What in God's name are you doing?" Laurence asked.

He had opened a flat cardboard box and taken out what she thought at first must be a pink inflatable cushion or a small rubber life raft. He had screwed the lead from the aerosol onto the valve. Now, as he pressed the button on top of the can, there was a hiss of compressed air and the thing slowly took shape, rising from its own folds, the creases popping as the air filled the rubber envelope.

Laurence stared as if mesmerized. She saw a painted eye, fringed with half-inch lashes, something that looked like a swollen household glove, a convex curve that gradually tautened until . . .

"Marc! Have you gone out of your mind?" she cried.

He kept on pressing, the hiss growing hollower, hoarser now, and jerked a thumb at the box. She turned it over. A lurid picture of a naked blond with a pubic triangle and improbable breasts. The words:

Inflate your (alter) ego with
FAITHFUL VIRGIE
You can let her down but she'll never let you down!
A playmate with everything you wanted but never
DARED
to ask for! Real hair.

Laurence was shaking with laughter. He was pumping up one of the life-size inflatable dolls sold to the sad men who frequent sex shops. "What the . . . ?" she gasped—but then laughter choked her again. She looked at the idiot grin on the pouting, red-lipped, half-open mouth. From the smooth rubber chest, first one and then the other breast thwacked out. When the figure was blown up tight, Dean ripped open a flat plastic package and took out a child's folded box kite.

"First childhood as well as second?" Laurence inquired.

He made no reply, assembling the square balsawood frame of the kite in the gathering dusk. As soon as the riggers were locked in position, he fashioned a rope harness to link the kite and the rubber figurine. "Would it be presumptuous," Laurence said, "to ask what the hell you're playing at?"

"Virgie is going to do a little job for us," Dean said.

"I don't know what you mean."

"It's called testing the strength of the defenses."

"I still don't—"

"Just do as I say. Be a good girl—like Virgie."

She shrugged helplessly. Under his direction, she took over the motor and opened the throttle, sending the outboard speeding along parallel to the cliffs. Dean took the spool of thin twine that came with the kite and began paying out the line, alternately hauling it in and then slackening his hold, trying to fill the kite with enough wind to get it airborne. "What we must hope for is what the delta-plane boys call a thermal," he explained. "An updraft of warm air that'll take her up to clifftop height."

"Oh, silly me!" Laurence said. "You're not so dumb after all."

For perhaps a quarter of a mile, kite and mannequin trailed along behind the boat, sometimes rising a few feet, sometimes dipping until the rubber legs kicked at the waves. They found their thermal as Laurence swung out in a wide arc to avoid a group of rocks jutting into the sea from the base of a headland. Traversing the shallow bay beyond, Dean felt a tug on the line, and the kite with its ludicrous burden rose abruptly skyward. He hauled in, paid out, tugged, slackened his grip again as the inflated figure sailed higher and higher.

Ten minutes later, she was being towed along, barely visible now in the Mediterranean twilight, level with the clifftop.

Rounding the next headland, they found that the breeze,

freshening from the west, had veered enough to carry the kite just over the edge of the rock face. Dean signaled Laurence to cut the motor. He stood up in the stern, jockeying with the line, allowing the wind to carry the kite and the mannequin farther still, keeping them bobbing a few feet above ground level, a little way in from the lip.

Suddenly there was a dazzling glare of light beyond the clifftop. Almost at once, from right and left, it was followed by the heavy stammer of large-caliber machine guns. The line went slack in Dean's hands. Immediately afterward, the light went out and the gunfire ceased.

Dean was winding in the line. There was a patter of small stones down the cliff face, a few splashes in the sea. And now, from some distance away, the sound of men shouting, question and answer. "Don't start the motor," Dean whispered. "Let her drift. If they heard us before, they probably thought it was a fishing boat, and I don't want them to know who or what the 'intruder' was." He dragged aboard the end of the line. The kite was riddled with holes; of the rubber figure, nothing remained but a few tatters of damp latex. "Sensor-actuated floodlights, followed by automatic machine gunfire directed by some kind of computer—so long as there's a body large enough to show on a screen," he said. "Most efficient." He laid the shreds of rubber on the duckboards and added, "Too bad. She was a good friend."

The current was carrying them slowly back to the east, but it was not until forty minutes later, when the puzzled shouts from the clifftop had ceased and they could see the lights of St. Florent mirrored in the dark water, that Dean started the motor and steered the dinghy back toward the harbor at the head of the gulf.

After dinner—Laurence had pleaded a headache and retired early—Dean wandered into a couple of waterfront bars and struck up conversations with the *garagiste*, the man who had rented him the boat, and one or two fishermen. But nobody seemed able—or willing—to advance any further information on Mansour Nessim and the expensive and curious establishment he was so careful to hide from prying eyes on the edge of the Desert of Agriates. There were a great number of visitors—Dean was at least able to confirm that—but it was impossible to say how long they stayed. They were collected from and returned to the international airport at Bastia in Nessim's chauffeur-driven limousines. One thing, however, was certain: they were invariably foreigners ("Not even French!" the boatman said disgustedly). None of which did any more than verify what Dean knew already.

"Short of battering down the gates with a Centurion tank and making a frontal assault," he said to himself as he walked back to the hotel, "I have to admit the damned place *is* about as difficult to get into as that citadel in Calvi!" There was, he reflected, no more he could do here now; until Laurence's helicopter arrived (presumably on secret loan from some base in France), they might as well continue their cover with the package tour, take note of communications in the other parts of the island, and liaise with Sean Hammer, who would be fact-finding in Ajaccio.

Dean climbed the stairs to his room, turned the key in the lock, opened the door, went inside . . . and froze.

The bullet-riddled box kite, dimly illuminated by the light filtering through the open window from the waterfront street-lamps, floated in the air above his bed. Beneath it, attached by an improvised rope harness, a naked figure slumped on the covers—a figure with painted eyes, a pubic triangle, and improbable breasts. Only this time the real hair wasn't blond; it was dark. This time the limbs weren't filled with air. This time it wasn't a rubber doll beneath the kite. This time it was . . .

"I can't promise I'll never let you down," Laurence said in a small voice, "but I'll try to do everything you want and in-flate your ego!"

Dean's burst of laughter shook the room. There was only one thing to say. "You *doll!*" he cried.

He unhooked the kite from the ceiling light fixture, slid the rope from her bare shoulders, and took her in his arms. "You crazy girl!" he whispered. "By Christ, this is the nicest gift Santa Claus ever unwrapped!"

She was breathing fast. Her fingers tore at the buttons of his bush shirt, unbuckled the belt at his waist. She held up her mouth and he kissed her, fiercely, almost brutally. His powerful hands cupped the firm, taut swell of those marvelous breasts, the thumbs caressing her stiff nipples. She had fallen back on the bed, pulling him on top of her. Her cool fingers slid pants and slip down past his lean hips, over the muscled curve of his buttocks. "Marc!" she choked. "Oh, Marc—take me now!"

For Dean after that there was nothing but sensation—the

65

hot clasp of flesh and the graze of hair, the fingers clenching on his shoulders, the delirious moist sliding of skin upon skin, the resilence of breast and belly and the warm breath at his ear. They came together as conclusively as an iron bar and a magnet. It could have been a minute; it could have been an hour. All he knew was that it was in another time and another place that at last he dared to ask sleepily, "But, honey, my splendid darling . . . why tonight?"

"And not last night?" Laurence nipped the lobe of his ear between her teeth. "I don't like to be taken for granted, that's why."

Dean was still wondering if he would ever understand the mind of a woman when they came in through the window.

There were four or five of them—he would never be able to say exactly. His brain had only just registered that there were intruders in the room when the edge of a hand, hard as a plank, chopped down on his neck at the base of the skull, and a fist slammed with murderous force into his back just above his left kidney.

He was half out on his feet when they pulled him off the bed retching for breath. Dimly he heard Laurence scream—and then cry out in pain as knuckles thudded into her naked flesh. He was striking out right and left, even in his semiconscious state landing blows that hurt and could cripple. But he was naked, dazed, and in the half-dark—and he was outnumbered by fresh opponents who were not only clothed but wore boots as well. Gradually he was beaten to the ground, and then they put the boot in. Through a red mist of pain, he heard the girl scream again . . . then something long and heavy glinted in the faint light, and the world spun away in a long, cold silence.

The first thing he was aware of when he regained consciousness was the odor of pitch: it was underlaid with the smells of fish, cheap tobacco, sweat, and hot candlewax. The next sensation signaled to his brain was cold: he was still naked. But both of these were swamped by agonizing pain as memory returned.

His whole body throbbed. His head ached abominably: his ribs, his kidneys, his face, and his genitals sent knives scything into his guts each time he drew breath. In addition to that, his jaw felt as if it was broken.

Warily, experimentally, he flexed muscles and made certain deductions. He was bound hand and foot with rough hempen rope and strapped to a plank that seemed to be laid between two trestles. The weight of his body on the hands bound behind his back was cutting the circulation and giving him cramp. The pain at the hinges of his jaw was due to a tennis ball that had been jammed into his mouth, forcing it open almost to the point of dislocation and effectively gagging him.

There were four or five men standing around the trestles—indistinct figures whose shadows undulated across wooden walls in the wavering light of three candles set on a crate near the head of the plank.

One of the men moved forward. Dean caught his breath as a rough hand seized his penis and testicles. "We're going to hurt you a little"—the other hand reached for one of the candles—"just to show that we mean business. When you've had enough and you can't stand any more, nod your head. Then, if you're lucky, we may take the ball out, and you can tell us what you're doing here, and who sent you, and why. If we ain't satisfied with your answers, back goes the ball and we hurt you some more. There's plenty of candles."

Even as the flame approached—even later, when the threshing of his bound body was making the plank bounce on the trestles—Dean's principal reaction was one of bewilderment. The torturer was speaking in heavily accented French. Earlier, during the fight in the hotel room and as he fought to dispel the mists of unconsciousness in here, he had heard them communicating in Corsican *patois*. That could mean only one thing.

These were not Nessim's men. He must be in the hands of some third party—presumably associates of people who had twice tried to murder him in Canada.

7

Jason Mettner

Naturally, of course, I heard the noise. Who wouldn't have?

I'll tell you: the *patron*, the desk clerk, the night porter, the kitchen staff, the chambermaids, and all the other guests staying at the Hotel Miramar, St. Florent. Too bad the package-tour guys and gals had left: not being Corsican, some of them *might* have registered the odd scream, the stamp of feet, or the sound of a two-hundred-pound bureau being overturned, and that at least would have saved it being a love game. As it was, nobody heard a thing; I was out of my mind; it must have been some other hotel; it was nine other guys. Zero.

I said a love game. That's what it looked like, too, when I kicked in the door of Dean's room and switched on the light. Laurence Chateauroux was lying on her back, sprawled across the bed. She was naked. She had a split lip, a black eye, and a gash in her forearm from which the blood was still running. The reddened patches covering her belly and breasts were already turning into purple bruises. "Jesus!" I said. "I knew he was a macho lover, but this is ridiculous!"

She was sobbing. "They took him," she cried. "There was nothing I could . . . It was so unexpected. They must have . . . through the window."

The window was still open. The drapes blew slowly out into the room and then subsided. The ladder was still against the wall outside. Considering the number of decibels involved, there wasn't too much to see: the upended desk, a chair overturned, a few splashes of blood. I picked a light-weight quilt off the floor and put it around her shoulders, taking care not to touch those savaged breasts. I have to stop myself saying any more about them: this piece carries an R certificate.

She looked up then and the one eye she could still use widened. "You again!" she gasped. "How do you . . . what are *you* doing here, for God's sake?"

I told her what I was doing there. Now I'll tell you.

I'd arrived, you see, toward the end of the evening . . . in a cab from the airport at Bastia, and at a price that was going to make the *Worldwide* accounting department call in the reanimation service when they received my expense account. Laurence had gone to bed (you can say that again); Dean was apparently out, the desk clerk told me. I'd been traveling all day and I needed a bath and shave before I faced the nightlife of St. Florent in the hope of contacting what Hammer would call your man.

In my baggage I always carry an electric razor with a plug at the end of the lead that is marked "Universal—Will fit any socket in any country in the world." Correction. When they come to put out the Mark II version, they'll have to add: "except the socket in the bathroom of Room 34 in the Hotel Miramar at St. Florent, Corsica."

Finally I found that if I unplugged the bedside lamp on the night table and moved the divan to one side, there was a socket that would take it in the baseboard at the foot of the wall. I was lying on my back on the floor, with my head under the night table, shaving, when they came for Dean. The razor doesn't make much more noise than a low-flying DC-10, but I didn't hear the sounds of conflict until I switched off at about 3:15 from my newshawk's nose. Even then there was a portion of chin still stubbly. But the evidence of battle was so pronounced at this point that it could hardly be ignored (except by the *patron*, the desk clerk, the night porter, et cetera, et cetera). By the time I'd finished quietening the girl and looked up at the open doorway, the passageway outside was about as crowded as the fireworks counter at Macy's on the fifteenth of July. Not one single goddamn soul was standing on tippytoes, trying to see over the heads, asking: What happened? What happened? To me that could only mean one thing, but I'll come back to that later.

Meanwhile the girl had pulled herself together enough to ask not only what I was doing there, but how come I got there in the first place. Why St. Florent?

The answer was too simple: because St. Florent was the nearest town to this guy Nessim's hideout with a hotel that was listed in the Michelin guide. But since Dean already suspected I was in some way connected with the assaults on his person (this was the fourth, after all) . . . and since I'd happened to show up inconveniently soon after all of them . . . and since this appeared to be Dean's girl now . . . well, I figured a more detailed explanation would be in order. Of course I didn't spill it all to her right away: the important thing was to go chase up the guys who'd abducted Dean. But you might as well have it now as later: flashbacks get in the way of the story if you keep them ganging around. Okay, so here's the way it shaped up.

I was in Paris, France, chasing some half-assed story about a dame from Albuquerque who'd bought a vineyard in the Champagne district and was aiming to undercut the French shippers on the American market—at least that was the story I'd drawn expenses on; in fact, I was following up the terrorist-college lead as hard as I could go. I'd promised not to write about it, but that didn't stop me collecting facts that I could use later. And I was approaching it from a different angle from Dean. He'd flown off with the luscious Creole chick and the retro circus; Hammer had disappeared. I was going to gather all the dope I possibly could on the Sheikh Abd el Mansour Nessim before I set foot on the island or went near his guerrilla retreat. To that end, therefore, Paris suited me fine: Tim Grayson, the *Worldwide* resident in the city, had the most comprehensive morgue outside the home office in Chicago—and he'd probably have more cuttings on Middle Eastern affairs, Nessim included, than we did Stateside. Plus he had the in at *Paris-Match*, the *Nouvel Observateur, Minute*, and several other ETO voices, which meant that we could milk their files too.

This would have worked out fine if the publisher hadn't taken it into his head to rent a stand at the Frankfurt Book Fair that year. He was already in Europe, ready to preside over the stand himself. The book fair is in mid-October, and that was still a month away? Never mind. The publisher was in Europe for the book fair.

Alvin Radczinski, that's his name. He's second-generation, but you don't tell any Polish jokes when he's in the room. Not if you want to stay in business. He's a lumpy man, with wrestler's shoulders, skin the texture of sandpaper, and a face like the front end of a bulldozer.

Maybe I should explain here that being a specialist feature writer on a magazine like *Worldwide* ain't as glamorous as folks imagine. Especially if the magazine happens to be based in Chicago. Especially if the publisher controlling the writer also has a desk with a plaque on it that reads "Alvin Q. Radczinski: Editorial Director." If your specialty is crime, for instance, you can find yourself writing about a lady trying to buy her way into the wine business.

What the hell—Radczinski was my boss. He told me what to do and where to go. He told me how much to spend. He told me what stories to cover and how much to write. The only thing he didn't tell me was *what* to write. Don't think he didn't try, but nobody tells me that; it was the first lesson my old man taught me: he called it the thick end of the proprietorial wedge. Weaken once and you end up a yes-man hack.

We had a certain amount of freedom, of course. You could nose out your own story and follow it up . . . so long as the other stuff you were handling wasn't too pressing. But you had to keep in touch, to let the office know where you were. In case they wanted a fast five hundred words on Radczinski's daughter feeding the pigeons outside Milan cathedral. You know.

So they knew I was in Paris. So I got an urgent cable telling me to report for a conference with Radczinski at the Hotel du Vieux Manoir at La Guerche-sur-l'Aubois, in the Cher *département*.

It's a small, pretty town—one long main street and a square off to one side—in the flat Upper Loire country between Nevers and Bourges, around 150 miles south of Paris. Outside a café in the square I eavesdropped on a conversation between two cab drivers. One of them thought St. Etienne would win the Coupe de France Football yet again; the other disagreed. But before they came to blows I was able to persuade one (he favored Paris St. Germain) to take me to the hotel.

There was no chance of anyone overhearing any conversation there. The Vieux Manoir was three miles out of town, on the road to Germigny l'Exempte, it said on the signs. It stood in about a thousand acres of pines, and if it had ever been an old manor house, it must have been during the feudal system existing in the mid-1930's. Radczinski and I appeared to be the only guests, but even if there had been others, the thick-pile wall-to-wall carpet, bathtub-size armchairs, and replica medieval tapestries garnishing the walls would have muffled our words long before they could have reached alien ears. I saw no evidence of any staff.

But my senses might have been dulled some. The cable had arrived in Paris too late—or too early—for me to catch the good trains. I'd had to change twice. From Nevers I'd been obliged to take a cab all the way to La Guerche (the cabbie was convinced *Monaco* would win, can you imagine!). And by the time I'd bribed the second one and bought my way out of his Peugeot, the hotel dining room was closed, the kitchen personnel had joined the Foreign Legion, and it was too late to eat. For a little light relief, Radczinski—who'd been given a ride in some oil king's private Cessna—had ar-rived at lunchtime and was mad as hell because I was late.

Don't ask me what he was doing in that hotel. He was my publisher. Probably he had friends with a château and he'd hit town earlier than expected. Maybe he didn't want the friends to find out the quality of the hired help. He was sit-ting there like Stromboli the day before an eruption. There were double chins all the way down the front of his blue gab-ardine vest, with a day's ration of cigar ash on each one. He wasn't smoking, either.

It was kind of funny, seeing him there in that phony, over-stuffed French hotel, away from the scissors and paste, the film-set galleys and litho pulls, the chatter of typewriters and the ringing of phones in the *Worldwide* copy room. He wasn't even wearing his green eyeshade. "This is one of the first times in my life I saw you wearing a jacket, Alvin Q.," I said. "It goes some way to make up for the lack of bodily nourishment. But talking of mental stimulation—what brings you to Europe a month before the fair anyway? Don't you trust the U.S. mail to deliver my copy and expense account anymore?"

"Wisecracks I can do without," he said, giving his celebrated impersonation of Al Pacino's grandfather on a bad day. "I got buddies in the wine business here, French guys, and it seems they're kind of steamed up about this dame horn-ing in on their market—especially if it's gonna bring the prices down. Some of these guys were considerin' they should put some money into the magazine: the Champagne families and the Sancerre people around here." He took a cigar from

his vest pocket and bit off the end. "They'd be happier doin'
so if we happened to run a piece tellin' the world this dame
was screwy—that you can't market a quality article at a bargain price. If that's the truth, of course. I wouldn't want to
influence what you write."

"Of course not," I said. "Who would even think of such a
thing?"

"So when you go visit the vineyard this broad buys . . ."

"Look," I said, and remember I hadn't eaten, "I already
been to enough vineyards to find out this racket stinks to high
heaven. The French are crazy: there's a big scandal when
they're caught out adulterating their fine Bordeaux; they sell
tickets and certificates of origin to the British, who slap them
on whatever crap they figure the trade will carry; because
there's a big demand in the U.S., they boost their prices so
high their own goddamned countrymen can't afford to buy
the stuff anymore; if they stopped artificially aging the wines
of the south, the West Indian sugarcane industry would be
bankrupt—"

"Mettner! I didn't want—"

"They cut their own product to hell, yet they pirate ships
bringing wine from Italy and set fire to tankers coming in
from Spain. Seventy percent of the producers could—and
should—be prosecuted under the EEC trade descriptions regulations."

"Mettner!"

"Yet these are the guys who dare to stand up and scream
about *quality*? Do me a favor each time the word 'quality'
comes up, and remember—"

"Mettner," Radczinski interrupted gently, "I'm your editorial director, not one of your readers. Sit down, man. Relax."

I dropped back into the leather bathtub. His cigar was in
his mouth, but it was unlit. I struck a match and held it out
to him. I lit a cigarette of my own. Fanning smoke away
from his face with one hand, Radczinski said, "Very interesting, all that stuff, just the same. Most informative. If our
California growers got as mad as you, we could have another
Boston Tea Party . . . with wine. I guess a lot of our readers
would find such a story fascinating." The glowing end of the
cigar stabbed in my direction. "But they ain't got much
chance, do they? You were saying about the U.S. mail, an'
it's true they don't favor me with your copy no more. Same
story with Western Union. I mean like no cabled dispatches

from our intrepid correspondent on the Champagne front. What gives, Mettner?"

"I'm following up a better story," I said.

"You're *what*?" He was halfway out of his chair. For a man of his weight, at that speed, in that kind of chair, the performance must have rated a mention someplace in Ripley or *The Guinness Book of Records*. "Don't hand me that shit, Jay. What the hell have you been playin' at since you hit this country?"

"I just told you. Following up a better story."

"What better story, for Chrissake?"

"One that'll have human interest, Alvin Q. What stories do you get these days? Only four. The nuclear story. The economic-finagling story, like your Champagne epic. The government-inflation-dollar-oil story. And local wars. Afghanistan. Iran–Iraq. Syria. Israel. Lebanon. Central Africa. Laos. And what do *they* amount to in terms of news? Some town fell here; another held out there. A siege was lifted, a hospital was bombed, some guys got killed and a nun was raped. Where's your human interest, your point of identification, in that kind of stuff?"

"You got human interest in the nun," Radczinski said. "Somehow folks always rate it worse when it happens to a nun."

"Oh, sure. Every time we run the story. Like once in every two issues. But you can't keep on dishing up the same bullshit, maybe with just the names and the places changed, and expect the readers to blow their tops with excitement. If the story I'm chasing comes up, it'll wipe those nuns off every front page in the world."

"*What* story? What the hell do you mean, 'if'?"

"It's a tough one. It's difficult. It may take time, because I have to wait for—"

"What story?"

I sighed. "Well, you see, that *is* the difficulty. I can't tell you."

"You . . . ?" Radczinski appeared to choke. "Protection of sources and all that," I said hastily. "Security of others involved; matter of life and death. If even one other person is wise to the setup, the whole deal's blown. Even you, A.Q. Besides, I gave my word."

"Are you out of your mind?" His shout was so loud that a youth in a white jacket materialized at the far end of the huge deserted lounge, peered nervously in our direction, and as abruptly vanished. "Listen: *I* decide which are the lead stories in this goddamn magazine! *I* decide who's goin' to cover what an' how it's gonna be presented! *I* hand out the assignments and make up my mind who's to be sent where! I don't need no jumped-up crime reporter to tell me what makes news and what doesn't. So cut out the crap and give: what is this earth-shattering story?"

I shook my head.

He laid the cigar in the saucer of an empty coffee cup on a low table by his chair. He leaned forward with his elbows on his knees and steepled his fingers. "Look, Jay," he said in a quieter voice. "Maybe we been workin' you too hard. Maybe you need to relax. Take a week off in Paris, and *Worldwide* will pick up the tab. Five days, anyway. But first I want you to do me this special piece on the lady from Albuquerque. I got a photographer standin' by at Rheims—"

"I can't leave this story now, A.Q.," I interrupted him. "It'll be a world-beater if it comes off, and I figure it's worth the risk. I'm sorry."

He stood up, slapped the creases in his vest, and disappeared behind a smokescreen of cigar ash. "Are you tellin' me . . . ?" The voice was incredulous. "Are you tellin' me that you refuse . . . that you *refuse* to carry out your assignment?"

"I'm telling you that you should trust my judgment. And trust me."

"Mettner," a voice said from out of the fog, "you're fired."

"Okay, so I'm fired. I'll sell the story to *Time* magazine. I'll sell it to *Stern* and *Oggi* and *Paris-Match* and *Al Ahram*, and it'll be syndicated all over the world so that the only stupid bastard who won't have it will be you!" I uncoiled myself from the airchair and stood up.

"You're not goin' outta here with damn near five thousand bucks of *Worldwide* expense money unaccounted for!" Radczinski yelled.

"Sue me," I said. "And if it's any help to you, I'll be going to Corsica. They tell me the wine there's just dandy."

"Corsica?"

This time the explosion produced two waiters at the far end of the room. I went up to the senior one—he must have been all of fifteen years old—and told him: "Call me a cab, will you? I want to get back to civilization. You can put it down on Monsieur Radczinski's account."

This does, allow me to say, have some bearing on the Dean story. First of all because it explains how I happened to be on the loose in St. Florent as a temporary free lance. I think it was the twelfth time Radczinski had fired me. It would take him a week to get over it, then he'd start bawling me out again as if nothing had gone wrong. But during that week I had to stay out of his way—so, second of all, I was denied the use of the Paris office and couldn't check out the files in the morgue. That's why, the next day, I went first to the Corsican tourist office near the Palais Royal, and then to the Institut Géographique National on the Rue de Grenelle.

And if I hadn't gone to the IGN, I'd never have run into Raoul Ancarani.

Run into? Let me rephrase that. I scarcely noticed him at first: a fortyish guy of medium height, farther along the counter. He was dressed in the middle-class Frenchman's nonvacation casual uniform: Terylene pants, canvas shoes, and a wool jersey shirt worn outside the trousers with the collar buttoned and the sleeves pushed up. The girl had given me some of the information I needed, but for the large-scale map of northern Corsica that I wanted, I'd have to go to their sales department in the Rue la Boétie, near the Arc de Triomphe.

The place was fairly crowded. It was while the clerk was looking for my map that I glanced around me and saw the same guy again. I was pretty sure it was the same guy. He had dark, thinning hair, cut kind of short, a long horse face, and a hairline mustache. That was odd. A coincidence. Maybe he was looking for maps too. But it wasn't until I walked out, crossed the Champs Elysées, and decided to treat myself to an expensive beer at Fouquet's that I realized my mistake. I mean like he hadn't been there by chance at all.

I had just opened the map when a shadow fell across the paper. I looked up. He was standing on the far side of the red linen cloth that covered the sidewalk. He held out his hand. "Ancarani, Raoul," he said. "Commissaire de Police. From Ajaccio in Corsica. Do you permit that I join you, Monsieur Mettner?"

"I don't see how I can stop you," I said, taking the hand and nodding at a vacant chair. "Especially as you seem to know my name." I was a mite sore, at that. I'd been looking forward to introducing myself as Mettner, Jason II. However. "What can I do for you, sir?"

Ancarani smiled. He had a brown face with tombstone teeth: when he opened it, his mouth looked like a war cemetery on the Somme. "You understand," he began, "there is nothing of the official in what I am about to say to you. One asks oneself, simply, how is it that an American crime writer interests himself so fully in one's territory?"

"Does one?" I parried. It wasn't the smartest retort I'd ever made. Maybe I'd improve with practice.

"There could be a number of reasons," he went on. "An article—a color piece, I think you call it—on the Unione Corse, our picturesque equivalent of the Mafia. A supplementary assignment to write a tourist guide. Perhaps even a wish to purchase a holiday home at a price considerably lower than those obtaining in France." He paused to signal a waiter. "A *pastis*. Ricard. No ice. . . . And yet, Monsieur Mettner, none of those explanations satisfied me."

I made no reply. I couldn't think of anything witty enough to cap my last intervention.

"A journalist on either of the first two assignments," Ancarani said, "would hardly visit the Ministry of the Interior to make exhaustive inquiries about building construction permits or public-utility surveys. Somebody in search of a property might . . . but they would hardly concentrate their attention on the most barren, inhospitable, visually desolate part of the island. Nor, one ventures to think, would they demand of the IGN which *cadastres* would hold architects' plans for properties *already developed,* and whether it was possible to obtain Cartes de l'Etat-Major* for the area in question."

He waited while the waiter set down a glass; then he poured water into the pale green liquor until it turned milky, sipped appreciatively, and turned to me. He said, "Just what, Monsieur Mettner, inspires your obsessive interest in the Desert of Agriates?"

Once again, it was a good question. I wasn't quite sure how to reply to it. Answers I had plenty—but which of them to give? I knew Dean had agreed to wipe out a terrorist-training school in the area we were talking about. I knew it was

*Very large-scale maps made for the army's general staff, which show every road, trail, track, footpath, and sheep run—even those on private property—which could conceivably aid the movement of men and materials in time of war.

run by this multibillionaire oil sheikh with an anti-West bias. I didn't know who was hiring Dean to do it (though I had my suspicions). I didn't even know if Dean knew. I didn't know how far he had gotten with his plans. Most important of all, I didn't know how much of this the guy sitting across the table from me knew . . . or if he knew any of it at all.

One thing I did know was that I was damned well going to stick like a leech to this story—which was why I'd been following up different leads in Paris in the hope that I might get a line someplace on the kind of fortress this guy Nessim had fabricated. Evidently I'd been less discreet than I should have been, and this cop had—up to a point—gotten wise to me. The point was: up to what point? Was it just gumshoe curiosity? Or did he know about the school? If so, did he know about Dean?

I decided to stall. "You seem very well-informed about my activities," I said, "especially for an officer almost a thousand miles away from his home beat. Since when has it been illegal for a newspaperman to ask questions?"

"It is not illegal, Monsieur Mettner. It is interesting."

"Oh, yeah? You just happened to hear me ask for a map, and you decided right off the bat to investigate?"

"I . . . happened . . . to be at the ministry, where your inquiries commenced. Since they were considered to be slightly unusual for a foreign journalist—and since they concerned a region for which I am partly responsible—I was informed of them as a matter of courtesy. I have been observing the sequel to them with great interest."

So this flatfoot had been tailing me all along! I wondered why—and then a sudden thought struck me. If he *was* a flatfoot. So far I had only his word for it. Was that really enough? I said, "You claim to be a police captain from Corsica. How the hell do I know that's true? Can you prove it?"

"But of course." He produced a plastic folder with a cellophane window, flashed it under my nose, and then shoved it back into his hip pocket.

"Look," I said, "that could have been a driver's license, some kind of credit card, a club membership, or even a one-shot mailing gimmick from *Reader's Digest*. All I saw was a photo and part of your name."

He laughed. It was the first time I'd seen him do it. The war graves spread over another field. "You are a suspicious man," he chided. "However . . . if you insist. . . ."

He produced the folder again and held it in front of my eyes. It was the genuine article, all right.

So I really was talking with a cop from Corsica! But what the hell—Dean had been warned that Nessim had a lot of French law in his pocket. I mean like he was covered. Just because this guy was a regular policeman, it didn't necessarily mean he was on our side: he could just as easily be on the enemy payroll. "What exactly do you want from me, Commissaire?" I asked.

Ancarani shrugged—one of those big Mediterranean gestures with the shoulders up to the ears and the arms spread wide. If I'd had any doubts about where he came from, that took care of them. "One is not," he said, "in a position to demand from you anything whatsoever. You are perfectly within your rights. One would, nevertheless, find oneself grateful for some indication of your intentions—why you make these queries, whether you intend visiting Corsica, and if so, why? For the record, you understand."

His English was good, almost accentless, but slightly bizarre because the syntax was translated directly from the French. "For the record," I said, "I am following up a story."

"For the record" was right! I was thinking maybe I should have a tape loop made of that phrase.

"Just so," Ancarani said. "A story. And doubtless certain . . . professional . . . considerations deny one the opportunity of knowing the subject of this story?"

"One is desolated," I said—now he had *me* doing it, for God's sake!—"but that is so."

He finished his drink, threw a couple of coins on the table, and rose to his feet. "It is probable that we shall meet again," he said. "In the interval, I would ask you, Monsieur Mettner, to remember three things. First, that a policeman in uniform and a policeman out of uniform are two different creatures, not always sharing the same views. Second, that the English aphorism 'Discretion is the better part of valor' applies today in a literal rather than a figurative sense. Third, that there is an old Corsican proverb that runs: 'He who would lift the stone must beware the scorpion.' " He nodded once, threaded his way between the tables, and joined the crowd strolling down the sunny slope toward the Place de la Concorde.

The next day I flew to Ajaccio. There was no trace in the official files of any construction permits granted for the Desert of Agriates. Okay, so I found a guy with a Piper

Comanche back at the airport and bribed him to fly me over the mountains in the center of the island to Bastia. From there I took this cab to St. Florent and checked in at the Miramar late in the evening. Radczinski would pick up the tab, all right, once I had the story.

You know what happened at the Miramar. I couldn't find a socket that fit my shaver. But all the way there, in the plane and in the cab, I was thinking of this character Ancarani and the last things he'd said. I felt like the fellow in that old story about the two psychiatrists. You know—two of these shrinks pass in the street, and one guys says brightly to the other, "*Good* morning!" And the second man stops, plucks his lower lip, and says to himself, "I wonder what he meant by that?"

8

Sean Hammer

To avoid anyone seeing them together and making a connection, Hammer had checked in at Ajaccio before Dean and Laurence went to Calvi. The Ulsterman spent two days cruising the northern coastline of Corsica in a power boat, and returned to the capital convinced that there were only two sites bordering the desert where an amphibious landing with a small but efficient force was feasible. These were the estuary at Peraiola and Saleccia Beach. Pearldu, the creek with the lagoon, was surrounded by marsh that could bog down anything on wheels—and according to the charts and his own observations, the whole of the rest of the area was fringed by steep cliffs and submerged rocks.

The final choice was not difficult. Peraiola was in view of and highway from Calvi to St. Florent. Even if his force could be landed there secretly, it would be faced either with a nine-mile advance across trackless granite upland or a frontal attack on the gates at Murenzana—which could only be done using the highway. Hammer preferred not to think about the reaction of the French authorities to a foreign assault group proceeding along Departmental Route 81.

Saleccia, on the other hand, was only just to the west of Nessim's land, and there was a mule track leading to the bluff that protected it on that side. Hammer was working on the logistics of a two-boat, forty-man attack when Dean—before he set out on his round of waterfront bars—called him and suggested they meet in St. Florent. The defenses, he said, were so strong that any seaborne assault would have to be supported by an air drop. They must get together at once.

The ninety-mile journey took Hammer four hours. The road, especially for the first twenty or thirty miles, was one of the hilliest and twistiest he had ever driven. Although the hired Renault 5 had automatic transmission, he was not yet used to stowing his artificial leg comfortably in so small a car. And a combination of daytime heat and humidity in the evening air had created a heavy mist that reduced visibility to twenty or thirty yards over the 4,000-foot Col de Vizzavona and again at Venaco and the Foreign Legion headquarters in Corte. He did not in fact arrive in St. Florent until sometime after Dean's abduction.

The scene that greeted him at the Miramar was not what he expected. The newspaperman, Mettner, was striding up and down the lobby shouting at a group of people in night-wear huddled around the desk. One or two were clearly hotel guests, but most of them appeared to be members of the personnel. A brigadier of the gendarmerie, who looked as though he had dragged on his uniform in a hurry and was still sore about it, stood red-eyed by the entrance doors. Laurence Chateauroux (and she, Hammer thought, looked as though she had just gone the full fifteen rounds with Muhammad Ali) sat wrapped in a quilt on the stairs.

"You're lying! You must all be lying!" Mettner cried. "I refuse to believe that there's not one person here who heard *anything*."

"Monsieur—" the gendarme began wearily.

"Mettner! What the hell's going on here?" Hammer said from the entrance. "What happened to *her*? Where's Marc?"

Mettner swung around. "Thank Christ there's someone here with a head on his fucking shoulders!" he stormed. "A hang of hoods broke into the hotel, beat up the girl, and took Dean away after a hell of a fight. And, believe it or not, not a single one of these *schmucks* saw anything or heard any-thing. Not one goddamned thing." He compressed his lips and then added, "And Steve Carella here's not being much help, either!"

"Monsieur," the gendarme protested, "I can do no more than take depositions. If these ladies and gentlemen have no evidence to give . . ." He shrugged his shoulders. "I already have the statement of Mademoiselle Chateauroux; a call will be put out following the kidnapping of your friend."

"Yeah, yeah," Mettner said. "Wheels will be set in motion. We know. In the meantime . . ." He turned to Hammer.

"Let's for God's sake you and me see if we can do something about this, huh?"

"Surely," Hammer said. "But why are you getting so steamed up about it yourself? If we did locate him, your man would probably think you had something to do with the snatch anyway. He might even think that was how you were able to find him! So why the honest rage, but?"

"I guess it's a thing called morality," Mettner said. "I just hate to see a whole gang of folks telling lies—and getting away with it."

It was one thing to talk of doing something; quite another to know where to start. It was only after Laurence had cleaned herself up as best she could and put on a pair of pants and a sweater that Sean Hammer noticed the mark on the dark wood of the windowsill. "Now, here's a funny thing," he remarked. "What would you say that was, at all?"

Mettner and the girl crossed the room. The mark looked at first like a long smear of cream. It was whitish, slightly frothy, but sticky. "I don't know," Laurence said. She dipped a finger in the substance and held it to her nose. "It's tacky . . . but somehow it's the odor . . . a familiar . . ."

"It smells like some kind of gum," Mettner said, "or a rubber solution."

"Of course!" she exclaimed. "Faithful Virgie!"

"How was that?" Hammer asked.

She explained about the inflatable doll, and told them how Dean had pumped it up from a puncture-repair aerosol. "There's finely divided rubber in solution in there too," she added, "so that any crack or tear in the punctured tire is repaired."

"Do you have the can in here?" Mettner asked.

"I . . . I guess so." She began to look around. "It was in here with the remains of the kite when I . . . that is to say, it was here earlier in the evening." She went into the bathroom and came back with a surprised expression on her face. "That's odd," she said. "I can't find it anywhere. It seems to have disappeared."

The two men exchanged glances. "Outside," Hammer said.

He fetched a powerful flashlight from the car, and they examined the ladder beneath Laurence's window and the ground near it. There was another smear of the rubber solution, almost dry, on one of the lower rungs of the ladder.

It took them a quarter of an hour to find the third. It was

on the top step of a flight leading down from the fortress and the hotel toward the waterfront. "He must have had enough sense left in him to pick up the can as they took him out," Hammer said, "and then loose off the occasional squirt as they carried him away."

"Like the old kids' game of hare and hounds," Mettner said.

It was a desperately difficult job, trying to locate and identify smudges and blobs of dried rubber solution on cobbled lanes and strips of macadam and stone walls in the dark, even with a powerful flashlight to guide them. Mettner had never realized before how variegated were the surfaces of masonry, how infuriating a stretch of graveled path—and how many imperfections in those surfaces could look exactly like a pale spot of dried-up rubber gum.

An alley ran right and left at the foot of the steps, and they had little difficulty there, for there was quite a large blob in the center of the pathway a few yards to the right. But after that, the trouble began. They had only the one flashlight, so they had to cast up and down each arm of every intersection in the network of passages behind the row of buildings fronting the harbor. Once they wasted nearly ten minutes in a cul-de-sac, misled just inside the entrance by what was in fact a wad of chewing gum. Another time it was Laurence, on her hands and knees, whose acute sense of smell led them to a minuscule smear on a flagstone.

There were seven deposits of the solution in all, not counting the one at the top of the steps. And then Mettner suddenly came across the aerosol can itself, lying in a gutter. "Is it empty?" Hammer asked. The newspaperman pressed the button. There was a hiss of compressed air, and a stream of white snaked out. "Then he must have lost consciousness," said Hammer, "an' let the thing drop. Else he'd of kept on givin' the odd press for sure. He'd only let go of it deliberate if there was not anything left inside, see."

They stood wondering what to do, where to go. Between two tumbledown buildings, a lamp at the end of the harbor mole cast wavering reflections on the dark water as it welled in among the boats. It was Mettner, with his newsman's sense of the anomalous, the fact that didn't quite fit, who noticed the black Citroën CX Pallas parked behind a boathouse in a yard full of abandoned lumber and discarded fish crates . . . and Mettner who realized that there was something odd, seeing the most expensive model of the up-market Citroën range in such a place. The car looked new, too: even in the shadowed yard, there were highlights reflected from the hood, the fenders and the edge of the long, tapering roof.

Perhaps it was the knowledge that during World War II a black Citroën inevitably spelled Gestapo to the French; perhaps it was the fact that the yard was only fifty feet from the waterfront, where there was plenty of parking space; perhaps it was just the sixth sense—the news sense that comes with experience—that tripped the alarm wires. Whatever it was, he froze and motioned the others to silence. "Switch off the flashlight," he whispered, "and listen. Something smells here—and it's not just the fish."

They held their breath and listened. Water lapped among the hulls of the moored boats and sucked at the harbor wall. Somewhere a long way off, a dog barked. Otherwise there was nothing.

And then, as they waited, and the myriad tiny night sounds manifested themselves as part of the near-silence, they did hear something. Beyond those barely audible noises—a dripping cistern, a faint snore, stays tapping an aluminum mast, and the creak of a shutter—there was a more sinister sound.

Faintly at first, then more distinctly as their ears became attuned: a curious, muffled thumping.

And was that a choked cry?

Hammer found the place—a deserted fish loft at the end of an alley that led off the far end of the yard. The houses on either side appeared to be empty, their glassless windows gaping. The double doors of the loft were outlined from within by a pallid glow that brightened and faded, brightened and faded as they watched. They heard a harsh voice speaking in French, a mumbling groan, and again that strange thumping.

There was an old-fashioned wooden latch securing the doors: they hadn't even bothered to lock them. Hammer twisted the weathered latch and pulled one of the doors fractionally open. There was a Browning automatic in his hand. He took in the scene with a single glance—the candlelit group around the naked, bound figure strapped to the plank; the man with the candle in his hand. Standing in the gap, he snapped in his heavily accented French, *"Les mains en l'air! Vite, ou je tire!"* Get your hands up, fast, or you're dead men.

For an instant—perhaps a tenth of a second—the tableau remained motionless, like a freeze frame at the end of a movie. Then there was a storm of action.

The three candles were extinguished as though by a single switch. Feet stamped on the stone floor and someone shouted. Hammer fired three times, aiming high so as not to hit Dean. In the triple flash of the explosions he saw figures scrambling for the rear of the loft. He fired twice again. A voice cried out. And then, as Mettner pushed past him and ran for the far end of the place, a door slammed and there was the sound of running footsteps.

A moment later the motor of the Citroën burst into life. Tires squealed. A further slamming of doors. And then the diminishing whine of gears as the car accelerated away into the night.

Mettner returned, panting, as Hammer and the girl relit the candles and started to release Dean. "No good: they got away," he said unnecessarily. "They knew the back way out and I didn't."

"Thank Christ," Dean said when they had shepherded him back, partly covered by Hammer's jacket, to the hotel. "Thank Christ they'd just started when you arrived. I must have been out for some time and they had to wait, obviously, before they began the interrogation."

"But, Marc . . ." Laurence said. "It looks . . . I mean, you poor darling! Doesn't it . . . ?"

"The hair will grow again." Dean smiled painfully. "As for the rest—okay, it hurt like hell; it's blistered and it still hurts, but it'll pass. Two or three days and . . ." He shrugged. "Wait and see," he said to Laurence.

Mettner coughed. "Unless you still figure me for the brains behind the attacks on you," he said, "how do you rate this latest number? Like, do you have any idea who? We know the *why* okay, but . . . ?"

Dean looked at Hammer. The Ulsterman nodded. "He knows about the assignment," he confirmed. "Seems regular. I got his word not to write about it until it's all over. If it ever starts."

"It'll start, all right," Dean said grimly. He reached up gently and touched the girl's bruised face. "Somebody's going to pay for that, for one thing."

"It's this shit about the goddamn hotel!" Mettner burst out. "Nobody saw anything! Okay, maybe. But don't tell me nobody out of all that collection of bums *heard* anything. Jesus!" He shook his head. "You see this kind of thing often enough in Chicago, but—"

"Sure, it's the same story entirely," Hammer interrupted. "It's like the three brass bloody monkeys. And why do these people see nothin', hear nothin', and say nothin', evil or otherwise?"

"Because they're shit scared," Mettner finished for him.

"Got it. And what does that mean, boyo?"

"It means," said Dean, "that the bullyboys at work here are local talent. That's the only explanation for a whole group of folks—and they're *all* local too, remember: the tourists have gone—for a whole gang of guys and dames clamming up like that. They won't talk because they're scared of reprisals. Right?"

"By local," Mettner said, "you mean . . . not connected with this Nessim character?"

"Not directly connected. I guess they're interested parties. They want to stop us putting Nessim out of business; they have to be the same people—or associates of the people—who were after me in Canada. I know they're Corsicans because I heard enough to prove it. But whether they're *employed* by Nessim, or in the game for reasons of their own . . . you tell me."

"We don't really know, do we," said Hammer, "if Nessim's wise to the fact that there's a contract out for him and his school—and that we're the guys hired to enforce it? I mean, look, either these Corsicans are in it for some reasons of their own or they're on Nessim's payroll. If they're on his payroll, it could be for one of two reasons: because *he's* on to *us* or because they have a general bloody mandate to check out and . . . uh . . . discourage *anyone* they find snoopin' around this area."

"If it's the same team as the one in Canada," Dean reminded him, "it has to be the first of those. According to Mettner here, the gorilla who was paid to beat the shit out of me was hired before I even knew about the mission."

"That's right," Mettner said.

"And according to that crooked barkeep," Hammer added, "the guy paid him to finger you was a Syndicate connection."

"Hey," Mettner exclaimed, "this begins to sound *interesting!*" He lit a cigarette, shook out the match. "And these local hoods, then—how do you read them?"

"The obvious connection," said Dean. "Mafia, Cosa Nostra . . . Unione Corse. It's the local equivalent, after all. The boys are always ready to do each other a good turn."

Hammer said, "What I do not get: first they try to beat you up, then they try twice to knock you off, and now they only snatch you and put the screws on you. Sure, the gorilla was just put in as a hindrance, like. When he fucked up and you met Mademoiselle here, they assumed you'd sign on the dear old dotted and tried the liquidation routine. But why back to the kid gloves again here?"

"Kid gloves!" Laurence exclaimed. "Can't you see—?"

"In a figurative way of speakin'. I mean, they could have killed you, easy, if they'd a mind to. But those guys weren't even armed, else they'd of shot back when I fired. They didn't as much as wait to see how many we were before they took a powder!"

"That's one of our good cards," Dean replied. "Clearly, these were lower-echelon soldiers, strong-arm boys from the neighborhood, briefed only to get information."

"One of our good cards?"

"Certainly. Think, Sean. They wanted to know who I was and who sent me; what the hell I was doing here. That means my cover held. It means they saw this academic character snooping around and got suspicious . . . *but they didn't know it was Dean.* If they had, on past evidence, they'd surely have killed me, as you suggest."

Hammer nodded. "That makes sense. Bully for the prof, then! And now what?"

"Now," Dean said, "we're going to shift up. I've seen the outside of the defenses, and they're tough. But thanks to Laurence, we're going to be able to see them from the other side of the perimeter too. We're going to borrow a chopper and survey Master Nessim's domain from the air."

9

Marc Dean

The helicopter was an old Bell UH-1 Iroquois—the prototype model that predated the Huey used so extensively in Vietnam. Dean, Hammer, and the girl picked it up in one of the perimeter pans at Poretta international airfield, Bastia. Rather to Dean's surprise, the machine was painted bright red, carried French civil markings, and announced in white lettering along the sides of its fuselage that it belonged to the fire department of the Alpes-Maritimes *département* based in Nice.

"That's not exactly anonymous!" Dean said as the jeep that the girl had somehow spirited past the security guards on the gates disembarked them at the edge of the pan.

"It's the best cover there is," Laurence assured him. "Because it's so underpopulated, there are always forest fires here in Corsica—especially in the interior. Sometimes landowners whose property is in a nondevelopment zone fire their own forests: once the trees have gone, they can get permission to build holiday villages for the tourist trade, you see. The whole island is constantly overflown by department overseers on the lookout for fires. If they're not caught when they start, hundreds of thousands of acres can be destroyed—in the center particularly, where the mountains are too steep for pumps and trucks to approach.

"You mean that so far as our friends are concerned . . . ?"

"I mean that a fire-department helicopter, flying low down, is less likely to be noticed—or make people suspicious—than any other kind of aircraft, anywhere in Corsica."

"Point taken," Dean said with a grin—but he was still unprepared for the second, and larger surprise that morning.

The UH-1 carried a two-man crew. In the navigator's seat, he saw with some astonishment, was the enigmatic Frenchman Maurice Duclos.

And at the controls, complete with leather flying helmet and goggles despite the fact that the cabin was enclosed in plexiglass, sat none other than the intrepid aviator Sir Daniel De'Ath.

He flashed a glance at Laurence—her mouth was still swollen but the black eye was hidden behind huge wraparound sunglasses—and raised his eyebrows. "Is that . . . ?"

"All right? Safe? Secure and discreet? Don't worry." She smiled. "It's all among friends. How do you think I managed to quit the circus and play Madame Professor so easily?"

Dean shrugged. She had organized the chopper. She was in a sense his employer. It wasn't up to him to question her choice of crew.

As soon as they had installed themselves in the six-man passenger cabin, the Lycoming T-63 turbine choked, whined, and then burst into life. The 44-foot rotors turned, and they lifted off.

It was a sunny day, slightly hazy, and the only clouds to be seen were low down on the western horizon. De'Ath took them northward along the rocky index finger of Cap Corse, flying at one thousand feet over the precipitous corniche road along which light still glinted, beetle-bright, on the coachwork of tourist traffic. The bare brown mountain ridge that formed the spine of the promontory, occasionally garnished with rolling woodland or patches of scrub, slid past below them and to the left. Only four tiny fishing villages broke the line of the cliffs plunging into the sea, and then they had passed over the Genoese watchtower on the foam-laced Ile de la Giraglia and were heading for France.

De'Ath flew some way out to sea and then swung the chopper around in a wide 180-degree turn to return a couple of miles off the opposite side of the cape. "Almost twenty miles," he said in answer to a query from Dean. "When we're about halfway, we'll right-face and then fly in from the bloody northwest, as if we were comin' from Toulon, what!"

"It would be the obvious way for any survey team to come," Laurence said.

Dean inclined his head. After so much time spent in planning and reconnaissance, he was seething with impatience to see with his own eyes the far side of the fortifications he had been unable to penetrate on land.

They crossed the coast slantwise near the thin strip of sand that Hammer had selected as a likely landing place. Beyond it was a silver thread of river and the mule track, barely discernible as a brush stroke against the dun-colored rock, zigzagging toward the granite bluff. "I must make it clear, Monsieur Dean," Duclos said from the navigator's seat, "that we make just one run inland, like this, and then—after we have landed someplace to allow a little time to pass—we fly out again as if returning to France, on much the same path. In this way we give the impression, not at all suspicious, that we are a fire-department plane which has come to Corsica for a specific purpose, some investigation farther south perhaps, and then to go home. What we cannot do is circle over the Nessim territory—there is, after all, virtually no risk of fire here—for that *would* be suspicious. But there is a special camera beneath us that will make a continuous photo record of the trip each way."

"That's fine," Dean said. "Just fine." Past a sliding panel in the plexiglass, he was scrutinizing through binoculars the land below. The clifftop batteries, together with the sensors and computer complex that had zeroed them in on Faithful Virgie, were so well camouflaged that he could locate none of them. Even the outposts behind the electrified fence below the lip of the bluff only betrayed their existence here and there by a fugitive gleam of metal.

Farther inland, the terrain was more instructive. On the eastern slopes of the granite ridge, small parties of men in combat fatigues were deployed across the rocky surface in front of a jeep carrying what looked like a film or television camera. Dean imagined they were being taught the proper use of ground cover—with a filmed or taped record to show them where they went wrong. Another group were being hustled past the obstacles of a battle course laid out between the sides of a shallow, scrub-covered valley. There was a firing range—not in use—in the center of a wood, at one end of which Dean recognized Russian RPG-7 rocket launchers, antitank rifles on tripods, and three different types of heavy machine guns. Several other ranges and installations he was unable to identify, but he did see a skid pan for automobiles and a number of semiconcealed entrances which could have led to a system of underground bunkers.

Not far from the public highway, but completely masked by the curve in the valley and the trees that grew densely on either side, was Nessim's central headquarters—the hamlet he had transformed, according to Duclos, into a veritable fortress. There was a stone citadel whose blank walls were built straight up from the sheer face of a rocky spur on one side—and which was approached on the other through a formal garden, complete with Olympic-size swimming pool, above a maze of alleys traversing the medieval houses of the hamlet. These, Dean could see, had all been expensively strengthened and restored so that the entire pyramidal complex resembled a single infinitely complicated structure.

He had time to notice, as the helicopter clattered overhead, that there were armed men climbing the pantiled roofs, swinging from ropes dangling down the face of the cliff, and edging along copings that clung to the ancient walls. Then De'Ath banked the machine slightly and he saw the strangest sight of all.

A mile beyond the citadel the valley opened out . . . and there in the center, not far from an immense edifice shaped like an airplane hangar, a complete city street was laid out. Beneath four- and five-story facades, Dean saw rows of shops, one section beneath a colonnade, with offices, banks, and an intersection controlled by traffic lights that was choked with cars, trucks, and even buses. One of the sidewalks was crowded and there was some obscure commotion around a flight of steps near the lights. But before he could work out what was going on—a simulated bank robbery, perhaps? a snatch?—they were over the southeastern border of Nessim's domain, flying above the brown-cotton shellbursts that marked the Foreign Legion artillery range.

They continued past the rectangular mountain mass that enclosed the Nebbio region and landed in a forest clearing high up near the peaks above the village of Vescovato.

"What I can't understand," Dean said as they sat in the shade of a huge chestnut tree, unpacking the bread and cheese and wine that Laurence had brought, "is how they dare carry out this training program so openly." He broke off a piece of bread and carved himself a slice of Niolo. "We can't be the only plane to have overflown the desert since Nessim bought his piece."

"By no means," Duclos said. "But you have to understand

the power that this man wields; the . . . connections . . . he has in Paris and Ajaccio."

"Half the powers-that-be in his pocket," said De'Ath.

"Meaning?"

"Meaning, Monsieur Dean, that he has been able to engineer things in such a way that no scheduled or commercial flights overfly his land. Not too difficult, this: the regular flight paths never did cross the desert. But Nessim has now managed the affair in such a way that it seems overflights are actually forbidden—at the request of the Legion, you see, because of secrecy concerning the weapons they are supposed to be testing in the adjacent artillery range. He is a man not only rich and powerful but also very astute."

"Okay. But, like I say, we can't be the only—"

"There is a second explanation," Laurence interrupted, pouring wine into paper cups. "When planes do cross the area flying low enough to see what goes on, they are usually gendarmerie or fire-department helicopters like ours, military-training aircraft, or private pilots waiting for permission to land at Calvi or Bastia. For them, should they ever ask questions, there is a perfectly satisfactory answer, a believable reason for men to be firing guns, hanging from ropes, or crawling over roofs. Nessim is shooting a movie. There is a production company, registered in Rome, bearing his name. He has in fact bribed his way onto the credits of films made by other people—as producer."

Dean said, "Very clever. And he even has cameras turning down there. For quite a different reason, of course, but it looks convincing."

"P'r'aps we could overfly the bally school in vintage kites next time?" De'Ath suggested. "Give the chap a bit of local color, Hell's Corsican Angels, the Dawn Patrol, an' all that." He smoothed the wings of his absurd mustache with a forefinger and uttered his braying laugh. "Maybe he'd even pay us: the circus business ain't exactly boomin', and I could do with the cash!"

Laurence reached up and pulled the goggles perched on his helmeted forehead back down over his eyes. "It's time we were on our way," she said. "This plane has to be back in France by four."

The return journey was much the same as the inward trip. There was, however, one significant difference. They had just flown over the citadel when De'Ath gave an exclamation of astonishment. "Well, I'm dashed!" he said. "Of all the . . . ! If that's not the rummest thing!"

Laurence leaned over his shoulder from the passenger compartment. "What is it, Dan?"

"The street, old thing! The houses and traffic and what-not! Have I gone bonkers, or have they bloody well vanished into thin air?"

They crowded to the starboard side of the cabin, staring out through the plexiglass panels. It was quite true. It was unbelievable, but it was true. The busy shopping thoroughfare they had all seen less than two hours previously had gone: the shallow valley to the east of the citadel was now as bare as the surrounding desert; apart from the aircraft hangar, there was nothing to see but low scrub along the upper edges of the depression and shelves of granite shimmering in the afternoon sunlight.

"That does it," Dean said to Sean Hammer later as they sat sipping *pastis* in a café overlooking the harbor at Ajaccio. "Whatever this guy Nessim has going for him in there, it's too high-powered—and too damned mysterious!—for us to risk an assault without we have a whole heap more information. And I mean from the inside."

Hammer unwrapped a stick of gum. Laurence had flown back to France with Duclos and De'Ath. Mettner—sore because they had refused to allow him to come with them on the helicopter—was supposed to be looking up some police captain in town that he said he knew. Dean himself, though he still retained his cover as a geology buff, had abandoned any idea of continuing with the next package tour. There was no point—especially as the mineralogist character had already aroused suspicion, apparently on the part of the local Mafia. "Just *what* do you mean . . . from the inside?" Hammer asked.

Dean answered the question with another. "You figured we should need two landing craft and forty mercs for an amphibious assault?"

"I did that."

"Okay. Let's say, in view of what we discovered today—and what the aerial photos confirm—that they need to be supported by another twenty guys parachuted inside Nessim's perimeter. That force will still need to be directed by someone *on* the inside. The place is too complicated for us to plan a successful attack without inside information."

"So we need inside information," Hammer said, chewing. "You got some bright idea on how we get it? You want someone he should talk the guys in at the right places like an airfield controller?"

Dean nodded. "I think Master Nessim's school for terrorists could do with a new student," he said. "Maybe an anarchist from one of the third-world countries in Africa."

Hammer's eyes widened. His weathered face split open in a delighted grin. "You don't mean you were thinkin' of sendin' Mazzari to school?" he inquired.

Once more Dean nodded. "For the second time in his life," he said, "Edmond Mazzari is going to find himself a preppie."

10

Edmond Mazzari

Edmond Mazzari was very big and very black and immensely strong. He had once been a sergeant in the Congolese Army—when there *was* a Congolese Army—and a grateful government had sent him to Oxford University, England, with a view to the "Westernization" of its future officer corps. Mazzari had never become an officer. The internal quarrels between Kasavubu, Tschombe, and Lumumba had seen to that. The next time he had been to the Congo was as a mercenary recruited by Marc Dean—as part of the force hired by President Mobutu to defeat the Katanga secessionists in the seventies.

From Oxford, he had emerged speaking a British English that recalled the ripest of P. G Wodehouse; from Katanga, he had emerged as one of Dean's closest friends, the man who, with Hammer, the combat leader liked best to have near him when the fighting was at its most fierce. They had soldiered together in the Middle East, in West Africa, in Brazil, and clandestinely in Europe. Once, in Haiti, they had found themselves temporarily fighting on opposite sides—but this had been due to a military confidence trick pulled on Dean, and they had finished the operation working together . . . and winning.

Now it was Dean himself who was organizing the confidence trick—introducing Mazzari into Nessim's guerilla-training school as a terrorist candidate, an anarchist who wished to overthrow the legal black government of Botswana. It was not a role that the huge Congolese ex-sergeant relished. But it was one that—with minor variations—he had played before.

In a previous adventure, he had posed as a Nigerian dissident and been accepted by the Soviets as a student, and potential agitator, to be trained at the University of Kiev.

It had taken some time, and apparently a great deal of influence, to arrange the discreet rendezvous in Gaborone at which Mazzari had first been contacted by front men working for Nessim whose task was to vet his credentials before there was any question of an interview with representatives of the school itself. Duclos, Dean's French intermediary, had flown down to southern Africa with him, feeding him the essential information he would need for his cover story. And it seemed that certain local figures in Botswana had been suborned to confirm that Mazzari was the author of a number of anti-South African demonstrations and one or two not very professional bomb outrages for which no rebels had claimed the responsibility. Then he had been asked to go north to Angola, where his bona fides had been subjected to a more rigorous examination by a three-man panel comprising a German, a Central American, and an Arab revolutionary whom Mazzari knew to be an ex-member of the Palestine Liberation Organization. He had quit because their aims did not seem to him extreme enough.

The interrogation had concentrated on Mazzari's own beliefs—or lack of them—and his aims. He had been well briefed on this. "You must," Duclos had told him, "give the impression of somebody embittered, malcontent, anxious for revenge. The world has treated you badly; you wish to hit back. But it must not be a small thing, the spite and envy of a *little* man. There must be rage and fury and a violent determination, a lust to destroy."

"None of your actual build-a-better-world stuff?" Mazzari had said.

"No, no. Their methods may be similar, but these people have nothing in common with Communist subversives. They do not wish to upset the social order so that it may be replaced by something they consider better; their aims are purely destructive." Duclos laughed. "Mansour Nessim—the last thing he would want would be a world organized by the working classes! He has no desire to distribute the cake more fairly; he is angry because his own slice was not big enough."

"But you said he is unbelievably rich?"

"Yes," Duclos said, "but *he* believes he could, and should, have been richer. So he uses these 'students' of his to make the world pay."

Mazzari had given a convincing demonstration of a man denied the place in the world to which his talents entitled him. He had summoned up a towering rage against the whites of western Europe, the system, the folly of the masses who allowed themselves to be duped by it, the uselessness of nationalism and the necessity of violence as the only weapon capable of piercing the world's armor of complacency. If only he knew how, when, and where to use it.

He had been rather pleased with the performance. Two days later he was told that he had been accepted as an elementary student at Murenzana.

The news was brought to him by the Central American, a tall, thin, seamed man with a heavy mustache who had lost the lobe of one ear during a shoot-out with military police in Guatemala. They sat drinking Coca-Cola in the diminutive lobby of a fly-blown back-street hotel in Luanda, where Mazzari stayed while he waited for their decision. The large blades of the ceiling fan were not revolving, and the leaves of the single potted palm were gray with dust.

The Central American, who called himself Ramon, said that there would be no fees to pay. But Mazzari must place himself completely in their hands. Students were entitled to no furlough, permission, or leave: once within the domain, they stayed there until graduation. "And graduation," said Mazzari, "is . . . ?"

"When you have taken part in your first genuine operation." Ramon paused. "Provided you comport yourself suitably," he added.

"What happens if one of your students flunks?"

Ramon caressed his mustache with three fingers of his right hand. "We have no place for failures," he said.

Mazzari nodded. "When do I leave?"

"Immediately. One of the Sheikh Nessim's aircraft is already on the way."

Mazzari rose to his feet. "Then I guess I'd better push off upstairs and collect my gear, and so on and so forth."

"Sit down. You will not need to go to the room again. You need bring nothing but the clothes you wear. A car will call directly."

"Yes, but . . . I mean, well, there's my passport . . . money . . ."

"I have your passport, the one you will be using from now on." Ramon tapped his breast pocket. "You will not need money. If the necessity should arise, some will be provided."

"You think of everything," Mazzari murmured.

"Yes. Everything." The Central American produced a sheet of thick paper, a small roller, and an inkpad from his briefcase. "If you would please allow me to take a handprint."

Mazzari raised his eyebrows, but he held out his hand obediently. "Nessim insists," Ramon explained, running the inked roller over the giant palm. "We cannot run the risk of any kind of substitution, the chance of an impostor . . . But you will see."

"Better clear out my room, just the same, don't you think?" Mazzari asked as his hand was pressed down on the sheet. "Look a bit fishy if a bloke disappears, leaves all his duds and papers in a hotel room, bolts leaving the bill unpaid, and all that."

"The bill has been paid. Your room is already empty."

Mazzari whistled. Nessim's people certainly had things sewn up tight! Clearly, from the moment an applicant was told he had been accepted, the instructions must be that he was never to be left alone. The precaution—what else could it be?—would effectively prevent any hostile person wishing to infiltrate the school from doing precisely what Mazzari himself had in fact hoped to do: get a message out to his control saying that everything was going according to plan. In the same way, the insistence on no personal belongings minimized the opportunity of smuggling undesirable objects—miniature radio transmitters, recording apparatus, and such —into the domain. If new arrivals brought no clothes and no luggage, Nessim's men had no linings to slit and no false bottoms to check out.

Fortunately Dean had foreseen the difficulty, and they had agreed on a contingency plan: if Mazzari failed to contact him by a certain time, it was understood that he was in—and would presumably be on his way to Corsica. Their arrangements for future contact were complex, because it had been obvious from the start that a project as sophisticated as Nessim's would be geared to the detection and elimination of would-be infiltrators. Dean had wisely ruled out any attempt, therefore, to sneak in anything that could be remotely suspicious. Which was just as well, Mazzari reflected, because his room, he was certain, had been thoroughly searched not once but several times since he arrived in Luanda. Thankfully he was one hundred percent clean. He felt nevertheless that it would be in keeping with the role he was playing if he made one complaint.

"There's only one thing," he said to Ramon. "My gun, you know. I would like to have that. I'm very fond of that little Stechkin: I've grown used to it, and it's helped me through a lot of scrapes."

"Then it's almost certainly traceable to you," Ramon said briskly. "Ballistically—through the work you have done with it—and otherwise. One of the things you must learn to reject, utterly, is any kind of sentimentality toward firearms."

"I don't know that I'd say *sentimental*—" Mazzari began.

"A gun is a tool. Nothing more. Once it becomes a possession, it becomes also a weakness. If it is used more than once, police and forensic experts can make a connection between the two events—and perhaps ultimately with you. But if you operate with a weapon you never used before, and dispense with it immediately after the mission has been accomplished, there is no chain of events to connect you with it. All our graduates—in any project involving loss of life—are issued with arms they have never handled and given the strictest instructions to dispose of them as soon as possible. They have, of course, naturally been trained on the same *type* and model of gun."

"Yes, but one gets used to the feel of a particular gun, the balance," Mazzari protested, "and when it's that familiar, your accuracy and speed are increased."

"For target practice and college competitions, perhaps." Ramon was scornful. "In our kind of work, accuracy—even speed—is less important than strength and willpower, the determination to kill."

Mazzari contrived a sigh—in fact the Stechkin automatic meant nothing to him: it was window dressing, a Russian model given him by Dean as a means of rounding out the character he was to play. "You're the boss," he said. "This place, now. How do I locate—?"

"I shall come with you," Ramon said.

The chaperoning was carried to extreme lengths. At the small airport, Mazzari was not even given his new passport: Ramon showed it with his own to the immigration officer, who had clearly been paid not to ask questions; he scarcely glanced at Mazzari. And the documents were held in such a way that Mazzari was unable to read the name on the one that was supposed to be his.

It occurred to him as the twin-jet Cessna executive aircraft lifted off halfway along the runway that this could turn out to be the most dangerous mission he had ever undertaken. He was smuggling himself, unarmed, into a hermetically sealed fortress protected by every refinement of modern electronics and weaponry, a school for slaughter where both teachers and pupils were killers who counted human life as of no value. And where nobody would have the slightest hesitation—or the slightest doubt about what action to take—if an intruder was discovered and it became necessary to eliminate him.

There was, moreover, no question of a student changing his mind once he had been accepted. He was himself now totally dependent on Ramon—he was a man without papers, without money, without even a name that he knew, and no possessions save the clothes that he wore. If Ramon were to disown him . . . well, it would be difficult. If the plane were to land and maroon him someplace, he'd have a hell of a time trying to convince anyone of *anything*. If they became suspicious and killed him, the corpse, if it was found, would never be associated with Edmond Mazzari. He had flown into Luanda under a false name. There would be no record of anyone of that name leaving. And nothing to connect either that name or the one on the passport in Ramon's pocket with Mazzari. Meet Mr. Nobody, he thought with an inward smile. The faceless triggerman destined to aim the assassin's gun.

The Cessna landed to refuel at a small airport somewhere in central Africa. The operation was carried out in a dispersal pan on the fringe of the perimeter track, by men who were clearly Arabs. But there was no way of telling what town the airport served. The control tower, surrounded by a collection of grass-walled huts, was half a mile away across a wilderness of dwarf thorn bushes that covered the flat land for as far as the eye could see in every direction. It could have been in Niger, in Chad, in southern Libya, or even in the Sudan. Ramon affected not to know. "The choice is the pilot's," he said.

"Good God," Mazzari thought it safe to say, "you fellows certainly cover your tracks, don't you!"

"It is a good habit to cultivate," said Ramon shortly.

The plane landed them at a small airfield outside Olbia, an estuary town in the northeast of Sardinia. "There's no landing ground at Calvi or Bastia?" Mazzari asked in surprise.

"You ask too many questions," Ramon said. "Nessim selects the most suitable route for each candidate. This way, no pattern of arrivals and departures establishes itself."

A taxicab took them 25-odd miles north to La Maddalena, at the extreme tip of the island, and from here they were ferried by a high-speed launch seven more miles across the straits to Bonifacio, the southernmost point in Corsica.

It was an impressive sight, approached by sea with the sun low on the western horizon. A honey-colored rampart surmounting two hundred feet of sheer white limestone cliff revealed itself, as they drew closer, to be a continuous line of houses, packed as closely as books on a shelf, rising vertically from the rock face. There was no jetty, no landing stage, nothing to mar the lacework of foam at the foot of the cliff. A single flight of steps cut into the horizontal strata climbed dizzily upward from the swell. "There are a hundred and eighty-seven of them," the boatman said conversationally. "Folks say they was cut in a single night by sappers working for the King of Aragon, when he had the place under siege in 1420."

Ramon made no reply.

The boatman shrugged and spit over the gunwale into the water. "There's the romantic type and then there are the others," he told the water. He spun the wheel, and the launch turned through ninety degrees to follow the line of the cliffs, heading straight into the dazzle of the sun. They passed beneath the huge bastions of an ancient fortress—and then suddenly there was an opening in the limestone wall, and beyond it an inlet that ran back parallel with the coast they had been following. The fort was in fact on the tip of a promontory.

The wheel spun again. The wake creamed in a graceful arc as the launch raced for the opening.

Within the anchorage—for centuries the impregnable refuge of pirate ships—it was already dusk and the deep water was ink-blue. The inlet was almost a mile long. At the far end, the town spilled down from the heights adjacent to the fortress to surround a triangular *place* where there were palm trees, rows of parked automobiles, and sidewalk cafés already crowded for the ritual aperitif. There was a customshouse in one corner of the wide, rectangular landing stage, but the doors were closed and the windows shuttered. Neither here nor anywhere else since they left Luanda had they passed through any immigration control or been asked to show their papers. Dean certainly knew what he was talking about when he said Nessim pulled some weight, Mazzari thought.

Ramon led him to a dingy back street from which a flight of stone steps mounted to a courtyard with a fountain. Here, in one of the tall, narrow houses whose peeling stucco walls reduced the sky to a distant oblong, Mazzari was handed over to two Corsicans. "These guys will drive you through the night to the school," Ramon said. "Don't try to get fresh in any way: they're kind of thick and obey orders to the letter. I mean like don't try to take any walks on your own."

"Well, thanks for introducing me to your friends," Mazzari said, wondering exactly what those orders were.

Like most gunmen, Ramon was completely humorless. "It's just part of my job," he said.

It was not one of the most entertaining nights Mazzari had spent. The Corsicans, as alike as two shells in a cartridge belt, were shorter than he was, but broader—220 pounds of hard muscle in each case, he reckoned. Their clifflike faces were blue-jowled, with expressionless eyes. One had a bald patch in back of his thin, dark hair. To each other, they spoke a *patois* that Mazzari was unable to understand; and his French appeared to be equally incomprehensible to them—unless that was part of the orders. Conversation until they left was therefore restricted to short phrases and monosyllables in their own heavily accented French. "We go now" . . . "Walk" . . . "In here."

"Here" was a black Alfa-Romeo GTV parked on the outskirts of town. Mazzari sat beside the driver and the man with the bald patch leaned forward between the front-seat headrests as if he was afraid the driver might lose the way. He chewed gum with his mouth open, filling the car with a curious odor that was a mixture of spearmint and garlic. Since conversation was impossible, and in any case gorillas such as these were unlikely to part with any information of use to him, Mazzari tried to sleep during most of the journey: he suspected that if he were able to see the hints of curves and precipices tunneled out of the night by the head-lights, he would be unable to speak himself.

The distance from Bonifacio to St. Florent is approx-imately 110 miles. Along the corniche following the eastern coastline of Corsica, the Alfa-Romeo made it in two hours and eight minutes. Snaking up to the pass that carried the road over the ridge behind Bastia, they left the lights behind. The gulf of St. Florent and all of the country on the far side of the saddle was in darkness. It was not long after midnight.

A few miles farther on, the car pulled up outside the gates where Dean and Laurence Chateauroux had so rudely been turned away. They had been driving for the past half-hour on dipped beams and Mazzari had seen nothing he could recog-nize again in the way of landmarks since they crossed the ridge. Was this, he wondered, another instance of Nessim's ex-traordinary security precautions—so that he would find it diffi-cult to locate the place at any future time in daylight—or was he reading too much into a simple situation that just hap-pened to dovetail with his previous findings?

Nobody was going to answer that question. Maybe he would find out later. Right now, two figures in Castro-style peaked caps were visible in the headlamp beams. Each of them carried a submachine gun, and one was opening the right-hand gate a few feet. His companion stood in the gap with his weapon at the ready as the two gorillas shepherded Mazzari out of the car and up to the entrance. The man with the bald patch exchanged a few words with the guards; Maz-zari was beckoned through.

The Corsicans climbed into the car and backed up. The Alfa-Romeo turned into the road and accelerated away in the direction of Calvi. Evidently the strong-arm men were used simply as carriers and were not part of Nessim's organization. Presumably they were associated with that "third party" re-sponsible (so Dean had told him) for the attacks in Canada and the kidnap of Dean himself . . . how long ago was it now? It had taken three weeks to make the initial discreet ap-proaches and then brief Mazzari at a border town between Botswana and Namibia, another three or four days while he waited in Gaborone. It must be almost a month. Hammer would be on one of the smaller uninhabited Greek isles, training his twenty paratroops and the forty seaborne assault men for the attack. And Dean? Dean would be back on Corsica, waiting until he figured the time was right to contact Mazzari and obtain the information without which the attack could not be mounted. How long did he have to get that information? Three days, maybe four, according to the last talk he had had with the combat leader.

One of the guards was thrusting a flashlight into his hand. "Walk up the driveway," he said curtly in English. "Two hundred yards beyond the curve, the village starts. Go to the first house left of the gateway and open the door."

Mazzari switched on the hand lamp. The driveway was newly laid macadam. "What do I do when—?" he began.

"On your way," the guard cut in. "Keep to the hardtop."

Mazzari shrugged. He walked away from the gates, keeping the beam of the lamp trained on the ground just ahead of his feet. Above all, he must avoid appearing inquisitive. He could stake out the approaches later, in daylight.

No lights showed in the village. The night was moonless, but a progression of serrated roofs and chimney stacks leapfrogging up the rocky spur toward the citadel was visible as a darker blur angling out the stars. A slight breeze rustled the leaves of invisible trees. It was unexpectedly cold after the heat of the day.

When the somber mass of the place towered over him, Mazzari raised the beam of the flashlight. The bright circle of illumination revealed a deep stone arch piercing an ancient building four floors high. The windows were shuttered and the arch closed off by massive wooden gates that must have been all of ten feet tall. But over the spiked tops he could dimly make out the slope of a narrow street zigzagging steeply upward. Buildings to the left and right of the gatehouse formed a continuous wall, like the clifftop houses he had seen at Bonifacio. Most of them were shuttered, but the one immediately to the left of the arch now had a low-power bulb glowing beneath a pantiled porch. He strode up and grasped the handle of a wide oak door. It opened outward.

Mazzari stared. It wasn't all that surprising but it was unexpected. Directly behind the door was a sheet of solid steel.

A flat, toneless electronic voice spoke suddenly from the shadows beneath the porch roof: *"Approach and remain still in center of step for physiognomy check."*

Mazzari obeyed. At once an activation light on a video scanner blinked on, directing its rays at him through a lens shoulder-high in the steel face of the second door. He whistled to himself. This was big-time stuff! He knew enough about high-echelon security systems to realize that somewhere inside Nessim's fortress a computer was extracting the essential features of his face as registered by the scanner and comparing them with data on file in its memory bank—and the data could only have come from a photograph . . . which Ramon must have taken, or caused to be taken secretly, sometime during their meetings in Luanda.

The automatic voice-response unit intoned metallically: *"Physiognomy match affirmative. Accepted. Proceed to enter handprint data. Panel at right of outer door."*

Mazzari looked. Just outside the doorpost, where an electric bell would normally be, a rectangle of dark green plastic material was mounted on the wall. He pressed his hand flat against it. Evidently the print Ramon had taken from him in the hotel had already been transformed into the plus-and-minus electrical fields that corresponded with the binary mathematics of the computer's data bank. The Central American must have raced ahead, either in another plane or an even faster automobile, to program the machine with photo and print before the gorillas delivered their package. Doubtless this was why they had waited some time before they left Bonifacio.

You will see, Ramon had said, inking Mazzari's hand before he took the impression. Mazzari saw. These characters were certainly taking no chances.

"Handprint match affirmative. Accepted. Access control now activated," said the voice. *"Five-second limit. Enter now."*

The winking scanner was extinguished. The safelike steel door swung noiselessly inward. Bright light illuminated a short corridor terminating in the trellised grille of an elevator. Beside the ironwork surrounding the cage, the lens of a closed-circuit monitor camera was trained on the entrance door. Otherwise the passage was completely bare.

Mazzari walked through in the six seconds before the armored door closed with a hiss of compressed air. He concertinaed the outer gate of the elevator and stepped into the cage. There was only one button on the control panel. He pressed it.

Taking him by surprise, the cage, instead of rising,

dropped silently beneath the level of the floor. Whatever lay beyond the far end of the shaft, he could already chalk up one alpha-plus: he had passed all the checks and he was on the inside of Mansour Nessim's castle keep!

11

Edmond Mazzari

The Sheikh Abd el Mansour Nessim was visually an impressive man. At sixty he still stood lean and hard and straight as a telephone pole. He was tall, too, and the white robe and white turban he wore, dazzling in contrast to his sallow, aquiline face, made him look taller. There were centuries of power implied in the curl of his lip, the droop of his eyelids, the arrogant flare of his nostrils. Rings flashed on his fingers, but otherwise there was no external sign of his wealth or his importance. It was all, as Edmond Mazzari reflected, in his mind.

Unfortunately that mind, incisive, imaginative, and brilliant in its own way, was just a little bit around the bend. By ordinary standards Mansour Nessim was crazy . . . and the immense fortune he had amassed permitted him to indulge his craziness; the Nessim millions were devoted to a single ferocious cause: the creation of a worldwide terrorist guerrilla which could shed enough blood to quench the thirst for revenge that his paranoia demanded.

He received Mazzari in the top room of the tower surmounting the old citadel. From the panoramic window that wrapped around three-fourths of the circular chamber, he could look out over the whole of his domain—from the firing range to the ridge, from the village to the sea. The place looked a little like the control room of a recording studio. There was an enormous flat-topped desk in the center of the glass arc. Behind it, Nessim sat in a white hide chair. The tooled leather top of the desk was empty except for a notepad and gold pencil, a single telephone handset, and a microphone on a short, flexible stalk. Farther back, covering the portion of wall that had no window, a bank of twenty-five or thirty video monitor screens stood above a complex electronic console busy with dials and switches and tape inputs and winking red, green, and blue pilot lights. Apart from two high-backed chairs in front of the desk, the room was otherwise unfurnished.

"Nothing that happens in Murenzana is hidden from me," Nessim said. He spoke in English, the baritone voice brittle with suppressed tension, his words loaded with an arrogance that only just fell short of contempt. "These monitors survey every corner of the property, inside and out. At the flick of a switch I can tune in to any area, any room, any sector of terrain. Through this microphone I can issue orders to any of the groups or individuals you see on those screens. And with the aid of those inputs I can record, if necessary, visually and aurally, anything that goes on."

He swung around in the swivel chair. Each of the screens, Mazzari saw, relayed a different picture. He distinguished a gymnasium, lecture halls, a firing range, the outside of a group of houses built on the rock, and a stretch of clifftop with the sea beyond before the Arab chief spoke again.

"I show you this not because it is supposed to be impressive," Nessim said. "Electronically it is as simple as the computer system regulating entry and exit, as the antieavesdropping sensors buried in our ferroconcrete walls. No . . . I show it to you, as I show it to every new student, to avoid . . . shall we say embarrassment? . . . in case an inmate should foolishly think of disobeying the regulations. As you see, it is not possible to do this without the risk, the very severe risk, of being both overseen and overheard."

Nessim touched a rocker switch with his forefinger. A blue light glowed above one of the monitor screens. It was repeated on the control of a rheostat beside the switch. He pushed the control slowly up the scale.

". . . *single-hostage situation out of favor now*," a male voice said with increasing volume from some hidden speaker. "*Except in a case where it is simply money that is required against the safety of the hostage.*"

Nessim indicated the screen with the blue light. It showed a small lecture hall with perhaps a score of students sitting at desks stepped in a half-circle around a podium. At the back of the podium, beside a large ground-glass rectangle on which

109

the floor plan of a building was projected, stood the man Mazzari knew as Ramon. *"It is clear,"* he said, *"that in a situation where only a single hostage is involved, there is a question of balance, of a gamble. But the stakes are not in fact the safety or life of the hostage on the one hand, the money or concessions we demand on the other. They are psychological. One kind of determination against another. We are gambling that we can persuade the forces ranged against us that we are prepared to carry out our threat; they are gambling that they can convince us of their readiness to sacrifice the hostage. Each party of course must have the will-power to do what they say. Otherwise they have lost before the game starts. But if they do convince us—what then? Either we kill the hostage—in which case we have lost, because we have nothing left with which to bargain. Or we don't—in which case we have lost even more. We have lost the object of the demands we made, and we have lost face as well. The only way to play the single-hostage game, if the demands are not met at once, is to resort to torture—if the opposition can hear the results—or partial destruction of the hostage: an ear, a finger, sent as an earnest of determination. Our Italian friends have successfully used this . . ."*

Nessim flipped off the switch and cut in a screen showing a sector of the ridge, the land falling away toward the more barren reaches of the Desert of Agriates. In the foreground were short posts bearing magic-eye beams, and a steel-shielded battery of rocket-grenade launchers actuated by sensors and aimed by computer. With the rheostat volume turned up full, there was nothing to hear but the thin whistle of wind among wild grass and thorn bushes. And then, off screen, a voice: *"Tu sais bien—fumer, c'est l'interdiction totale!"*

And another, deeper: *"Les interdictions, je m'en fous."*

Nessim was back at his desk, pressing a button, speaking into the microphone. "Kerim? How many times do I have to drum it into their thick skulls? One of the Frenchmen on F-6 is smoking. I won't have it. I want a full report by thirteen hundred hours."

He returned to the console, stabbed another button, took up a hand mike. "Maruani and Colbert? You are observed. Report to the duty officer immediately your trick is over and await my decision." He looked over his shoulder at Mazzari. "You see what I mean?"

Rapidly he made a tour of some of the other video scanners. An empty dormitory, another lecture hall, the commissary—half a dozen blue-chinned men sat over coffee, discussing in Spanish the latest moves in the Basque separatist campaign—a battle course laid out among trees and scrub with the instructor yelling: *"MOVE, for Jesus' sake! This is live ammunition being fired at you, but the gunners aim to miss; imagine they were CRS or an Israeli patrol or thugs from Britain's Special Air Service out to get you. . . ."*

Nessim switched back to the first lecture hall. Ramon was saying: *"So, you see, the multihostage project—a bank taken over, a restaurant, a hijacked plane—has much to recommend it. You can eliminate one, two, three, a dozen people to create an effect, and still have your bargaining counters. Killing is always a satisfactory ploy anyway: it shows we mean business; and it arouses world opinion. 'Whatever the cost, these innocent victims must be saved!'"* Ramon sneered. *"Nobody is innocent!"* he cried passionately. *"We are all part of this putrid society—and thus we are all victims too. All that the media imply by such emotive terms is 'nonengaged.' But those of us strong enough to become engaged must remember: public outrage is an invaluable weapon . . . for us."*

Nessim switched off the monitor. "An admirable teacher," he said.

"Fascinating!" Mazzari agreed with what he hoped was the right amount of enthusiasm. "How many different lecture courses do you . . . we . . . have? Apart from the practical, I mean?" It was the first chance he had had to ask questions. Two taciturn Arabs had escorted him from the foot of the elevator shaft, when he arrived the previous night, through a network of subterranean passages to a self-service bar where he ate a solitary meal. Then they had taken him to a small bedroom in a house halfway up the hill toward the citadel. Either the two men had orders not to speak, or they could understand neither English nor French, for Mazzari was unable to get a word out of them. In the morning a sultry dark girl, whose name was apparently Fawzi Harari, brought coffee to his room and made a note of much of the background cover he had learned from Dean and Maurice Duclos. Fawzi was some kind of official receptionist (although, he saw now, there were in fact female students on the course), for it was she who took him to a quartermaster store, where he drew and put on Castro-style battle fatigues like all the other students, male and female, and she who eventually led him to the tower. By nine o'clock he was with Nessim . . . and he realized that Dean had been right, saying that the entire village had been transformed into a single complex redoubt: not once, from the moment he walked through the entrance door to the opening of the elevator cage outside the tower control room, had he reemerged into the open air.

"How many courses?" Nessim said. "Every theoretical lecture has its practical counterpart—even those on holdups and getaways. We teach you the best way to use firearms, how to conceal firearms, and how to make improvised firearms. We advise on the smuggling of arms past customs and security checks, on remaining unnoticed in a crowd, on the arts of violence and surprise. There are also courses on explosives, timing mechanisms, threats and menaces, the selection of hostages, kidnap routines, unarmed combat, burglary, torture, and the need for ruthlessness. The assassination lectures now include information on hydrocyanic acid, the alkaloid poisons, and the new minimum-dose nerve reagents developed by the Russians. Psychologically, we try to suggest 'disciplines,' as the French call them, to counteract the mental pressure exerted by the forces ranged against us in a kidnap or hostage situation."

"If I could ask a generalized question . . . ?" Mazzari began.

"Generalized? Well, what is it?" Nessim was suddenly wary.

"It's just . . . Well, you're helping people like me, helping people with grievances, who want to purge their countries of the rottenness and corruption ruining them." Mazzari felt it was safe to lay it on thick. He said: "But do you have any plan for us to work on a global scale? Maybe it's selfish of us, accepting your help so we can do something about our local problems, when these are trivial compared with the world situation. Isn't there any way *we* can help *you*? I mean, a highly trained, fearless band of men and women such as you produce here . . . deployed in strategic places, couldn't they be a powerful weapon for the revolution that—"

"Nothing is trivial," Nessim interrupted. "Not if it means, however minimally, cleansing the putrescence that destroys our civilization. Everything that sears, that cauterizes, that cuts out and eliminates, is good." There was now a fanatic light in his eyes. "Sometimes the writings revered by superstitious followers of the so-called Western religions have a certain validity, especially those which are in fact no more than the reframing of tenets held by the ancient Arab philosophers. One such phrase we have borrowed and made it our watchword. 'If thine eye offend thee, pluck it out.' But we cannot go that fast. Every individual act of annihilation, every outrage, every *défi* counts. Yet the opposition, however corrupt and disorganized, is strong. To attempt anything on a global scale at this stage . . ." Nessim shook his head. "Expending our fire and our energy in too many different directions, we would lose the impetus of our anger. No, what we have to do first is encourage, by our example, those antisocial elements in all countries who wish to tear down the existing social structure. It is not, after all, up to us to suggest anything to replace it. Something will emerge . . . and it cannot help but be better. For the moment, the command is simply: Destroy."

Nessim sat down behind his desk. "One of the things you will learn here," he said, "perhaps the most important, is that the Western world is run according to a set of rules, framed by the men who stand to gain the most from them—but that when we pit ourselves against these self-seeking individuals *we are not obliged to follow those rules*. The pursuit of power is not like a game of rugby football.

"In the same way, 'civilized' people"—the quotation marks were noticeable —"are expected to subscribe to innumerable effete and idealistic concepts dreamed up by so-called liberals (and usually perverted by the rule-makers for their own ends). Equality. Freedom. Liberty of expression. The *sacredness* of human life—oh, especially that!" Nessim was scathing. "One of the most useful weapons in our psychological arsenal is the total inability of these same liberals to believe that intelligent human beings can exist who do *not* subscribe to these concepts. They cannot conceive of a person being killed without a specific reason, particular to that person. It seems to them outrageous; it puts them off-balance. They prate of the horror involved because that person was 'innocent.' But this is nonsense: as you heard Ramon say, nobody is innocent. Our graduates who planned and carried out what is known as the Lod airport massacre were no more 'guilty'—to use their nauseating term—than the aviators who

113

destroyed Dresden, Coventry, or Nagasaki, killing people they had no cause to dislike and about whom they knew nothing."

Mazzari said nothing. The Arab continued: "The fact that we make our own rules gives us a unique advantage. Because when they get over their stupefaction at the discovery, the fools *still* play by their own outmoded rules . . . so we are always one jump ahead. Arrest, caution, extradition, trial, proof—they go through the whole damned charade. Yet if they had any sense at all, they would know that the way to beat us would be to play by *our* rules, or lack of them: shoot us on the spot and the hell with a trial. But nobody dares do that because of that holy fiction, public opinion. What stupidity!"

Nessim shook his head. He said, "Soon we shall have enough people recognizing our rules to change the nature of the game. But before that happens, we have to get a really unbreakable system going. And the only way to achieve that is to breed a race of guerrillas for whom human life has no value. One death, a dozen, a hundred, must mean no more to them than the mowing of a cornfield to a farmer." Mazzari was treated to a frosty smile. "Remember one thing, though," the Arab added. "The dangerous man, the really dangerous man, is he who sets no value on the lives of others—but places a very high value indeed on his own!"

Mazzari was left with a single thought as the girl Fawzi conducted him back to the fortified houses of the village: the most important thing to destroy, and that as speedily as possible, was the Sheikh abd el Mansour Nessim himself.

He saw no reason to reconsider his opinion during the rest of that day. Fawzi showed him to the six-man dormitory he was to share in the row of village houses converted into a barracks, and then one of the Arabs who had received him the previous night took him to a lecture hall for his first class. It was on the manufacture of fake ID papers and the falsification of passports. "Never forget," said the lecturer, a heavily mustached Libyan, "that the wisest thing to do in the case of awkward questions during an identity check is to shoot to kill. Thrust any thoughts on the so-called sanctity of human life ruthlessly from your mind. Why do you think Carlos is still at large?"

There seemed, Mazzari saw during a frugal lunch in the commissary, to be about a hundred students, five-sixths of them men. There was a minimum of personnel. Aside from the instructors, a handful of Arab servants, and a permanent detail guarding the gates, the students themselves were charged with the day-to-day operation of Murenzana, including—on a shift system—the policing of the perimeter.

Small groups of men and girls—Palestinians, Lebanese, Africans—who had evidently enrolled as existing units, talked together in low voices, but otherwise the students showed little desire to communicate. Mazzari was happy to leave it that way, and he cultivated a demeanor as surly and suspicious as most of his fellows. Clearly, in such an environment, he could learn more by watching and listening than he could by talking. It would have been difficult, in any case, to have imagined a collection of individuals with whom he wished to converse less. The girls, mainly lesbian so far as he could judge, were militant feminists—and, paradoxically, like so many libbers, spectacularly unfeminine. (Along with many of his contemporaries, Mazzari believed firmly that most intelligent women were "liberated" anyway, and didn't need to join a hate club or an anti-man movement to prove it. "But, crikey," he said to Marc Dean later, "you should have seen this lot, old man! Talk about fishers of men: they should have been chucked straight back in again, the moment the net came out of the water, honestly!")

The male students fell into three distinct categories, which Mazzari mentally classed as fanatic, psychotic, and chip-on-the-shoulder misfit. ("They were so obviously around the bend," he told Dean, "that I'm amazed any of 'em ever got past an immigration check! But then, I suppose that's where old Nessim's pet theory helped: they weren't playing our rules, so they could get away with murder, in every sense of the word.")

There was nothing helpful to be gained from such contacts. But Mazzari did at least solve one mystery that first day.

The disappearing city block was in fact no more than a huge and elaborate movie set, the components of which, dismantled and then towed away by tractors, were stored in the hangar Dean had observed from the helicopter. The buildings were not just facades shored up behind by buttresses: each one had four walls and a roof, complete with balustrades, coping, and stackpipes. But except for a replica bank, a jeweler's store, and an administrative interior that could have been part of an embassy, they were all hollow. The paramilitary exercises rehearsed there, with the students taking it in

115

turn to play the roles of guerrillas, police, and members of the public, were concerned with holdups, rooftop escapes, and street pursuit rather than forcible entry or the burglary of rooms. Such trivia could in any case be attended to in the houses of the village.

Dodging between automobiles and cabs crowding the artificial street, Mazzari in his first role—as a traffic cop—could from his own not inconsiderable experience have suggested a number of improvements to the schema outlined by the instructors. But it was no part of his real-life role to improve on the antisocial designs of these evil men, and he dutifully remained silent and followed orders. What *was* important to his real-life role—and vital to the success of Dean's mission—was the continued concealment of the one physical secret that had so far eluded Nessim's security checks. This was a tiny round plastic box, a quarter of an inch deep and no bigger than a silver dollar, that was taped high up on the inside of his thigh . . . so high up that it was hidden by his genitals, even when he was standing naked in the shower.

The box had been modified from an ordinary "bleeper," of the kind used to contact hospital personnel and White House security men. But the talkback microphone had been removed and the incoming signal, instead of being audible, was tactile. Inside the plastic cover there was a miniature pulsator that could transmit either a continuous vibration or an intermittent series of short or long impulses to the sensitive skin of the thigh.

And this device—since it had been impossible for Mazzari to smuggle any kind of transmitter in with him—was the sole means of communication (and then it was only one-way) that Dean had with his undercover agent.

116

12

Jason Mettner

Sometimes they fall right into your lap. It doesn't happen often, but when it does . . . boy, you take advantage of it, because it's going to be a long time before the next one comes along!

I was kind of burned up, the way Dean and Hammer took a powder along with this chick right after I hit the northern part of Corsica. I mean, okay, I couldn't talk my way onto the helicopter shuttle they planned to run over this guy Nessim's property. So I hightailed it back to Ajaccio to see if I couldn't locate the flatfoot, Ancarani, that I'd met in Paris, and get him to come across with something more than island proverbs. And, okay, he wasn't home yet, or if he was, he'd gone out again. Or he was on indefinite vacation. Or he was maybe shooting pool with some buddies in Melbourne, Australia. Whatever. The point was, so far as I was concerned, it was three strikes and out. He wasn't there.

Wasted journey, all right? Just the same, Hammer at least could have told me they'd had to postpone the hit on account of they had to train a whole team. After all, I was sitting on their story, the way I promised. And I could have made the front page with it, even the way it was then.

What the hell. I'd lost them, and that was that. Right then, of course, I wasn't wise to the fact that they, were raising a team. All I knew was that the more I looked for them, the way it says in the kids' teddy-bear book, the more they weren't around. And I'd no way this side of Jupiter finding out when they'd be back; if they'd be back. No way.

So what does Mrs. Mettner's boy do? Shit, I figured, I

might as well fill in time, go chase up the goddamn story about the dame from Albuquerque who'd bought the Champagne vineyard. That way Radczinski would at least pick up the expenses tab (sure, sure, I was on the payroll again: a phone call at the right time fixed everything. I mean, I told you, didn't I?). And maybe if the story didn't turn up mud, I could chisel a week's vacation out of *Worldwide*—hell, the guy had *offered* me one, hadn't he?—and sneak back to Corsica in the hope of picking up the trail someplace. It didn't seem that Dean was the kind of guy to let the contract drop through the floor. I didn't know any reason why he should have vanished, but I guessed he'd be back sometime or other. It was just a question of my being there when he was.

So.

Paris, France, and then that great big wide town called Rheims, where all the bosses in the Champagne Mafia hang their hats. I'm there two weeks, making what we call discreet inquiries (which is to say bribing employees to break confidences), when I get the break. Some old guy, a chief cellarman who'd been fired and was sore as hell about it, gave me the line on a café on the outskirts of Epernay. He knew all about the American lady, and good luck to her if she could soak the *salauds* who made too much money out of the indefensibly high prices that the U.S. market could command. The only thing was—a crabbed finger laid alongside a nose that the wine looked upon when it was red—the bastards could only be undercut if the organization doing the undercutting did it in bulk. There was a complicated fiscal reason for this, which it took all of three Armagnacs and two strong coffees to explain, and still it meant nothing to me. I guess, roughly, that it added up to the supermarket syndrome: buying in large quantities is cheap, so it's worth taking a smaller profit margin with a bigger turnover because you make more money in the end. The only thing was, in the case of the American lady, the vineyard she had bought was not sufficiently *important* for those parameters to apply.

There was, of course, no chance of her expanding or buying more land in the area: the wine Mafia, once her intentions were known, would see to that. But the American lady, my new friend said, was indomitable. She was determined. If she could not undercut on the accounts side, she would cut on the side of the product.

"Meaning exactly ... ?" I asked.

"Oh, monsieur! Monsieur cannot be so naïve!" The old guy was half cut himself by now. "The lady will make up the required amount by adding cheap wine from another region and falsifying the *certificats d'origine*. It is, after all, what the *vignerons* of Bordeaux do when there is insufficient supply to meet the demand. This is well known in the business."

And where, I asked, would the cheap wine come from? If I could find out, and get the facts confirmed by the guys selling the cheap stuff, and trace it back to Champagne, it wasn't a bad story at that. It could even make the publisher look kindly on my vacation request.

There were a number of regions where a white wine that could be faked up as though treated by the *méthode champenoise* could be bought, the old drunk told me. Spain, Italy, the Loire, parts of the Côtes du Rhône near the town of Die, the Languedoc. In this case, however . . .

Don't tell me. You guessed it already? Yeah, that's right.

Corsica.

The most likely areas, the guy tells me, are the Balagne, near Calvi; the Sartenais, which is right down south; or the Nebbio. This last would have suited me fine—it's a flat, fertile area south of Bastia and St. Florent, between the mountains and the sea. It's also about ten minutes' drive from Nessim's playground. But the old boy had no idea which one the lady was using. For that, he tells me, one would have to go oneself to the island.

Nothing would suit me better. I hare back to Paris and take the first plane out, waiting only to phrase a cable to the office, telling them what I am doing . . . and why. This way, I figure, Radczinski may even think there's a connection between my previous insistence on Corsica and the way the wine job is turning out. Maybe I can kind of slip it in subtly that I suspected this Corsica-Champagne tie-in but didn't want to let on until I was sure. Would he fall for that? Probably not. But it gave me an honest-to-God reason for being there—a reason he couldn't quarrel with because he himself had laid the story on me—and that was all I needed.

The first thing I had to do, though, was check out which of these areas was selling wine to a lady from Albuquerque. And if the deal was undercover, that might not be too easy. For starters, I tried the Maison des Vins in Ajaccio. This is kind of an information bureau, financed by a cooperative of wine growers, programmed to hand out publicity material on

Corsican wines. You can taste them there, you can buy them there, you can even drink them with a meal there, on a terrace overlooking the sea. You can find out All a Gastronome Wants to Know about the harvest, the pressing, the bottling, the maturing, and even the different types of vine cultivated. They'll give you as much promotional material on the virtues of Corsican wine as you can carry. What they won't give you is the name and addresses of the folks who buy the stuff in bulk.

"But that is confidential material, monsieur," the broad behind the desk told me. "It concerns nobody but the parties involved."

"It concerns me," I said.

"May one ask in what way?" She was about forty years old, thin, flat-chested, and colorless. Pale chains looped down to her neck from the transparent frames of her glasses. I handed her some fancy line about a special supplement, a California restaurateur specializing in Mediterranean food and a behind-the-scenes piece I was supposed to be cooking up. They always fall for it if it's California.

Except, it seemed, at the Maison des Vins in Ajaccio. I scored zero. She handed me a list of 173 proprietors of vineyards on the island and suggested I make my own inquiries. I tried another tack. Which of these guys, I asked, produced a wine comparable to the *blanc-de-blancs* of the Champagne district?

Corsican wines, she told me, were in a class of their own, not to be compared with the products of any other region. The same could have been said for her: her lacquered hair was the color and consistency of the steel swarf that curls away from a lathe in a machine shop. She looked as though she had never been asked out on a date in her life; worse, she looked as if she didn't care. She was vain about that hair, just the same. She patted the crimped waves complacently as I turned to leave. "Mind you don't cut your hand," I said sourly.

Outside on the sidewalk—it was almost dusk and the steamer from Nice was black against the red sky beyond the port—I almost bumped into a cop in uniform. He was a tall guy with a horse face, a hairline mustache, and a certain amount of gold splashed around on *képi* and shoulder. "Ancarani!" I said. "*Now* he shows up!"

"*Pardon?*" For a moment he looked puzzled, and then his

face cleared. He said, "Ah! Monsieur Mettnair! The journalist chasing the so mysterious story. What brings you here at last?"

"I was already here three weeks ago," I said. "But you weren't. I looked for you all over town."

"Possibly." He favored me with that shrug again. It was a good performance. "One has one's exterior duties."

"Anyway, there's nothing mysterious about the story"—I figured I could telescope the two, the way I had with the office—"it has to do with an American woman buying into the wine business. And there's a Corsican angle, for your information."

"Indeed. How interesting. A *criminal* angle, do you mean?"

"I already told you: I don't handle only crime stories," I said irritably. I wasn't sure if I could take him into my confidence. I knew that passing one wine off as another was illegal in France. But what if it was going abroad? I didn't want to interest him too much, in case there should be a police crackdown on the deal—which would leave yours truly with no story. I decided to stall for the moment. "I want to interview a producer who's selling in bulk to this lady," I said, "but right now I don't know which of the 173 guys in the business qualifies."

"Why don't you ask the lady?"

"I would if I knew where she was, but I don't. I guess you wouldn't be able to help? It's a white wine. Is there any special area more likely than another? I mean, if I knew the region, I could narrow down the search some."

He shrugged again. "It depends on what grapes . . . They grow Muscat on Cap Corse. But then there are the Malvoisie, the Nielluccio, the Sciaccarello. They are starting a big-time commercialization on the eastern-coast plains. But this is mainly Grenache—"

"Yeah, yeah," I said. "Could it by chance be from the Nebbio area?"

The cemetery teeth were suddenly unveiled. "Ah, yes," he said. "The Nebbio. Of course, the Nebbio."

"What do you mean, 'of course'?" I said uneasily.

"Nothing, nothing." He looked up at a clock set into a church tower across the street. "My duties call me. Perhaps another time we may drink an aperitif together? If you are thirsty in the meantime, there is always the Coco Club."

"The Coco Club?"

"A *boîte*. The vintage is recently terminated. It was a good year and the wine will be good. The producers go there sometimes to spend their money and celebrate. Perhaps there you would find . . ." He left the sentence unfinished and turned to go back toward the *commissariat*. "It's in a narrow street behind the port," he called over his shoulder. "If they tell you the Nebbio, watch out for those scorpions!"

The Coco Club was a long bar with a big guy sitting at a table just inside the padded doors. There was a bouncer standing behind him with a face about as expressive as the north face of the Eiger. I reckoned I'd play it straight and flashed my press card. "Glad to have you with us, friend," said the character on the door. "Gentlemen of the press always welcome. Bar's straight ahead, sir."

The bar was crowded. Most of the drinkers were men. Big, well-fed men wearing city suits beneath their farmers' faces, some of them with Bonnie-and-Clyde shoes in brown and white. They were talking quietly for the most part, the chuckle rather than the laugh. These were guys who had made it . . . and intended to keep it.

There were one or two girls around, but the action was evidently in the cellar below. From the top of a flight of stairs I could hear a group down there playing pretty groovy music—for Corsica. And crowd sounds that meant the scene was jumping. All very nice, but how the hell was I going to find out which of these growers sent their invoices to Albuquerque?

"Too bad you couldn't find out about the white wine," a girl's voice said behind me.

Telepathy yet! I swung around. She was leaning against the bar—a tanned beach broad with frizzy platinum hair, a scanty sequined top, and an impudent bottom. "Hi, handsome," she said lazily. "You look like I could do with a drink. What you gonna buy me, man?"

"I always did go for the subtle approach," I said. "Keep me in the dark a little while longer and order for both of us."

The bouncer had followed me in. He whispered in the barkeep's ear. This was to wise him up that I was press, and save me from the stuff they served the tourists. In fact the rye-and-dry I was handed was cold, it was good, and it was genuine. I ordered a couple more, just to make sure. I was right the first time.

"How did you know?" I asked.

"The bureau. I work in the outer office."

"In those clothes? With Miss Frosty?"

She giggled. "No, silly. White shirt and respectable skirt in there."

"How come an American girl . . . ?"

"Earns her living in the Ajaccio Maison des Vins? I'm here on vacation and I run out of the necessary. So because I speak French and English *and* some Italian I get me a job until I have enough loot so I can split. I help some with the tourists. You know?"

"I'm not certain that I do," I said. I was lying. I know a hustler all right when I see one, even if she does work at the Maison des Vins in Ajaccio in her spare time.

"You like to dance?" the girl said.

"Is that a question or statement?"

"What question isn't basically a statement? Come to that, what statement, scientifically speaking, isn't a question?"

"I like to dance," I said. "I majored in Eng. lit., and that gave me enough Gertrude Stein for a lifetime."

"That's not Abner Stein's sister, is it?"

"I don't think so. Countrywoman of ours who lived in Paris. The story is that on her deathbed she asks: 'What is the answer?' And when none of the mourners gathered around can think of a reply, she says: 'All right then: what is the question?' "

"Oh," the girl said. "Paris."

Her name was Candy and she must have been all of nine-teen years old. Downstairs, she hooked her forearms over my shoulders and draped four-fifths of her body, from the tips of the sequins to the tips of her silver sandals, against me. The top fifth leaned back and looked me in the eye. At least, that's my guess: I couldn't actually see her doing it, because there were about eight hundred people jammed into a space the size of a Mercedes 600. The short-chassis version. And the only light in the place came from a single lamp above the piano keyboard. "Dance" was a euphemism. We stayed pressed together and swayed while the four guys on the stand earned their money. The music wasn't bad, quiet enough so you could talk, but plenty of drive. Fiddle, bass, piano, and electric guitar, with the guitarist really wailing. "Where are you from, Candy?" I asked during a bass solo. Mettner the brilliant conversationalist.

"Albuquerque," she said absently.

I stopped swaying. "Albuquerque, New Mexico?"

"Where else? How many other Albuquerques do you know?"

I let that one go with the tide. I said, "Those bulk consignments I was asking about—if you heard the whole routine—they're invoiced to a woman from Albuquerque."

"Why mess with her when you can dance with me?" Candy asked.

"I have a message from her mother in Wichita, Kansas," I said.

"I could add a P.S. that would make you forget the message."

"And how would that read?"

She hummed a couple of bars of the evergreen that the guitar man was ornamenting. Her fingers laced together behind my neck. "Candy kisses," she said meaningfully.

It was about this time that the music was drowned by the stamping of feet overhead. This was followed by a succession of sounds I had gotten familiar with in my years on the crime desk: the noises of combat—like splintering wood, breaking glass, shouts, and curses. A communal tremor passed through the dancers packed in front of the stand. "My God, it's not another police raid, is it?" someone near me asked plaintively. "More like the Unione again, if Ricardo hasn't paid his dues," another voice replied.

Abruptly light flooded the room from wall brackets on three sides of the floor. I took a quick glance around. Being a private club, the premises were exempt from fire regulations. Apart from a narrow doorway that led to a dressing room in back of the band, the stairway was the only exit.

There was a lot of yelling up there in the bar now. Some of the men on the floor ran for the stairs. At least one of them was carrying a knife. A few girls screamed. The band had already played Harry Houdini, but the bouncer was standing on the edge of the stage, telling everybody not to panic, please, everything was okay. I was figuring him for an optimist when all the lights went out, including the one above the piano.

In total darkness there was a moment's frozen pause in which the mayhem above sounded unnaturally loud. Then, beneath the resumed uproar bursting around us, I was aware of a purposeful undercurrent, a whispering, a shuffling of feet. My arm was seized; I was shoved toward the stage. I tripped over the edge, cursing, and Candy's hand, which had stayed in mine, jerked me impatiently forward.

Surprisingly, the stage was clear. The musicians and—with the exception of the piano—their instruments had disappeared. It's amazing how they do it: the first hint of trouble, and they already left, it was sixteen other guys, the place never had any music. And they always get the instruments, even drums if there are any, away with them. I think they must have to pass some kind of a test before they can join their union's local.

A cool breeze blew through the door that led to the dressing room. There was quite a crowd of folks pushing through, but there was no jam-up—just an occasional staying hand, a murmured "Easy there, lady!" . . . "No cause to panic!" . . . "This way, now." The dressing room was minute. Beyond it, signaled by the odor of carbolic, was a pint-size washroom . . . and yet this continuous stream of guys and gals seemed to be piling in there.

A conveniently placed stepladder stood beneath an open trapdoor in the washroom ceiling. And those in the know, aided by the club stewards, simply climbed up and disappeared into the night. Clearly it was an established getaway, arranged to aid members who wished to avoid embarrassing encounters with the law—or the Unione Corse. With organization like that, who needs fire regulations!

We surfaced in an alley behind the adjoining block. "Well, honey," I said when the outflow had thinned some, "it seems I owe you the other half of that drink we left back there. Where do you want to go?" In the street lighting, her lips were the color of ripe plums, and I was crazy for summer fruit.

She steered me to a second-floor dive over a bakery where they were already at work on tomorrow's bread. "You'd never guess why they opened over a bakery," Candy told me when I'd bribed my way in and ordered.

"No complaints about the noise, because bakers work at night?" I offered. The place was half the size of the Coco Club, with about 112 times as many people shrieking and braying between the walls, and the waves of conversation crashed around us like there was a force-nine gale behind them. I use the nautical metaphor deliberately. Most of the customers were what Côte d'Azur residents call "yachties"—a collection of weirdos crewing the rich men's boats berthed all year round at Cannes and Antibes and Menton and Juan-les-Pins. They come from all over, though there's a preponderance of English—dropouts from the rat race, advertising whiz kids who didn't stay the course, failed salesmen with an IQ of minus nine, and artist hippies whose work just ain't commercial. No connection with genuine mariners, though. But the yachties all have three things in common: loud voices, an excessive consumption of liquor, and a puerile sense of humor. On calm days in summer they take their floating gin palaces cruising, when the owners fly down friends they wish to impress from London and Paris and Bonn. The rest of the time they draw fat paychecks, cheat their employers on the revictualizing invoices (which they split with the local tradesmen), and loaf around pouring bonded liquor into the nubile camp followers you always find where the living is easy. The employers are London property dealers, Danish shipping magnates, Ruhr industrialists, French arms dealers—and of course, increasingly, oil sheikhs. For all I knew, half the red-faced beer drinkers in cute yachting caps were on Nessim's payroll.

Okay, okay, so I'm jealous. Who's denying it? Candy was saying, "The noise was one reason. But the main one was the smell."

"It's pretty bad," I agreed, "but I don't quite see—?"

"No, no!" she shouted. "You can't tell charge from tobacco over the odor of baking bread. Not for sure. Did you know that?"

"Charge?" I yelled.

"Quiet, or you'll have the legionnaires over there out the window! I mean like smoking. Shit. Grass. Hash. Charge."

I shook my head. I hadn't known. You learn something every day. I said, "So the jolly old crowd lights up as soon as the ovens are fired?"

"Or before. Talking of which, I could go a bundle on a smoke right now."

Acting dumb, I fished out a pack of Camels. If the place had run a competition offering prizes for the miming of pejorative epithets, Candy's reaction would have won three years running and gained her the trophy in perpetuity. The words chosen by the successful candidate were Scornful and Derisive. "All right," I roared peaceably. "All right. It just happens that I'm not in the habit of crossing frontiers with my pockets stuffed full of marijuana. Where I come from, the weed just happens still to be illegal."

"Here too, silly. If you want to be stuffy. If you want to please the lady you're with, you go get some from Joe."

"I see. Joe."

"The guy in the men's room," she explained impatiently.

The door was hidden behind a scrimage line of big block-and-tackle men wearing soiled white jeans and striped shirts with anchors aweigh. I ducked past right tackle, made some yardage, and went for six.

The attendant in the men's room was a bald, fat Moroccan. By the time I'd waited around for the place to be empty, hedged about some, slipped him a couple of ten-franc pieces, and finally put the question, I had an eight-thousand-word Sunday-magazine-section piece on his life story. Even then, he only shook his dark head. "I am desolated," he said, "but it is impossible. Tonight it cannot be done."

"But I thought . . . ? They told me . . ."

"Sure, sure. Of course, monsieur. Any other night. But I cannot sell you what I do not have, *n'est-ce pas?* My supplier has let me down."

"That's too bad," I said with some relief. "I was hoping . . ."

"I know, my friend. Others too. But Margie didn't show this week. Some inconvenience in the north, I believe."

"Margie, Margie, it's you," I sang in my pleasing light baritone. The Moroccan stared at me. "Don't worry," I said. "It's not important."

"It is to some people," he growled.

He was right, of course. Everything's important to someone. And to me, at that moment in history, it was lips like ripe plums. Which just shows how even a newspaperman can get his priorities wrong.

"That's too bad," Candy sighed when I returned to the table with the bad news. "I guess there's nothing else to do: we'll have to go back to my place, then."

I sighed too. With satisfaction. Maybe with a little . . . er . . . intimacy, she'd be able to tell me what I wanted to know about the wine business. She did. Later. And it was the Nebbio, too.

I woke up the next morning with three headaches. One because rye and marijuana didn't mix. Two because, even if the wine story did take me now near to Nessim's territory, I still didn't see how I could use the situation to progress the Marc

Dean story. Three because they don't issue invoices or receipts for sin, and now there was another hundred bucks I had to fake somehow on my expense sheet.

The apartment I was in was one of those "bohemian" studios with sloping ceilings, damp marks on the wall, and candles stuck into Chianti bottles. So far as I could tell, I was alone in it. There was a depression in the second pillow on the divan (navy-blue sheets with a printed Indian cotton bedspread), so unless I really did have two heads, it hadn't all been a dream. I guessed that . . . what was her name? Cindy? No—Candy . . . I guessed Candy had gone back to work enlightening the world about Corsican wines. That was what I had to do, too. I must find out the quickest way to get to the Nebbio.

I swung my feet off the divan and shuddered upright. My head hit one of the slanting beams that kept the roof off the ceiling. I picked myself up and padded in search of coffee. There was nothing but instant in the kitchenette. Through the small square window I had a knockout view of Ajaccio laundry hanging in tiers from the shuttered balconies of the tall, narrow, grimed facades of the houses three feet away on the far side of the street.

Did I say knockout? I figured the coffee could wait. I couldn't. I went looking for the john. You had to go through a clothes closet to get there. They had a tasseled bathrobe cord instead of a chain. Very cute.

Next on the list was the bathroom. No dice. Finally I had a hunch and opened the entrance door. There it was, against the wall at the stairhead—a shallow earthenware sink with a single dripping faucet. Cold water, of course.

Back in the love nest, a brassy blond who looked like she once sang in a Western saloon grinned at me from out of one of those oval silver frames folks used to give as wedding presents in the 1920's. At the foot of the photo, above the litter of discarded nylons and a torn brassiere on top of the bureau, I read the words, scrawled with a thick felt-tip, "For my little girl, with all the love in the world—M."

"Momma," I said, "you shoulda taken a return engagement at that saloon and done better for your little girl than this." I decided to make a second run for the instant.

Judging from the odors floating up through the open window, Ajaccio was a fishing port. I put down the jar, figuring maybe I'd be better off at a sidewalk café.

128

That was my mistake. It also brought me my fourth headache. As I turn_d to go back into the *salon*, someone dropped a mountain range on the back of my head and I pitched forward into a roaring blackness.

13

Marc Dean

The sirocco was blowing off the northern coast of the island, and Laurence Chateauroux's dark, glossy hair was teased out like banners against the pale, clear sky. From the ground where he squatted at the rear of the panel truck, Marc Dean stared up at her racy silhouette. As she stood at the edge of the low cliff, the wind plastered her dress against her thighs, shadowing the subtle curve at the base of her belly and sculpturing the outline of her breasts. Dean sighed and shook his head.

She turned and smiled at him, the teeth brilliant in the dark face. "What is it?" she asked.

He smiled himself, ruefully. "I was just thinking," he said, "how nice to be an oil sheikh, with all the money in the world, no need to work, and all the time in the world to spend with girls like you."

"Girls like me don't like oil sheikhs," Laurence said. "That's one reason why we're here, isn't it?"

"I guess so. What's good about today is that you *are* here." He turned back to the machine he was assembling from a crate in the truck. The shape was familiar; it was the size and scale of the device that made it bizarre.

It stood on four splayed, stove-enameled feet terminating in rubber cushions about half the size of a clenched fist—a miniature remote-controlled, pilotless helicopter. The body, checkered in yellow and black, looked like a circular soup tureen. It was twenty-four inches in diameter and sixteen inches deep. From the center of this rose a thick shaft about one foot high, carrying two five-foot, variable-pitch rotor blades at right angles to each other. The top of the shaft was no higher than a point halfway between Dean's knee and hip.

"It's incredible," Laurence said. "And you say it's powered by two motors from a *lawn mower*?"

"Not exactly," Dean said. "But motors on exactly the same principle: two-stroke gasoline engines, each driving one rotor. It can fly at eighty miles an hour or hover completely motionless."

She shook her head. "Wherever did you get hold of it?"

"They're commercially available. From the Westland airplane company at Yeovil, in England. It's called the Westland Wisp. It seems they do a pretty fancy export trade."

"I would think so. The spy in the sky."

He nodded. "That's what they call it. There's a television camera housed in the body, and the pictures it relays show up on a monitor screen that forms part of the remote-control panel. Plus of course you can record the whole trip on videotape."

"How high does it fly? Won't they try to shoot it down?"

"Probably," Dean said. "Once they realize what it is. But by that time it should have done its job. It's got very low radar, infrared, and noise signatures. So, if we send it in low, it shouldn't register at all on their detection equipment; the alarm won't be given until they actually see it with their eyes. And it may take a while for them to get wise to the implications even when they do."

He rose to his feet and took the control panel from the truck. The wide plasticized deck carried dials and switches and graduated tuning wheels as well as a slot for the introduction of the HT batteries that worked the radio control mechanism. An eight-foot telescopic aerial pulled out at one side of the hooded viewing screen, and the whole complex was slung from two shoulder straps like a match-seller's tray.

Laurence came toward him. The light had changed a great deal in the few weeks since they first came to Corsica. Now it was autumn; the sun's trajectory was low; although the rocky outcrops bordering the Desert of Agriates were hard and clear in the late-October air, already at noon hollows out of the direct rays brimmed with dusky shadow. The girl's face, too, when she turned away from the sun, became mysterious and indistinct, its fine lines blurred in the refracted light. The wind, whistling through cistus and juniper where they had parked near the creek at Peraiola, blew a lock of hair across

131

her eyes. She put a hand on his shoulder. "It will work, won't it?" she asked. "Even if it doesn't come back, it will send the pictures of the terrain that you need? With the help of the pictures, you will be able to organize the attack you plan? It is very important."

"I never like to count my chickens," Dean said. "It should do that."

"Unless this evil thing is destroyed, more and more the world will become a dangerous place—perhaps in time too dangerous for girls like me to meet men like you on a clifftop in the sun. Too dangerous even for the oil sheikhs, who will be unable to stop what they have started."

Dean kissed her. Lightly on the eyelids and at the corners of her mouth. "We'll pull out every stop, honey, I promise you," he said gently.

There were three removable hatches, about the size of coffee saucers, in the body of the mini-helicopter. Reaching in through the top two, he started the motors and then replaced the covers. The third, underneath the body, between the four legs, he left open to reveal the lens of the television camera.

The idling motors made a barely discernible hum. "Okay, honey, stand back: we're gonna take the air!" Dean said.

As she moved away, he slung the control panel in place in front of him and twisted a knob. Slowly at first and then with increasing speed the rotors began to revolve. There was a faint whine as gears meshed, and the engine note became slightly more obtrusive.

Dean's fingers were busy as a pianist's during a Bach fugue. A red pilot light flashed and then held steady on the section of deck reserved for the radio controls. A fraction at a time, he turned the largest of the tuner wheels.

The tiny chopper's engines climbed the scale. The whirling blades were transformed into a single flashing disk. Dean thumbed a switch, a green pilot glowed, he clicked a knob.

As the pitch of the rotors altered, the machine, as if pulled on invisible wires, rose slowly into the air. As soon as it was a few feet above the roof of the truck, he sent it skimming around in a wide circle, testing the radio controls. When he was satisfied that everything was working satisfactorily, he maneuvered it up to a height of about fifty feet, directing it toward the three-mile distant ridge, the shadowed crest of which was already a dusty purple in the autumn light. The Wisp sped away across the bare rock outcrops and the pockets of stunted *garrigue*. When it was no more than a speck, barely discernible against the windswept blue of the sky, Dean switched on the TV scanner. "Come and look," he called to Laurence.

She had been standing with her back to the truck, staring out over the three lines of white breakers foaming in to the crescent of sand below the bluff. Now she turned and peered over his shoulder at the tiny monitor screen. "My God," she said, "that's incredible!"

On the pearled surface of the cathode tube a faithful representation of the barren countryside flashed past. Outliers of granite in mauves and pinks and grays, green carpets of moss clinging to the rocky shelves, the dun spikes of desiccated scrub, all raced across the rectangle in a blur of movement.

"I'll have to take her higher," Dean said. "Much higher. The camer's too close to the ground to show anything in context—it has to be at some distance if we're going to get a clear picture of the terrain as a whole." He manipulated controls. The bare undulations of desert receded on the screen. "In any case, we have to make several hundred feet to get her over the ridge. There's a summit near the road to St. Florent—the Col de Lavezzo—that's over three hundred meters."

"Won't you lose a lot of detail at that height?" Laurence asked. "I mean, if there's a bunker or something you want to check out, or some part of the defenses you'd like to study closely?"

He smiled. "Like all good cameramen, we have a zoom lens." He twisted a knob, and Laurence gasped, instinctively moving a pace back as a jagged mass of rock appeared to leap toward her out of the screen.

A dial on the control panel repeated readings registered by altimeter equipment on the miniature helicopter. As the ground represented on the screen began to rise, Dean slotted in a cassette recorder and directed the machine to climb. When it was overflying the lower slopes of the ridge— "Look!" Laurence said. "Isn't that the stream where you did your geology number?"—he pressed another button and switched the receiver to "Record."

The altimeter needle swung steadily across the dial. At an indicated six hundred feet, the lip of the ridge slid from top to bottom of the screen. Here, clearly, they could see a lookout post half-buried in the rock, some kind of multiple-barrel gun behind a steel shield, an astonished face turned upward as the chopper passed over a guard outside the bunker. "Those short posts, like undersize pylons, are supports for the sensors," Dean said. "That sentry will be in contact with the citadel by now, either by phone or walkie-talkie, to report the presence of a UFO in his sector."

"They'll try to shoot it down, won't they?" Laurence said again.

"Probably. But we may have time to make a couple of passes before they get organized. In any case, the computer-operated guns won't have a traverse that will permit them to fire into the sky. They aren't geared up to repel airborne attacks, after all. Small arms, a machine gun, SMG's, or possibly a bazooka—that's all the Wisp will have to contend with."

"Even so . . ." She looked dubious. "If the machine is so low, eighty miles an hour isn't all that fast—and it will be well within range."

"Sure, honey. But they have to have the guns where it'll be. I mean, I'm doing the entrance and the village citadel on this first run. That's where there's likely to be a concentration of weapons. And I hope we'll be away before they get around to using 'em. After that I plan to crisscross the property at random, maybe taking a second flight over the coastal cliffs, and then a diagonal, from someplace out along the ridge to the far corner by the Legion firing range. They won't be able to deploy whatever arms they have across the property at eighty miles an hour. Nor, when they get a sighting, will they be able to predict the course the Wisp will take. We'll be too low for their radar to warn them."

Dean circled the citadel once. A man in white robes standing by the huge swimming pool . . . figures in combat gear moving up the steep streets below a jumble of tiled roofs . . . Land Rovers in a motor park. The helicopter flew over the firing range and battle course toward the shallow valley beyond. The hangar was still there, but there was no sign of the mysterious city street. Dean had begun to doubt that he had ever seen it at all.

On the return leg, by a wood off to one side, half a dozen men ran out into the open and starting firing submachine guns at the chopper. They could see puffs of smoke and a twinkle of flame against the dark background, but the Wisp flew on unscathed. Sending it slantwise across the property near the sea, Dean discovered a landing strip he had not suspected. A twin-jet Cessna stood in a dispersal pan, and there were evidently underground strongpoints at each end of the strip. "With the money he's got," Dean said, circling the machine over a buttressed stairway he had spotted that led below the earth, "he could have the latest RDF and talkdown equipment for that plane down there."

"What exactly are the plans?" Laurence had been back to France to see Duclos and the people she still referred to as her "principals" while Dean was visiting Africa to sign up Mazzari, and arranging with Sean Hammer the recruitment and training of their assault force.

"Make a map of Nessim's territory, so far as it's possible, from the recording of what we're watching on the screen. Get the map to Sean, so that he can fill in the guys on what they have to expect and brief them on alternative tactics. Then— this is the most difficult—contact Mazzari and supply him with ground beacons—"

"Ground beacons?"

"They emit a radio signal on a fixed frequency, a beam, and anyone with a receiver tuned to the same frequency can home in on the beacon. If Mazzari can place them at strategic points—where the defenses are . . . I won't say at their weakest, but at their least strong—then our paratroops will avoid the risk of jumping into a hornet's nest of hostile gunmen. They should be able to reform and advance as a proper striking force before anyone knows they're there. The same goes for the overland soldiers: with beacons in the right place, they don't have to get cut down like targets at a fairground shooting stall when they break through the perimeter."

Laurence was frowning. "Yes, but how *do* you contact your man Mazzari and get these beacons to him? If, as you say, the so-called students never leave the domain . . . if there's no way of getting in from the outside . . . ?"

"Just a minute, honey." He was bending over the small screen, his brow furrowed in concentration. Quickly he twisted, pressed, pushed. The helicopter appeared to be circling again, sometimes over the bare rock, sometimes just over the sea. Dean took the machine lower, actuated the zoom lens. A granite outlier that rushed up into focus revealed itself as the cover for a partially concealed pillbox, surmounted by the revolving wire skeleton of some kind of radar antenna. "Shit!" Dean breathed. "It looks like they have more sophisticated equipment than I thought." He widened the circle. "That looks like a modified Wurtzburg Bowl, that saucer-shaped thing there. It's much smaller than the usual model, but . . ." He paused in mid-sentence.

"Is it serious?" Laurence asked.

"Depends. If everything's right up-to-date . . . But no! Jesus, surely they couldn't have . . . ? I was going to say they might even have some kind of ground to air missile. But I don't think—"

"You don't mean nuclear . . . ?" She sounded alarmed.

"No, no. Conventional HE. But with that kind of equipment, you could maybe expect stuff programmed, for example, to home on the heat from a plane's motor. They certainly have the computer capability."

"Even little tiny engines like this?" She indicated the screen.

"Even little tiny engines like this," Dean said. "I reckon we have as much as we need now: it's time to bring Wisp home to Dad." He turned again to the controls. The barren ground receded from the screen and slid past more rapidly. But the maneuver was too late. They saw the steel shutter sliding back into the rock. The missile was small, a slender tube less than four feet long: it emerged from the launcher quite slowly, accelerating with breathtaking speed as the second motor was engaged. "An SA-7," Dean said grimly.* "Our only chance is to try to duck below its minimum range."

On the screen, the ground rushed up once more as he reset the controls. The missile was foreshortened now, a gray oval streaking toward the chopper. For a hundredth of a second they saw it like a ball being hurled at them from the monitor. Then the screen went blank.

*The Soviet-made SA-7, or Grail—a man-portable antiaircraft weapon —was first used in the 1973 Arab-Israeli war. When the operator aims the launcher at the target, the thermal battery is switched on. As soon as the target is picked up, there is an audible warning and a light glows. A second trigger is then pressed and the first motor ejects the missile from the launcher. The second is a booster and the third a sustainer. The missile weighs twenty pounds and carries a small high-explosive warhead with a graze fuse. The bore of the weapon is less than four inches. Its maximum range is two miles, its minimum operational altitude 165 feet.

Dean sighed. "Too bad." He held up his hand before she could speak. Faintly, from beyond the ridge, the echo of a distant explosion rolled.

"I hate it," Laurence said. "Even a machine, even something without a pilot, just a mess of metal and plastic and wires. All destruction is so . . . so . . . such an indignity. I almost felt I had gotten to *know* the thing!"

He shrugged. "It had done its job. Practically everything we want to know should already be here." He patted the video cassette. "You were asking how I planned to contact Mazzari and deliver the beacons just now. What we've just seen made up my mind for me. I'd thought of borrowing your fire-department chopper again, but no dice."

"Well, how *do* you plan to do it?"

Dean countered the question with another. "Are you still in touch with your erstwhile employer, Daredevil Dan De'Ath, the Death-Defying Diver?"

"Yes, of course. I think he's barnstorming somewhere in northern Italy. Why?"

He smiled crookedly. "Have you ever done your wing-walking number on a glider?" he asked.

Dean was about to stow the control panel in its case at the rear of the panel truck when he heard the voice.

"What the devil do you think you're doing?"

He backed out between the open doors of the vehicle. Two uniformed gendarmes were standing watching him. Fifty yards away, at the edge of the track leading to the road, there was a bright blue Estafette with a flashing amber light on its roof. "Pardon me?" Dean said.

"You heard. What are you doing here?" The man's voice was neither friendly nor respectful. He was almost as big as Dean, a coarse-faced individual with a heavy black mustache. His companion was slightly shorter, clean-shaven, with small eyes and a prominent chin.

"Do I have to be doing anything?" Dean said mildly. "So far as I know, we're not on private property. There's no sign saying that parking is illegal. The military restricted area is miles away. I'm enjoying your beautiful Corsican scenery: I do like to be beside the seaside."

"Your papers." The gendarme evidently had no knowledge of Victorian music-hall songs. He held out a peremptory hand.

Laurence came around from the front of the truck. "What's the trouble?" she asked.

"I wish I knew," Dean said. The papers he was carrying were his own genuine ones. He produced them—passport, visa, French residence permit, gun license.

"Yours," the gendarme with small eyes said to Laurence. She produced her French passport and he handed it to his companion.

The taller man turned over the pages of all the documents slowly, sometimes riffling back several leaves, occasionally looking up to compare a photo with the face before him, reading every word. "This gun for which you have a permit?" he said. "You have it with you?"

"No."

"Why not? Where is it?"

"I have a license to possess the gun," Dean said, mastering his temper with an effort. "So far as I am aware, that does not oblige me to keep it in my pocket."

"Where is it?"

"That is entirely my business, and I have no intention whatever of telling you," Dean snapped.

"Very well." The man closed the documents, turned on his heel, and began walking toward the patrol wagon.

"Hey! Where the fuck do you think you're going?" the combat leader shouted. He started forward. Laurence raised a hand and called out some kind of warning. Small Eyes unbuttoned the stiff flap of his white hide revolver holster. "Stay where you are," he said.

"Just what is this?" Dean demanded angrily.

"Routine check."

"Routine my ass! This is some kind of—" Dean caught the girl's eye and subsided into silence. As clear as if she had signaled it by semaphore, he read in her expression: Cool it. Don't push it. We just have to grin and bear it.

The tall gendarme had unhooked a radio microphone from under the dashboard of the wagon. He stood outside, one elbow resting on the sill of the open door, reading off details from their ID papers. He kept them waiting a long time.

At last he sauntered back. "All right," Dean said. "You checked back with Bastia or Ajaccio and you found we're not on the wanted list for bank robbery, murder, or incest; we haven't stolen this truck; we have not—so far, at least—

knocked off any policemen's *képis* or spat in their stupid faces—"

"Marc!" the girl said. "Please—"

"—so perhaps now you would have the incalculable goodness to return our papers and let us get on with our day," Dean finished.

The taller gendarme shoved the documents into the side pocket of his jacket and buttoned the flap. "Have a look," he ordered his companion, jerking his head at the panel truck.

Small Eyes half-pulled the control console from its case. "What is this?" he demanded.

"A combined electric shaver and dishwasher," Dean said savagely. "Don't you recognize a gadget when you see one? Or have your eyes gotten too screwed up reading the fine print of the law so that you can find an excuse to make an arrest?"

Laurence sighed audibly. Small Eyes had flushed. "Don't you know it's against the law to operate a radio transmitter without a license from the Minister of Posts and Telecommunications?" he said.

"Certainly I do. So what?"

"Where is your permit for this apparatus?"

"That's not a radio transmitter."

"No? Perhaps you would explain what it is?"

"It's a . . . like a toy . . . a model. For model airplanes. You know: remote control while they fly. This is the control board."

"Indeed? And where is the airplane it controls?"

Dean was silent. The taller gendarme said, "Do you deny that the controlling of this machine—if it exists—is effected by radio impulses?"

"No, but—"

"Then you are operating a transmitter. Without a license."

"The law is framed to regulate those who *broadcast*—who make transmissions of speech or music," Dean said with asperity, "and you know it."

"Technically, you are transmitting with this apparatus. That is highly irregular. We will have to investigate further."

"If these people are suspicious characters," Small Eyes said, "we must remember the burglaries."

"What the hell are you talking about?" Dean raged. "Suspicious characters . . . burglaries . . . you know damned well—"

"You are right," the taller gendarme cut in. "The robbery

at the big property near St. Florent. The thieves were seen but not caught. A foreigner and a woman."

"Perhaps it would save time if we were to take these individuals there now, so that an identification could be made?"

"Exactly. You will come with us." There was a gun in the taller man's hand now. He jerked his head toward the patrol wagon. "Get going, both of you."

"We will take this with us. It may be stolen." Small Eyes began easing the remainder of the control panel out of its case.

"Take your hands off that," Dean said quietly. The video cassette, with its irrecoverable record of the terrain over which the Westland Wisp had flown, was still locked into the slot beside the monitor screen. He was not going to run the risk of that tape being sequestered, held as evidence, run through, perhaps damaged or destroyed by some dumb Corsican flatfoot.

Small Eyes' gun was also unholstered now. "Hold out your hands in front of you," he ordered. He unhooked a pair of handcuffs from the white belt around his waist. The other man moved in threateningly.

Dean held out his hands, palms downward. An instant before the first steel bracelet snapped over his wrist, Laurence uttered a soft cry and collapsed to the ground.

Involuntarily the tall gendarme turned toward her, bending slightly forward. She bounced up like a rubber ball, seizing his gun arm in both hands and sinking her teeth into the wrist. At the same time—Small Eyes too had instinctively glanced away—Dean seized the handcuff and jerked sharply downward, kicking up with one foot at the pistol in the officer's other hand. The weapon flew from his grasp. But a lanyard looping down from the belt was attached to a steel ring in the butt: the gun swung away and then dropped back, still within the gendarme's reach. Unbalanced by the tug on the cuffs, he was groping for it when Dean leaped tigerishly forward and struck him backhanded across the biceps with the edge of his palm. The blow had all of the mercenary leader's 180 pounds behind it, temporarily paralyzing the man's gun arm. The handcuffs dropped to the ground as the gendarme's other arm came up to defend himself.

Dean was at close quarters now. He slammed a ferocious punch to the solar plexus, and then, as his adversary folded forward, grabbed the gun and jerked forcefully downward, trying to snap the cord. But the lanyard was too tough . . . and it was too short to allow Dean to turn the weapon against its owner. He had to rely on his fists to keep the man's hands off the weapon.

The gendarme with the mustache was yelling, trying to shake Laurence free of his savaged wrist. There was no lanyard on his gun and it had dropped to the ground. She kicked it spinning away beneath the panel truck and hung on to the arm, the blood flowing salty in her mouth. Finally he drew back his other fist and hit her heavily on the temple. Her head snapped back and he pulled free, cursing. She tried to knee him in the groin, but he was strong and he was agile. He twisted away, hit her again, on the shoulder this time, so that she spun around—and then he closed in, fast, seized her from behind, and put a half-nelson lock on her as he reached for his handcuffs.

Dean had wedged a forearm beneath his man's chin, forcing the head back while he struggled to keep his hand off the gun. The gendarme's eyes bulged. He made a supreme effort and got his fingers around the chamber and trigger guard of the revolver, straining to bring up the barrel. But Dean's steely grasp closed over the hand, turning it away and squeezing.

The gun went off—a loud report, the slug scoring the rock at their feet before it whined into space.

Dean's numbing grip, on a hand already affected by the blow to the biceps, was weakening the Corsican's hold. But he slammed in punishing blows to the head and shoulders with his other fist—short-arm jabs that were nevertheless powerful and could ultimately tell. It was no time for Queensberry Rules. Dean jerked his knee violently up into his opponent's crotch, and then, as the man groaned and folded forward, he relinquished the gun hand, laced his fingers together, and brought his locked hands crashing down on the back of the gendarme's neck.

The man dropped to the ground like a felled tree.

Bent forward in the crippling lock, Laurence was desperately hacking at the tall gendarme's shins with her heels. But he had already snapped the handcuffs around one of her wrists and was slowly forcing the other up so that he could close the second bracelet.

Dean hurled himself across the intervening space and hit him on the side of the head. It was a tremendous roundhouse blow, a punch that came up from the ground, thrown with all the American's force and lent additional weight by anger. The gendarme released the girl, staggered away, lost his balance, and fell to the ground. Dean was on him before he had time to shake his head. His heel caught the man on the point of the jaw, to send him sprawling on his back. All that was needed then was to bunch together the front of his jacket, haul him a foot or more off the rock, and slam another murderous left to his jaw.

The second gendarme collapsed and lay still.

Dean put a toe beneath the unconscious body and turned it over. He unclasped the ring of keys from the man's belt and unlocked the handcuff around Laurence's wrist. He unbuttoned the jacket pocket and retrieved their papers. Then he fetched Small Eyes' handcuffs, and using both pairs, locked each man's right wrist to the other's left ankle. Finally he walked to the edge of the bluff and threw the two key rings as far as he could into the sea. "That should keep those two bastards occupied for a while," he panted.

"Marc, you're crazy!" Laurence was dabbing the tall man's blood away from her face with a handkerchief. "You don't know what you're doing."

"I know what *they* were doing," he said grimly, "and I don't like it one little bit."

"What do you mean?"

"*If* they were genuine policemen—and it's possible: we know Nessim has certain ministers and some of your cops in his pocket; we know he's covered—if they were genuine, they were certainly working in with our Arab friend. Either he got wise to our chopper earlier than we expected and sent them down here to bring us in, or else they had been watching us for some time and decided on their own initiative. In either case, no way was I going to allow us—and our cassette—to fall into their hands."

"But . . ." She made a helpless gesture. "One of the conditions of your contract was that you should—how do you say?—that you must keep your nose clean, isn't it? You . . . you can't go around disarming policemen, and knocking them out, and stealing their keys. Especially in Corsica."

"Try to stop me." Dean grinned.

"Darling, we are supposed to keep a low profile. If these are genuine gendarmes—and they probably are, you know— the whole island will be on the lookout for us as soon as they get free. Don't forget they already radioed our details some-place. There will be no trouble identifying the aggressors: they have our names, descriptions, passport numbers, every-thing. We shall be unable even to—"

"Look," Dean interrupted. "Of course you're entirely right—or you would be, in the normal course of events. But this wasn't normal." He shook his head. "All that crap about radio transmissions and licenses, the routine-check shit, and most of all the so-called burglary at a big house near St. Florent. You know where that would be, don't you? Muren-zana. They were just casting around for any excuse to get us into that wagon, so they could take us along and hand us over to Nessim. And if anyone ever asked, those two guys never saw us. We just disappeared."

"You really think so?" She still sounded dubious.

"I know so," said Dean. "I know a crooked cop when I see one. That's why they're always so damned unpleasant—be-cause they know they're way out of line, so they have to blus-ter, to convince themselves as well as the victims."

He walked across to the truck and shoved the control panel back into its case. He slid the case out and stood it up against the fender. "I just couldn't let it happen," he said. "Whatever the consequences. Not with that videotape as a witness against us."

"But . . . why would they want to hand us over to Nessim, even if they do work with him? They wouldn't know who we were, and even if they did, they'd know nothing of the mis-sion."

"I told you," Dean said. "Either because Nessim has long-distance lookouts and he knows we were responsible for send-ing the chopper over. Or else because those cops have orders to fake up a charge against *anyone* behaving in a way they don't understand. Here—give me a hand with this merchan-dise, would you?" He was attempting to lift up the mustached man and push him into the back of the truck, where the con-trol panel had been, but the second gendarme manacled to him was making the task too cumbersome.

"What are you doing?" Laurence sounded alarmed. "You're not taking them with us?" She heaved and pushed. At last, between them, they manhandled the unconscious men inside. Small Eyes was stirring and beginning to groan already.

Dean slammed the doors shut. He picked up the panel in

its case. "No," he said. "We're not taking them with us. Come on." He started walking down the track toward the gendarmerie wagon.

"*Marc!* You can't . . . ? You're not going to . . . ?" She hurried after him, aghast.

"Not going to compound my crimes by stealing a police vehicle as well?" Dean replied cheerfully. "I certainly am." He climbed up into the patrol wagon and settled behind the wheel. "Come on in."

"But . . . The truck . . . ? Why should we—?"

"The company we rented the truck from will get it back. No, don't interrupt; let me finish." He pressed the starter and the motor throbbed to life. "If we take that truck and split, the moment those two goons wake up, all they have to do is hobble down to this buggy and unhitch the radio mike—then, like you said, the whole goddamn island would be on the lookout for us. They'd have roadblocks on every route before we even got to the next main intersection."

The wagon rolled forward, and Dean steered them out onto the road. "This way, it could be hours before anyone even finds them: they can't get much farther than this, hog-tied the way they are. And when they are found, they still have to get to a phone. Plus they won't be able to get loose before someone comes out from the station house with a master key. And during that time, we should be able to get back to Calvi, junk this buggy, check out of our hotel, and go to ground someplace where we can turn that tape back there into a map."

"Go to ground? Just where do you figure we could do that, with half the island after us?"

"In a boat. A little way offshore. A boat with a radio, so we can keep in contact with the others."

Laurence sighed again. "You win," she said.

"It's a habit I like to cultivate," said Dean.

14

Jason Mettner

I woke up with a sore throat all over my body. Inside my head it was dull and empty; I felt as though I had been asleep for several years. The sore throat bothered me, just the same. I ought to suck a lozenge, otherwise it might get worse. It felt as though it was going to get much worse.

The sun was very bright. It hung from four brass chains in the center of the white sky, hurting my eyes. I lay on my back and stared at the sun, praying for rain. I moved my right arm to shield my eyes from the glare. Something heavy hung on to my arm.

Bedclothes?

I spread my fingers and touched myself. Coarse flannel pajamas, county-hospital pajamas, rough material that hurt the skin where it touched, and it touched all over. I was sweating. I shouldn't be out here in the sun wearing nothing but pajamas; I might catch cold. Shit, I had this sore throat already—or was it just the flannel chafing my neck?

I began to remember who I was, and sweated some more. Matchless Mettner, man of the moment. Ace crime writer tells all about terrorist training school. You too can be an investigative journalist and expose the dog beneath the skin. Just mail your check for our correspondence course. Six easy lessons. For a dollar seventy-five extra we send you flannel pajamas in plain wrapper, complete with sore throat to fit.

I raised a hand and touched the throat, the side of my face. Pain lanced through my skull, but my fingers only felt more coarse flannel. The hand was no good. It must have come with the six lessons. I'd read it somewhere: mail-order hands. No substitute for the real thing.

My head was swathed in bandages.

In a way, it was a relief: I never did like insensitive fingers. I drew a deep breath . . . and butcher knives sliced through me from shoulder blades to chest. The sweat soaked into the bandages. I wished a cloud would cover that sun: it was far too bright. Then I remembered: they'd sent me eyelids with the reporter's kit. Hinged at either side of the nose. I closed them and the sun set in a crimson sky.

When I opened my eyes again there were three suns hanging above me. The bright one receded and the others advanced to hover in the air over the hospital bed. I blinked the eyelids—they worked better now: maybe I hadn't read the instructions carefully enough the first time. I tried to focus the lenses. Two faces, one long and dark, with graveyard teeth under a hairline mustache, the other one kind of crumpled, with a mouth like a mailbox slit. "He's coming round," Sean Hammer said.

"You thought that yesterday," said the cop, Ancarani. "But you were mistaken, monsieur. However, perhaps this time . . . ?"

I licked my lips. The tongue swept over the edge of a bandage. The lips were thicker than the ones I was used to. Somebody else's voice came out from between them. "Jesus," it said, "I feel like I was run over by a beer truck."

"You look like you was run over by a beer truck," Hammer said. "They put sixteen stitches in a gash across the back of your head. You got two shiners, a broken nose, three cracked ribs, and what it says here on your fever chart is multiple contusions. Which is to say, someone beat the bejasus outta you."

I tried to smile. It hurt too much and I filed the idea away for action at some future date. "Maybe I *was* run over by a beer truck," I offered.

"Yeah. Question is—who was the driver, Mettner? Who was the driver, but?" Marc Dean's Number Two pulled a chair from beside the night table and lowered himself into it. Ancarani perched on the other side of the bed.

"You were found naked in an alleyway behind the port, Monsieur Mettner," Ancarani said. "Apart from the beating, you had lost a lot of blood and you were suffering from exposure. The nights are cold at this time of year, and you could have died. If my *brigadier*—the man who found you—had not known something of first aid, that could well have occurred."

"When was this?" I croaked.

"The day before yesterday. I should add that although your clothes had gone, your wallet, keys, money, identification papers, and an address book were found beneath your body."

I began to give a sigh of relief, but the butcher knives came out again, so that scheme too went into the pending tray. All the same, it was good to know about the little book: a newspaperman without his list of personal contacts is like a power boat without a wheel. All right—a dinghy without a rudder.

"I just have one question," I said. "Why?"

"We may be able to answer it," said the *commissaire*. "The manner of the attack at least gives us a lead."

"No kidding! Let me in on the secret."

"The severity of the treatment, coupled with the fact that all your possessions were untouched, suggests two things: one, that robbery was clearly not the motive; two, that the beating must therefore have been intended simply as a warning—an admonition to keep off. After all, they could easily have killed you if they wished."

"Okay," I said. "Sixty-four-dollar question: keep off what?"

"We were hoping *you* would be able to enlighten *us* on that point. I know that it is a matter of pride with men of your profession to keep their secrets to themselves"—Ancarani smiled frostily—"but perhaps if you were to tell us what story you were following up . . . ?"

I hesitated. In the books, the tough reporter always refuses to come across with what he knows, leaving a surprise for the reader on the last page. I saw no reason to hold back anything. My hesitation was because it was me that was surprised: what was Hammer doing here, and how much of Hammer's business did Ancarani know?

Hammer himself misinterpreted the pause. "It's all right," he said, feeding a stick of gum into that mouth. "Your man knows the score. There was a bit of a hooley up the desert between Marc and a coupla lawmen that was seemingly in yon Arab's pay. Marc had to take a powder, see, and wait outside the three-mile limit a day or two. So I figured it'd be no bad thing to have a member of the constabulary on our side too."

"Where does this guy fit in?" I asked.

Hammer pursed his lips. It didn't stop him chewing. "I'd say his professional duties, what his superiors require him to carry out, don't always fit in with his views as an individual."

I remembered then. *A policeman in uniform and a policeman out of uniform are two different creatures.* It was Ancarani himself who had told me that, at Fouquet's in Paris. And he'd added something about discretion being the better part of valor. There was a third piece of homespun, but I couldn't at that moment recall what it was. I could see what he meant about discretion, though. I said, "Just what do you want to know?"

"Everything about your investigations and your movements—and the story you were following up."

I glanced at Hammer. He nodded. On his say-so, I spilled the lot, right from the overheard conversation at the flying club in Joinville Falls, Ontario, to the morning I woke up in Candy's bed. "So who," I asked Ancarani at the end, "is it warning me to lay off?"

"The method is classic," he said. "The honey trap, the beating that stops short of killing, the possessions carefully left to signal that this is no mugging but a warning: next time it will be for keeps. It has every sign of the Unione-our local Mafia."

"Yeah," I said. "The only thing is: I wasn't following up the Dean story. Haven't been for weeks. I was on some dumb lead about an American dame trying to undercut the French wine market. I told you when I saw you the other day."

"Yes," Ancarani said, "you did tell me. But I thought it was what you call a stall—especially as you seemed interested only in the Nebbio region, which after all is where this Arab has his property."

I nodded, and stopped quickly because it hurt. But I remembered the way he'd repeated the word, all right, and the way I'd questioned that at the time. "Okay," I said. "I admit I hoped my wine story would take me there . . . but only in case I might stumble on a lead if I was on the spot. I wasn't following it up or asking any questions on the Dean thing here in Ajaccio."

Ancarani's horse face was intent. "That is very interesting," he said. "Very interesting indeed." He turned to Hammer. "You see the obvious inference, monsieur?"

"I do that. You mean, if the Syndicate boys put the boot in here . . . and if your man was only chasing the wine story here . . . then the warning must have been *to lay off the wine story*; that the beating had nothing to do with Nessim and Dean?" I told you there was a brain working in back of that battered face.

The cop was looking grim. "I agree with the first part of your proposition," he said, "but I would take it farther: to me this implies that the wine story and the *affaire* Dean must in some way be connected."

I stared to laugh, but changed my mind as soon as the obliquus internus abdominis started to contract: those muscles are linked to the intercostal nerves and it's hell if they're bruised. It was a gas, just the same. Here was Radczinski, trying to veto my pet story and sic me onto some dog he'd dreamed up himself; there was yours truly, doing his damnedest to dump the boss's piece and follow up his own leads . . . and all the time the two of us, unknown to each other, were into the same goddamn thing! Beat that one for irony.

"Just what is the strength of this wine story, Monsieur Mettnair?" Ancarani was saying.

I remembered not to shrug. "It's just some broad bought a Champagne vineyard and then found she didn't have enough product to sell as cheaply as she wanted, so she aims to spike it with wine she buys here." I told him the rest of the story so far as I'd researched it.

"And this lady, you say, is American?"

"Sure. Crazy dame from Albuquerque."

His eyebrows rose. "Albuquerque, New Mexico?"

"Where else?" I said wearily. "How many other Albuquerques do you know?"

Hey! Wait a minute, though! Where had I heard that line before? It wasn't even original. "Hold on," I said. "A little back, you mentioned a honey trap. You don't mean that it was part of the routine? That this girl Candy . . . ?"

Ancarani nodded. He could afford to. "Candide Henschel, yes," he said.

"*Henschel?*" I almost jumped out the bed, bruises and all. That was the name of the woman who'd bought the vineyard: Martha M. Henschel. I'd almost had the headlines ready: Martha's Vineyard. "No wonder they both came from Albuquerque," I said. "Yeah, yeah—New Mexico."

"Mother and daughter," said Ancarani. "With the girl, one supposes, staked out at the Maison des Vins to head off any inquiries—or tip off her mother if they became too persistent."

"Kick me now," I said. "Persistent like mine, you mean?"

"I'm afraid so."

"And all the time I figured it was my irresistible charm! Tell me one thing: would you know what the M. in 'Martha M.' stands for?"

He took a small notebook from his hip pocket and riffled through the pages. "Ah!" He wedged a forefinger in, somewhere near the center. "Margery," he read out. "Martha Margery Henschel. Lately the . . . er . . . companion of one Billie-Boy Graziano. Head of a Mafia family working the American Southwest."

"Who doubtless plans to shift the hooch, when it's ready for consumption," I said. "Oh-oh-oh, this is really getting someplace. Tell me, *Commissaire*, this Margery M.—would she be a brassy blond, the barmaid type, looks like a saloon singer in a western movie?"

Ancarani nodded. "A very good description. I thought you had not met the lady?"

"I saw a photo," I said. *For my little girl, with all the love in the world,* it said at the bottom of the picture. And the M. could as easily stand for Margery as for Mama. And then I remembered the fat, bald Moroccan in the men's room, and another piece of the puzzle clicked in place. *Margie didn't show this week . . . some inconvenience in the north . . .* I'll bet there was, with Dean stirring it up around Nessim and me shoving my big nose in down here: she probably had to tell the people running the Nebbio vineyard that they never heard of her! "Would I be out of line if I suggested this lady was also in the drug business?" I said. "A pusher and a wholesaler?"

"We have been keeping her under surveillance for some time," Ancarani said. "And the daughter. That is why we raided the Coco Club as soon as the man I had in there reported that the girl had picked you up. Unfortunately, we were too late: you had escaped the back way."

"Well, thanks for trying," I said.

"What is so interesting about your contribution, Monsieur Mettnair—and so helpful—is that it provides the link we require. It is the first time the woman Henschel has been linked, even indirectly, with the Arab at Murenzana. But if, as you say, she has this wine connection nearby, and if the Unione is connected with her drug trade and will be connected with the wine . . ." The policeman spread his hands. "They already supply the arms for the so-called school run by Nessim—and for its graduates—so we have at once a three-way link-up."

"Is that so? About the hardware, I mean." Hammer suddenly sounded interested. He even stopped chewing. "That will be a reason why they are so keen on keeping His Excellence in business—and why they asked their Syndicate buddies Stateside to stop Marc taking the job. It would be a useful market dried up, would it not?"

"Maybe we shall be able to put him out of business ourselves—if we can tie his organization in with the drug racket," Ancarani said.

I said, "I'm surprised you can't do that already."

"Officially, I am instructed to help the distinguished foreign visitor in every way I can. This includes the removal of any person or persons who threaten to . . . er . . . invade his privacy. Today I am off-duty: I am here talking to you in an unofficial capacity."

For the first time I realized that Ancarani was wearing a white turtleneck sweater and tan gabardine slacks. "A different creature," I said. "I remember."

"Evidently you forgot about the discretion, nevertheless." He smiled. "I will for a brief moment do the same. What I am about to tell you now will be denied on all sides. You are not in any way to use it professionally. If necessary, I should deny it myself. It is because Monsieur Hammer knows something of it already that I permit myself to speak at all. In my unofficial capacity."

"You made the point," I said. "It's off the record."

"Good." He pushed himself up off the bed and walked across to the window. He had a good, lean, muscular body. He must have been quite an athlete in his day.

"This, roughly," he said to the blank wall outside the hospital window, "is what you would call the scenario. As in the days of Machiavelli, there are two factions at work, both semiofficial, both French. Your friend Dean, through Mademoiselle Chateauroux, is being employed on secret government and EEC orders to . . . effect a certain commission. The SDEC, our French secret service, is aware—again unofficially—of the contract. For internal political reasons concerning Corsica, neither they nor the army nor the Legion can be seen to have anything to do with the affair.

"There is also—you may or may not have heard of this—a second force, largely autonomous, with the sinister name of the Parallel Police. This body, designed originally to oversee the normal security services and ensure that no corruption blunts their impartiality, is by its nature answerable only to a very few specialized persons. It spies on the spies and polices the police, all in dead secret. None of the regular officers in either service, however high up they are, know who is or is not a member of the Parallel Police. The commissioner himself, for all he knows, may be under investigation.

"By its nature also, the Parallel Police is itself peculiarly susceptible to corruption. In the case we have here, it is being used by a handful of unscrupulous ministers, all of whom have been suborned by the man Nessim, to encourage the Unione Corse and the Mafia to block Dean at all costs. The crooked politicians in Nessim's pocket have let it be known that, in return, ministerial blind eyes will be turned toward certain rackets—protection, prostitution, drugs, and so on."

"If they're on different sides, how did these ministers and their Parallel Police know that Dean had been hired in the first place?" I asked.

Ancarani brought another of his shrugs out for an airing. "Nessim has a great deal of money," he said. "Most men have their price, and it would be fairly easy to copy the minutes of the meeting at which it was decided to seek outside aid."

"And your own position?"

"Is equivocal. Officially, as I say, I am instructed to warn off any outsiders who appear to threaten the status quo in the north. From another, equally important department, I am ordered to put a stop to the drug business here. Unofficially . . . well, I am here, am I not? And your own story could be the breakthrough. If Nessim can be linked with drug-running and an illegal *Corsican* wine deal, nobody would dare complain if a local policeman took action—or looked the other way while someone else did. Not even even our bribed ministers."

He smiled. It was kind of a warm smile for a cop. "It

would be a nice *cadeau d'anniversaire*, a splendid birthday present for me," he said. "The day falls at the beginning of next week—and by a really excellent irony of fate, I see from the dossier that the date is shared by none other than Madame Henschel, M!"

"My God!" I cried, remembering what date it was. "Scorpio! You're both born under the same astrological sign—the scorpion!" And of course that was the third piece of homespun he had handed me—here and in Paris too. *Beware the scorpion*. And he'd said especially in the Nebbio. "Well, happy birthday!" I said. "And many of them!"

He inclined his head. "If it is, it will be thanks to you."

"Maybe you done somebody some good at last, Mettner," Hammer said genially, plastering his wad of gum to the underside of my night table. "Even if you don't get to publish the stuff."

"No, no," I said. "Not me. The guy who wrote the song. He should get the credit; he fingered the connection years ago."

"What guy? What song, for Chrissake?"

" 'Margie, Margie, it's you!' " I explained.

Hammer and Ancarani exchanged glances. "I guess maybe we stayed a mite too long," the Ulsterman said hurriedly. "That Sister said not to tire him out an' all. See you, fella. Take it easy . . . and get some rest, huh?"

They went out as if they were walking on eggs.

III

Fox

Peel's View Halloo would awaken the dead
Or a fox from his lair in the morning.

—Old English folk song

15

Edmond Mazzari

"Intolerable!" Mansour Nessim stormed, striding up and down the immense sitting room beneath his tower control point. "It is quite intolerable. With all the security systems and electronic aids at their disposal, the fools allow the machine to cross and recross my property five or six times before they manage to bring it down—a simple device only a few feet up, flying at less than a hundred miles per hour! It didn't even have any antimissile equipment."

"You know what the machine was?" Margie Henschel asked.

"Of course I know what it was," he said impatiently. "It was a British gadget first shown at the Farnborough Air Show as long ago as 1976. So far as my people can discover from what is left of the wreckage, it flew under the simplest form of radio control and was equipped with nothing more than a television camera and video relay. That is what it was designed for, after all: sending back pictures of terrain that may be inaccessible to the viewer."

"And you think it was controlled by the man and the woman who bested the gendarmes at the other end of the desert?"

"Of course it was. And quite clearly it is the same couple . . ." Nessim paused in his angry walk and threaded his way toward a desk in Oriental marquetry. The vast room housed a priceless collection of antique chinoiserie—decorated settles, hexagonal tables in gold-painted lacquer, silk screens, and pots from the Ming, Tang, and Sung dynasties on elaborately carved wooden stands. He picked a sheet of paper from the desk and continued: "The same couple who attempted to gain entry via the main gates, according to this report, last month; the same couple who were observed, at about the same time, in a boat below the cliffs when there was an inexplicable burst of fire from the clifftop batteries, although no intruder was found; the same couple who stayed in St. Florent, posing as geologists." Nessim let the paper fall back on the desk. "The couple whose male member was captured by your Unione Corse friends—and rescued by an armed band before any information could be extracted from him."

Margie Henschel had once been attractive in a blowsy way, a voluptuous Diamond Lil with curves full of sexual promise, but the good living with her Mafia boss had softened the resilience of her flesh and now the muscles at the side of her jaw sagged and the skin linking chin to collarbone was loose and flaccid. Her mouth too had changed. What had once been sultry and smoldering was now just ill-tempered and mean. "You know who they are, this goddamn couple, and what they're at?" she asked.

"Oh, I think so." Nessim was almost genial. He was dressed in a beautifully cut Western suit, and his upright carriage and patrician features lent him an air, especially in profile, that reminded her a little of a not-too-benevolent eagle. "They are clearly professionals," he said. "As evidently they have been investigating my defenses, testing their strength and efficacy. Why? Obviously because they wish to get on the inside. Now, thanks to the incompetence of those who should have known better, they will have a fairly complete picture of the whole domain—a picture from which they can easily make a detailed map. This is annoying, but it will hardly help them break through the perimeter."

"You don't think they're some free-lance bums, planning a heist?" Margie said. "Face it, everyone knows you're loaded."

He shook his head. "No, no. I have little doubt now that the man is, or is employed by, the imperialist mercenary, the hired killer who goes by the name of Dean. It is unfortunate, most unfortunate, that your friend Graziano's employee— Klein, was it not?—failed to arrange for his death in Canada."

"And you figure this guy plans some kind of attack here?"

"According to our ministerial friends in Paris, decisions

were taken—there and in Brussels—that he should be employed (clandestinely, of course: nobody has the courage to act openly) to do just that. To mount an assault and destroy my work." For a moment, the veneer of arrogance and sophistication vanished, and the outrage of the nomad threatened with the loss of his tent was visible.

"What do you plan to do?" the woman said.

Nessim strode to the window and looked out over the formal gardens at the top of the bluff, past the limousines and the huge swimming pool, to the barren country below and beyond. A group of men were learning how to jump from a fast-moving automobile, firing submachine guns as they fell. "I do not intend to allow several years' work to be negated by some Western military whore," he said savagely.

She shifted in her seat. It was a fifteenth-century carved wood settle inlaid with peacocks and dragons in ivory and mother-of-pearl. "It'd be too bad if anything loused up the drug connection we just got going," she said. "Graziano'd be sore as hell. The wine deal, too—that could be something if it was allowed to develop."

Nessim made an irritable gesture. "You only think of money. I have money, more than enough for everyone. It is the chance to act that is important, the opportunity to train enough enthusiasts, to cause enough outrage to wipe the smug and complacent smiles from the faces of the hypocrites who for too long have had the reins—"

"Okay, okay," she said. "So what do you plan to do?"

He turned back to face her. There was a feverish light in his eyes. "I have an idea," he said. "As soon as I learn what action these mercenaries propose to take against me, as soon as I know what these impudent dogs hope to achieve, I shall take steps to ensure that the attacking force, however large it may be, is obliterated, annihilated for presuming to move against me . . . and all without any loss, without any engagement even, of the guerrilla force I train here." The smile with which he completed this statement bore the stamp of true fanaticism.

"Oh, yeah?" Margie said practically. "As soon as you know?"

"I shall know; I shall find out," Nessim cried. "I have just had installed here an associative-memory computer. Do you know what that is?" When she shook her head, he continued:

"An ordinary computer is specific. It will answer specific questions according to the information programmed into its data bank. It will adduce correspondences or relationships between objects or ideas—provided you pose the right questions and the material from which the replies derive have been programmed into it. What it will not do is *suggest* such correspondences without these detailed questions. An associative-memory computer will do precisely that: it will produce—as near as a machine will ever produce—an informed guess."

Margie rearranged her skirt and crossed nylon-clad legs that were still far from ugly. "You don't say?" she observed.

"It is too complex to explain in detail," said Nessim, "but in effect it will supply, in certain circumstances, an answer to questions that have not in fact been asked."

"So what's this wonderful machine going to do: give you a rundown on the guy's plan of attack?"

"Not in so many words. Although, given enough information on his previous actions, his psychology, and our defenses, it might do just that. No—I shall simply feed in every smallest item of intelligence, every scrap of gossip, the gist of every press cutting, all the information we ourselves have gleaned on the man, his work, our work, and anything else touching on any of those things since we were first warned by our friends in Paris that a decision had been taken . . . and I shall see what the computer comes up with. I shall give it some simple generalized instruction—a key word such as 'attack' or 'plan' or 'operation,' coupled with 'Dean'—and wait for the printout."

"A machine like that," Margie said, "must have set you back some."

He shrugged helplessly. "Yes," he said. "It costs a lot of money."

Seventy yards to the northwest and fifty feet lower down the hill, Edmond Mazzari was dismantling, cleaning, oiling, and reassembling the components of a Soviet-made Kalashnikov AKM assault rifle. On either side of him, seated on benches in front of a long scrubbed wood table, a dozen men, most of them young, performed similar tasks with revolvers, automatic pistols, and several types of submachine gun. Among them were three Cubans, an Irishman, two South

Americans, several Arabs, and an elderly black man from East Africa.

A woman in camouflage battle fatigues walked up and down the far side of the table supervising the work. She was tall and flat-chested, with short fair hair, steel-rimmed spectacles, and no makeup. She stopped opposite Mazzari. "It is correct to well oil the parts," she said, "but as much as possible should be wiped off before reassembly." Mazzari couldn't place the accent. It was certainly Central European. "Superfluous oil," the woman said, "can leave giveaway stains on clothing. Smeared on the fingers, it can mark surfaces with easy-to-find prints, and on a telescopic sight could fatally blur the vision at the time of a hit."

Mazzari nodded and picked up a wad of cotton waste. She moved on and stopped by the Irishman. "The Skorpion Vz-61 is useful because it is so short—only ten inches—for a machine pistol," she said, picking up the frame of the dismantled Czech weapon. "But the fifty-five-yard range when it is in this form is a grave disadvantage. With the wire stock extended, the range at once increases to two hundred and twenty yards—although even then, on single-shot, you empty the whole twenty-round clip in thirty seconds."

"Sure it suits me down to the bloody ground," the Irishman said. "I'll not even be needin' fifty *feet*: the bugger opens the door an' I zap him from the gate: one, two, three, an' the shooter in the belt of me trousis. Three seconds an' I'm away outta there. It's not as though it was like a president or somethin', you see—a particular man has to be clobbered, that needs time and plannin'. Any fucker will do for me, just so long as he's a flamin' Prod."

"Admirable," said the woman. She moved on to the next student.

Later, the Irishman joined Mazzari, the man from East Africa, and three Palestinian girls, all of them fairly new students, on the battle course laid out at the edge of the wood. Stopping every dozen yards to loose off a short burst at targets set up among the trees, they carried their Uzi submachine guns over high walls, beneath barbed-wire entanglements, through barrels suspended on wires, and across a greasy plank over a stream. During the whole exercise, grenades exploded on either side of the three-hundred-yard course and heavy machine guns on tripods hosed a stream of lead behind the laggards and over the heads of all of them. The course was run three times, with a camera mounted on a jeep filming the actions from behind the brown smoke of the grenades and the dust hazing the sun-drenched air as slugs scuffed up the trodden earth.

In the evening, the film was run before the entire school, with frequent stops while the lecturer—Ramon again—pointed out faults or dwelt on points of expertise. Mazzari's head was spinning with the information already pumped into it by other experts in various classes during the day.

"There are three proven ways of getting small arms past the security checks at passenger airports. Two are foolproof . . ."

"In the case of the plastic grenade, the disadvantage is . . ."

"In the psychological subjection of hijacked hostages . . ."

"Provided an assassination attack comes from an unexpected quarter—Sadat is a good example—the operative can rely on two to five seconds of stupefaction before the security forces act . . ."

"When we drew up the plans for the execution of the British parliamentarian Airey Neave . . ."

"If a car bomb also kills bystanders, so much the better . . ."

There was another reason why Mazzari was unable to give his full attention to the lecturer's analysis of the exercise captured on film. Just before he went into the lecture hall, the tiny pulsator taped to the top of his thigh began to vibrate. It was the signal that Dean would be transmitting a message wthin the next half-hour.

Halfway through the first reel, the vibrator started the series of alternating dots and dashes that signified a message about to start in Morse code. The students were encouraged to take notes during the course, in the belief that to write something down was to commit it to memory, though all papers had to be fed into a shredder before they quit the class. Mazzari was therefore able to intersperse the letters of Dean's message between the words of a supposed digest of Ramon's lecture. The first letter was three dots: an S. It was followed by T . . . A . . . N . . . D. The word "stand." The whole message, when Mazzari was able to assemble it, read:

STAND BY RECEIVE BEACONS AIRWISE 0300 HOURS EXGLIDER 650 YARDS WEST FIRING RANGE ON GRANITE BOSS AT EDGE OF WOOD STOP FURTHER INSTRUCTIONS WITH MESSENGER END.

Deep within Mazzari's huge frame a Vesuvian chuckle started. His whole body began to shake. So that was all they wanted him to do, was it? Slip out of a dormitory he shared with five other guys at dead of night, quit the ancient village house where he was billeted—which was in fact a steel shell within the medieval walls, where doors were sensor-operated and monitor scanners blinked everywhere—then cross roughly a mile of open ground that was constantly patrolled, and wait for an air drop on the most exposed point of the whole site! They weren't asking much, were they! And it was only after that little task had been accomplished that he would receive his "instructions."

He managed to suppress the chuckle before it broke surface, but he was unable totally to control his features. "There is something humorous perhaps in the manner of my discourse?" the acid voice of Ramon inquired, seeing the sudden bright flash of teeth in Mazzari's dark face.

"Not in the discourse, chief," the big man said hastily. "I was just thinking: Blondin went over Niagara in a barrel; it looks there"—he gestured at the screen—"as though we could be repeating the dose over Wall Street or Piccadilly or the Kurfurstendamm!" It wasn't brilliant, but it was the best he could do in the time.

"You would do better to ask yourself why you made much the slowest time on that part of the course," Ramon said with a scowl.

"Yes, sir," Mazzari replied. But he was careful to make sure the shredder was churning before he dropped in his wadded paper on the way out of the hall.

Nessim was watching a sunset of Oriental splendor from the panoramic window of his tower control room when his secretary-receptionist, Fawzi Harari, buzzed him on the intercom to say that the operator in the computer complex had come up with something that might interest him.

Nessim took the elevator six floors down into the heart of the rocky spur on which the village was built. Here, in a network of soundproofed rubber-tiled corridors whose construction was based on the innermost A Ring of the Pentagon in Washington, were the multimillion-dollar nerve centers of the sophisticated security systems the Arab had built for himself. Fawzi was waiting for him as the elevator doors slid soundlessly apart. She was a short girl, rather wide, with fleshy curves and a down of dark hairs on her upper lip. Nessim found her attractive because she had very large nipples and her pubic hair was silky.

There was also the additional advantage that, except when they were in bed, she treated him with the greatest deference and her attitude never progressed beyond the formal. Today, however, her dark eyes gleamed and there was an air of suppressed excitement about her. "What is it, Mademoiselle Harari?" Nessim asked. "What treasure has Yussaf unearthed?"

"You will see, sir," she replied. "In the Associative Memory Room. I think you will find the visit worthwhile."

Like all the systems terminals in Nessim's redoubt, the chamber was in fact three ferroconcrete boxes, one within the other. Neither sounds nor electronic signals could filter through those walls, and no eavesdropping device could possibly penetrate the interior. A bearded Sudanese in a white laboratory coverall was seated in front of the gray steel computer console that was the only piece of furniture in the room. The program bays and data banks, together with the infinitely complex universe of diodes and transistors and wire that united them, were housed on a lower level.

The Sudanese turned around as they came in, and then rose to his feet. "Good evening, your Excellency," he said politely. "I believe we have a positive result for you here."

Nessim nodded. "Very well. Let us have it."

Greenish letters formed a crowded printout on the computer's screen. The Sudanese punched out instructions on the keyboard, and the lines of electronic information twinkled, rolled away, and reformed as quickly as summer lightning. Finally the screen went black and then four separate lines unrolled, to remain there flickering slightly as they read:

DEAN, MARCUS MATTHEW—ASSOCIATES SM2/180793 PROJECT 967
2. MAZZARI, EDMOND, CONGOLESE, D/B UNKNOWN TRUSTED LIEUTENANT ††† KNOWN TO HAVE BEEN INFILTRATED UNIVERSITY KIEV POSING AS AFRICAN SECESSIONIST.

The operator's fingers danced over the keyboard. The lines telescoped, fused, reappeared, vanished. This time the final printout was three lines only. It read:

164

MAZZARI, EDMOND—SM2/180795 SUB-PROJECT 967/2
PARTICULARITIES ††† BLACK, 74 INCHES, 200 LBS, SHORT
HAIR, SPEAKS BRITISH ENGLISH PRONOUNCED OUTDATED
OXFORD STYLE.

16

Marc Dean

A cold night wind blew up from the southwest before Dean and Laurence installed themselves in the old Waco glider. Nobody knew from what secret stores Sir Daniel De'Ath had dredged up the vintage sailplane: it was reputed to have been used in the American airborne attack on the south of France in August 1944, and there were certainly patches on its stressed-fabric wings that suggested hasty repairs of damage caused by shrapnel or slugs. Now, however, it was painted an overall matt black and it bore no identification marks whatever. It had probably been used in Korea and Vietnam and possibly even the Sinai desert as well, Dean said cheerfully as they settled themselves in the narrow hull; the important thing was that the controls still functioned well. That and the strength of the wind, which would allow him a much greater choice of maneuver.

They took off from a small grass field used by a gliding school between Callian and Seillans, in the Var *département* of Provence—there was, they were told, less likelihood of any busybodies noticing and then shooting off their mouths in such a place. Also, since he had received such positive evidence that at least some of the police were in Nessim's pocket, Dean was unwilling to initiate any more moves in Corsica before the actual assault.

The machine in which De'Ath had chosen to tow them was a twin-engine De Havilland biplane, variously known as a Dominie and a Rapide. It was an elegant ship, with nonretractable landing wheels half-concealed in the faired engine nacelles, and slender, tapering wings. Until the end of World

War II, in the Rapide version, the plane had been used to carry mail between England and Ireland, while the Dominie, once on the London–Paris commercial run, was a favorite transport of high-ranking staff officers. "Where the hell does he get them?" Dean asked in wonderment as they waited for takeoff. "Some of these crates must be worth a fortune, in rarity value alone. And I mean apart from museums."

"He has contacts," Laurence said vaguely. "Daredevil Dan could have any plane he wanted out of any museum, just for the asking, anytime at all."

"But . . . ? Is he *that* good a pilot, for God's sake?"

"It's nothing to do with his skill—though he *is* a good pilot, as it happens. No, he gets what he wants because of his value as a . . . because of the valuable information he contributes."

Dean swung around in his seat and stared at her. "You don't mean . . . ? You're not telling me that this . . . this jackass is in some way connected with intelligence? With the British intelligence service?"

Laurence nodded. "A very useful and highly placed agent, I believe."

"And he's part of the . . . one of the 'principals' in this project we're involved in? Ah, c'mon, honey"—Dean's voice was a mixture of outrage and disbelief—"the guy's a cretin, a dope, one of those silly-ass jerks that went out of style fifty years ago."

"Exactly—an effete, laughable figure of fun. Can you think of a better cover for a particularly acute secret agent?"

"Yeah, but . . . Jesus!"

"This absurd vintage air circus: it's the perfect front for such a man. He's mobile; he can go anywhere, do anything. Anything unusual, they put it down to eccentricity—that crazy flying fool. But let me tell you . . . well, one day, maybe I will." Laurence smiled. "An old piston-engined machine laboring through the sky; the whole world's going to think: Madison Avenue sky-writing to push some new brand of cigarette; some kids learning to fly can't afford a more modern trainer; it can't be that prize *schmuck* back with his lousy circus again!"

"Okay," Dean said. "Okay."

"They treat the old boy with contempt—not even a good-humored contempt; he's been smart enough to make himself a club bore as well. But do you think Nessim would as easily dismiss a pursuit ship or an executive jet if it was towing us? Not on your sweet life, Marc. Remember, too, that the vapid, brainless facade behind which there lurks a penetrating intelligence is something of a convention, a British specialty. Did you never hear of Albert Campion, of Lord Peter Wimsey, of Raffles' friend Bunny Manders?"

"That's fictional material," Dean said shortly.

"So is Sir Dan, if only you'd realize it. One of the most convincing fictional characters in years . . . and still nobody believes he's true!" Laurence settled back in her seat and adjusted her goggles over the leather helmet she wore with her nylon/kapok ski suit. "What's the matter, Marc? You're not usually edgy—I could almost say bitchy—like this."

Dean looked a little sheepish. "I'm sorry, honey. I guess it's . . ." He shrugged. "I don't know: this is not the kind of mission I go for. Most times, there's two sides fighting it out someplace, and one side hires me and my buddies to come in and zap the other side, in the hope that we'll win. Or there's a certain objective to be overcome or pacified or taken, and we go on in and do it. But in each case the basics are simple: we make a plan, then it's quickly in, do the job, and quickly out again. Finish. All this to-and-fro shit; acting cagey so we don't tread on anyone's toes; keeping the whole deal under wraps in case the natives complain; whatever else, to keep the nose clean—tell you the truth, it's not my style. I like to be in there where the action is, so I know where I'm at."

Laurence nodded. "They're signaling us for takeoff," she said.

He turned back to stare out through the plexiglass screen. A green light was blinking on the De Havilland's tail group. Dean slid a green filter over a powerful electric torch and signaled his own readiness. The biplane lumbered across the grass and rose into the sky, dragging the glider behind it.

In a few minutes they had crossed the dark bulk of the Esterel and were flying slantwise over the coruscating loops of bright light marking the coastline between Théoule and Juan-les-Pins. Away to the left, a whole firmament twinkled beyond the sea where Nice lay spread out below the foothills of the Alps.

They had chosen a moonless night because of the assault that was due twenty-four hours later; stars shone in the gaps between high drifts of cirrocumulus. De'Ath kept below two thousand feet for the whole of the 130-mile flight, but it was penetratingly cold in the motorless, unheated glider. Dean was thankful at last to see the long finger of Cap Corse pointing across the dim, wrinkled surface of the water.

Flying over the promontory, they made a wide circuit above the sea beyond, and reapproached the island in a shallow dive from the east. When the Gulf of St. Florent was still only a paler indentation in the darkness ahead, a red light began winking from the De Havilland. Dean signaled back with the green filter over his own torch and the crimson blink settled into a steady glow. He reached down and operated the lever releasing the shackles of the towline.

As the line fell away, the glider, no longer being hauled through the atmosphere by the thrust of twin screws, soared momentarily higher, meeting the resistance of the air. Then Dean eased forward the stick, the rounded nose dropped, and they were winging their way down toward Murenzana and the desert.

The steady beat of the biplane's motors receded; the tiny points of flame from its exhausts dwindled and then vanished into the dark; for a short while the whining of the wind through wires and stays and the struts of the Waco's undercart was startlingly loud.

Dean's plan was to circle lower and then make his run from the landward side of Nessim's property. Since the glider would have no heat and no noise signature, he hoped that it might make no more impression on the radar scanners than a large flock of birds. There were, however, some tricky maneuvers to make. And for these he would need all the lift he could get. For that reason the wind and the coolness of the night after a hot day were advantageous: they should create a thermal which would sweep up the steep face of the ridge. There should also be both dynamic and undulatory currents caused by the interrelation of thermals with the abrupt contours of the inland mountain mass. But until he was lower down, he would be unable to gauge the use—or the strength—of these currents.

The glider swooped and soared, swinging around the barren desert terrain in narrowing spirals. Second time over the outer confines of the ridge, Dean felt the sudden upward lift of the warm air, and he turned around and signaled Laurence that it was time to start the most perilous aerial acrobatics of her career. She nodded and prepared herself for the ordeal.

In front of the narrow seat, secured in a burlap container

like a mailman's sack, were the six ground directional beacons that had to be delivered to Edmond Mazzari—each one a small cone on a square base, resembling the red-and-white markers used to block off a traffic lane during highway repairs. The girl hitched the sack to a harness belt with a quick release catch and slid back the transparent canopy above her. She leaned forward and thumped the combat leader on the shoulder. He turned briefly and nodded, holding up a gloved hand with the thumb pointing skyward.

Quickly he tested each of the control surfaces, flicking the sailplane from side to side. The maneuver he was about to perform, dangerous for anything as unwieldy as a glider, with no power to pull it out of trouble, was a slow roll. As the ship revolved in a clockwise direction, Laurence was to emerge from the cockpit and crawl over the hull counterclockwise in such a way that she was always on the highest point of the fuselage. When the glider had turned through 180 degrees and was momentarily flying on its back, she was to crawl forward until she was between the undercart oleos and grasp the axle that Dean had fitted between them. He would then complete the roll, leaving her hanging, complete with sack, like a trapeze artist beneath the plane.

The whine of the wind rose to a shriek as the airflow hit her. She leaned out of the cockpit nacelle and seized the rope grips that had been specially inserted along the smooth, stressed curve that was rolling, rolling toward her as she dragged her body out of the safety of the interior and into the slipstream.

The wind numbed her flesh and plucked ferociously at her clothes and stifled the breath in her throat. One of the glider's wings, canted skyward, momentarily blacked out the stars between two patches of clouds as it swung over . . . and then she was hauling herself over the sharpest part of the curve onto the belly of the plane.

Spread-eagled flat on the smooth, doped fabric, she gasped and choked for breath while the roaring wind tried to dislodge her. It was only a few feet from there to the undercart—the ship was still slowly turning over—but it seemed like a hundred miles. At last, however, she was within reach. Eyes streaming, she raised herself high enough to grasp the axle with one hand.

But she had left it a fraction of a second too late. There was a sudden momentary drop in the air pressure. The glider plunged, completing the last part of the roll more quickly than the first. Gravity and the force of the wind snatched her off the plane's belly as it swung away and above her. Her body dropped into the roaring void, supported only by that single hand clenched desperately around the axle.

The shock almost dislocated her shoulder and wrenched the arm from its socket. She cried aloud with fear and alarm, but the relentless wind tore the sound from her lips and it was lost in the dark. For an eternity she hung there, streamed out behind the wheels like a drogue, fighting to force her other hand back and up to the axle. Her tortured muscles were screaming. Time and again she almost made it; once she touched the cold steel tube with the tips of her fingers; once she thought she was lost when an extra strong buffet sent the glider lurching sideways. But at last her hand touched solidly, wrapped around it, held fast.

Sobbing with relief, she dragged herself up and jackknifed over the bar. Below her—one hundred feet? two hundred? three hundred?—the blurred outlines of the desert raced past.

Dean had to pilot the ship with great skill now. He must keep her low enough—and slow enough—to make an accurate delivery to the man waiting below. Yet he must retain sufficient speed and lift to carry them out beyond the desert and ditch in the sea, where Sean Hammer would be waiting to pick them up in a launch.

Above Laurence, a green light glowed in the floor of the hull. She unfastened the sack from around her waist, hooked the backs of her knees over the improvised trapeze and hung head downward beneath the plane, holding the sack ready as the ground wheeled up to meet them.

There was no way Mazzari could leave the dormitory through the door. He would have to pass three other beds to get there. Behind his own bed there was a window—open because guerrilla fighters were supposed to be tough, open-air types, and anyway, the building was unheated. He reckoned he could probably leave that way once the other men were asleep: so far as he could judge, it was out of shot for the video scanner above the door; there was no moon, so that for the brief moment the opening would be blocked by his body, there would be no appreciable difference in the quality of light—certainly not enough to awaken a sleeper; generally speaking, after a strenuous day in the woods, on the range or the battle course, the students slept heavily.

Mazzari fumed with impatience, waiting for the moment when he could be certain there was nobody left awake. The rendezvous was for 0300 hours, but he had agreed with Dean when the project was first discussed that they would allow a quarter of an hour leeway on either side of whatever time was finally chosen. He must therefore be at the appointed place at 0245 . . . and he had no idea how long it would take him to get there. The first—and possibly the most difficult—task would be to get out of the village itself. The outer ring of houses encircling the rocky spur at its lowest level had effectively been made into a continuous wall and the few entrances were all electronically controlled. The only way to do it, Mazzari thought (and this had determined his choice of the window), was to use some of the expertise they had been taught on these very walls and make with a kind of cat-burglar number in reverse.

It was after one o'clock when the last of the snort-and-start sleepers had settled into the stertorous breathing of the more deeply unconscious. Mazzari stole up and down between the beds a few times, keeping out of range of the camera, to test the sleepers' awareness. Nobody stirred. He thrust his head and shoulders out the window and then hoisted one leg over the sill. For a moment he paused, listening.

The wind was blowing quite strongly. Somewhere above him a loose shutter creaked. Away below the houses, branches threshed on either side of the driveway leading to the gates. Otherwise he heard nothing. There were no lights burning. Even Nessim's control room above the citadel was darkness.

A narrow ledge—what architects term a string course—ran below the window and separated the dormitory floor from the story below. One of the lessons they had been taught and retaught was how to use just such a projection as an escape route. He swung his other leg over the sill and turned around so that he was facing back into the room, then lowered himself until his feet were resting on the ledge. It was about four inches wide, not big enough to permit a traverse of any distance without handholds, but just sufficient to hold him while he reached for a stackpipe six feet away from the window embrasure. He grasped the hard terra-cotta tube, using it as a support while he lowered himself once more to the point where he could hook his fingers over the string course and hang from it at the full stretch of his arms. From there he worked his way hand over hand, as though the ledge was a rope, to the corner of the building.

The house was about halfway up the hill. From the corner he dropped lightly onto the roof of the commissary, which was entered from a lane at a lower level. The pitch of the roof was shallow: it was easy enough, taking care not to dislodge one of the curved tiles in the dark, to move to the gable end and use another stackpipe to reach a roof that was still lower—on the outside rim of the village. The second stackpipe led past the open window of a dormitory used by some of the school's male instructors. From inside he heard the sound of heavy breathing and a faint snore. But apparently the rustling, scraping noises of his descent sounded no alarm bells at the back of the sleepers' minds. No lights blazed on; no shout disturbed the steady rushing of the wind.

Two minutes later, Mazzari was at the edge of the last roof—a pantiled slant on the outermost edge of the village, rather more than a hundred yards north and east of the porch through which he had first entered. He had chosen his route well: the house was only two stories high, a squat stone edifice with walls that were three feet thick, dating probably from the Middle Ages. By the time he had let himself down for the third time and hung from the guttering at the full stretch of his arms, his lower extremities were no more than twelve feet from the ground. He landed with catlike agility and stole away into the night.

His route lay past the firing range, across the battle course with its barbed wire and swaying barrels, and through a belt of woodland to the shallow valley where the city-street movie set was still in place. It was an uncanny feeling, treading the deserted macadam below the blank windows of those tall facades, with only the moan of wind through the superstructure to accompany the pad-pad of sneakers on his feet. The cars and trucks and buses were parked fender to fender in a lot on the far side of the hangar. He threaded his way between them, the odors of gasoline and diesel sharp in his nostrils, and then he was climbing through the scrub toward the wilderness of granite that stretched between the valley and the rocky butte that was his target.

It was tough going in the dark. The granite slabs were seamed and fissured; he had to feel every yard of the way; a false step could land him with a broken leg or fatally twist an ankle. He had taken care to make himself known to the guard dogs that patrolled the domain at night, and so far as possible to make friends with them, but he saw no signs of the animals, nor did he hear any of the mobile nightwatch details that the students manned on a rota system as part of their training.

He made the granite boss with ten minutes to spare. While he was climbing the steep slope of scree to the summit, he heard the drone of a piston-engined airplane somewhere out to sea. The low-pitched throbbing moved slowly from west to east and then faded away over the invisible mass of Cap Corse. By the time the De Havilland had turned and was making its approach run, Mazzari was on the bare rock platform, several hundred yards across, that surmounted the butte.

This time the plane passed several miles to the south, over the foothills beyond the Nebbio. Mazzari knew that the glider would have cast off sometime before, but although he strained his eyes upward, squinting into the night sky in the hope perhaps of seeing a vague shape momentarily blot out a group of stars, in fact he saw nothing of Dean's preliminary circling.

He waited, listening to the distant sighing of the sea, a surf of autumn leaves as the wind tossed the trees in the wood beyond the butte. The engines of the plane were now inaudible.

He was expecting it—every nerve was tensed in expectation—but the glider's approach still took him completely by surprise. There was a rush of air, something increasing in volume almost to a subdued roar . . . and then the great bird shape swooped over him. He was dimly aware, some thirty or forty feet overhead, of the inverted figure hanging batlike from the undercart, of the darker mass beneath it. Then the sack landed with a soft thump some way to his left, and the sailplane was gone, soaring up on the thermal that Dean knew would be rising up the steep western slope of the butte.

Mazzari hurried over to the sack. The beacons, cushioned in polystyrene formers, were lightweight and had not been damaged by the drop. There was a miniature flashlight taped inside the neck of the sack. Shielding the lens with his fingers so that only a narrow beam escaped, he read the attached note. The attack was to be at midnight, in twenty-one hours' time. He was to position the beacons immediately—they

174

would transmit continuously for twenty-four hours—hiding them wherever, after his sojourn at the school, he considered it safest for small groups of paratroops to land. It would be too dangerous for him to try to get back into his quarters in the village; he was to conceal himself someplace in the wood and join up with Hammer's seabourne assault force when it broke through from the west.

He retied the sack and began working his way down the slope of scree. He had already figured out where to locate the beacons, but it would take him all the time he had before daybreak if he was to get back to the wood while it was still dark.

The nearest site was on the far side of the wood. At the foot of the slope he walked hastily toward the trees.

White light blinded him. He froze, dazzled into immobility by the searing beam of a searchlight mounted on a jeep parked beneath the canopy of branches.

He stood there, a huge, absurdly guilty figure—like a strip-cartoon baddie caught red-handed, still clutching the swag. He was aware, squinting away from the agonizing brilliance, of movement among the trees, of the low growl of a guard dog.

And then Mansour Nessim's suave voice: "Mr. Edmond Mazzari, I believe?"

17

Raoul Ancarani

A great number of things happened in the eighteen hours immediately preceding Marc Dean's assault on the terrorist school at Murenzana. Not all of them directly concerned Commissaire Raoul Ancarani, and of those that did, there were some of which he preferred to remain officially in ignorance. The borderline between that which was official and that which was unofficial was a sinuous one, constantly shifting, in his case . . . and in his place. Take a pace in any direction: one day the foot would be on this side of the line, another on that.

There was, for example, the case of the Arab. Many Arabs came within Ancarani's jurisdiction, both resident and transient. This particular Arab was resident but he had the right only to be transient. It was, like so many things in France, an affair of papers. The man formed part of the small permanent staff at Murenzana, but unlike the other Arabs working there, he had no work permit. Unlike the students, all of these Arabs—perhaps because, at however low a level, they were of the same race as the sheikh—were permitted to leave the domain during the time off that the law required their employer to grant them. Again unlike his fellows, the man with no permit—his name was Hassan—spent much of his free time with Ancarani.

As the policeman had pointed out to Mettner, most men have their price. Hassan's price was not exorbitant. It required only that the official eye be looking in a different direction when there was a question of the illegal transfer of his earnings to his native village in Tunisia, that certain reports be filed and forgotten, that the matter of work permits be conveniently shelved. In return, Ancarani was furnished with an unofficial eye—on the inside of the protected area owned by Nessim. It was not, after all, only the Parallel Police who could play this particular game.

"A black man, a very large black man," Hassan told him. "It was Ahmed and myself who admitted him when he came. He seemed a student like the others, but last night they caught him in the open when a great bird passed and something fell out of the sky. Is something the matter, Excellence?"

Ancarani had uttered a stifled exclamation. "It is nothing," he said. "Continue."

"The pasha was extremely angry. But instead of executing the man at once, he ordered that a hunt be prepared, like the British with a fox. It would be an exercise for the students, he said. The black man would have his hands manacled behind him, but would otherwise be free to conceal himself or run within the domain. Thirty minutes after he has been loosed, the students may start the hunt, with a prize for the first to shoot him down."

"Poor bastard!" said Ancarani.

"Sir?"

"Go on. This thing that fell from the sky? What happened?"

"I do not know exactly. But whatever it was did not please the pasha. Ahmed tells me that the contents are to be thrown away. He overheard the man Ramon giving orders that they should be distributed over the Foreign Legion artillery range next to us. Clearly they wish them destroyed."

"What!" Ancarani exclaimed. And later, talking to Jason Mettner at a sidewalk café overlooking the port, he said, "It appears obvious what has occurred. With the sack and the beacons, which were probably accompanied by some form of message, Nessim will now realize at least in principle what Dean's plans are. And the wily old fox has thought up a very smart way to foil them."

"I'm not sure that I understand," Mettner said. "What's with this artillery-range deal?"

"Hassan overheard the sheikh making a phone call to someone 'very high' in Paris," Ancarani replied. "He suggested that it might be a good idea if a Legion exercise planned for tonight in the Corte area were transferred to the Casta range, near St. Florent. What does *that* suggest to *you*?"

Mettner shook his head—and winced. He was still suffering from the beating he had received. "Search me," he said.

"Come, now, Monsieur Mettnair, you are usually more acute."

"They only let me out of the hospital an hour ago," Mettner said. "Why don't you show me how acute you are?"

"If the directional beacons are placed on the firing range, concealed . . . and actuated," the policeman explained, "Dean's airborne force will home on them and drop the paratroops there. How do you imagine a force of the Légion Etrangère on a night exercise would react if armed men dropped out of the sky and began shooting at them—because the paratroops will of course assume that the legionnaires are Nessim's men."

"Christ!" Mettner said. "I see what you mean."

"And if a discreet word had been gotten to the officers that some crazy band of desperadoes—Corsican separatists maybe—were likely to attempt a putsch, a coup d'état, a revolution . . . Well, you can see the headlines, can you not? 'Foreign mercenaries attempt a commando-style raid on French territory! The Legion under fire—in its own backyard! Disgraceful, unprovoked aggression by American-led irregulars!' "

"My God!"

"It is the two sides again, you see: one arranges, as promised to Colonel Dean, that the Legion will be in another part of the island on the night of the assault; the other insists on a contrary arrangement . . . and sows the seeds of suspicion for good measure."

"What are you going to do about it?"

"I?" Ancarani shrugged his shoulders. "I am a policeman. I receive my orders from the Préfet. Officially, you must remember, I know nothing of this escapade. On either side."

"Yeah. Well . . ." The newspaperman looked at his watch. "I guess I'll be . . . that is to say, I have one or two things to attend to. See you around, huh? And thanks for the coffee." He rose stiffly to his feet, waved, and strode away into the crowd along the waterfront.

Ancarani smiled. He raised a finger, and a young man in sunglasses, seated at a nearby table, laid down his copy of *Corse-Matin* and joined him. "He will probably hire a car and go straight to the Agriates," the *commissaire* said. "Keep him in sight—don't lose him on any account—and report to me by radio every hour. All right?"

He left some coins on the table, walked to his office, and called his chief. "I have two days' furlough owing, sir, from the last Easter vacation," he said. "Since there is not much doing at the moment, I wondered if I might take them today and tomorrow? . . . What?. . . . Oh, no, sir. Nothing like that! . . . The hunting season is open: I thought I might drive up into the hills and try my luck."

As soon as he had received the Préfet's okay, he went into an anteroom and changed out of his uniform into slacks and a sweater. Then, after he had given certain instructions to one of the plainclothes inspectors whose office was outside the teleprinter room, he left the building, collected his car from the underground parking lot, and drove rapidly northeast on Route 193.

Out at sea, fifteen miles south of Genoa, Sean Hammer walked around two DUKW-353 amphibians on the lower deck of a small car ferry that acted in summer months as a supplementary transport for tourists visiting the isle of Elba from the mainland port of Piombino. It had not been too difficult, given a persuasive tongue and the right amount of lire, to hire the craft for a one-off operation. She had been built in the early fifties and was due to go for scrap anyway. And the odd little Irish-American had promised that the amphibs, each of which carried twenty rather tough-looking men, would be off-loaded from the ferry ramps well outside Corsican territorial waters. It was not the harbormaster's business to comment on the combat-style clothes worn by these hardbitten tourists—or to speculate on the contents of certain extremely heavy crates that were winched aboard and stowed in the DUKW's.

A similar indifference characterized the well-paid immigration officers at a small south Italian airfield later that day when Sir Daniel De'Ath took a score of supposed film stunt men aboard a veteran Dakota transport.

Dean and Laurence stayed in bed in a room above the local *trattoria* until the last moment. "I'm sorry, darling," she said, "but I just can't make it." Dean lay beside her, late afternoon sunlight filtering through the slatted shutters gilding the outlines of his lean, bronzed body. He was coiled taut as a spring, she knew—and she sensed that he wanted her ferociously, possessively, the way he always did in the last moments of calm before the action. "It was the trapeze act," Laurence said. "First the extra weight, then flying all that way out to sea to the launch where Sean was waiting. The hamstrings in back of my knees, and the muscles behind my thighs, are so stiff that I can hardly move."

"Me too," said Dean.

She raised herself painfully onto one elbow and shook her head. "When a combat leader is reduced to making jokes that bad," she said, "a girl knows it's time she has to do something about it!" She leaned over him until her full, firm breasts lay against his hip, and then lowered her open mouth toward his loins.

Before sundown, he climbed up into the old tail-on-the-ground Dakota to talk with his twenty men. Kurt Schneider, from Schleswig-Holstein; Novotny, the naturalized Pole; Wassermann, the Seventh Avenue sharpshooter; and other mercs with whom he had often worked before, were all with Sean Hammer's seaborne force; but these jumpers were mostly ex-regulars recommended by friends, soldiers he hardly knew. "If the beacons lead us, as planned, to the dead areas between strong points and patrols," he told them, "we'll have time to orient ourselves with our maps. After that, we play it by ear until we make the link with Hammer . . . and then it's back to the tactics you rehearsed with him in Greece, okay?"

In Corte, an ancient town spilled over a three-hundred-foot rock spur halfway between Ajaccio and Bastia, an artillery major stalked up and down the parade ground of the Foreign Legion barracks perched on the highest point of the hill. "It is absurd!" he cried angrily. "What are they thinking of! We only just got here; this blasted exercise has been planned for weeks. And now, before the men have even disembarked from the transports, here's a signal instructing us to go back home to the Nebbio to take part in some damfool *infantry* maneuvers on *our* firing range! What do you make of that, Lefèvre?"

His opposite number, who was adjutant to the officer commanding Legion forces quartered in Corte, shrugged sympathetically. "You know Paris," he said. "Typewriter generals. RHIP and all that." He stared out at the heavily wooded mountains surrounding the town. "If I were you, I'd thank my lucky stars I didn't have to run up and down those babies, chasing my guys all night!"

On the far side of the mountains, Martha Margery Henschel sat in the back of a black Cadillac limousine speeding south across the flat coastal plain on the side of the island that faced Italy. She had removed her shoes, put her feet up on the occasional seat behind the chauffeur, and opened a box of chocolates she held in her lap. It was almost dusk. Beyond the bronze and blood-red geometry of harvested vines, sea and sky merged into a violet haze.

"I don't see why Mansour has to send us away just now," she complained to her daughter. "And to Sicily, would you believe it! Mr. Graziano will be sore as hell: there's guys in Sicily don't like him."

Candy was crouched on the far side of the bench seat, with her long, slender legs tucked under her. "He's still paying, isn't he?" she asked.

"Sure he's still paying, but money ain't everything, my chick." Margie Henschel popped a Rose Creme Delight into her wide mouth. "That would have been a good connection, that wine deal, if only I'd been allowed the time to pull it off. But because Mister Middle East suddenly gets other ideas, I have to choke off the grower here just as we're gettin' down to the details. And there's that shipment of leaf'll be standing off in the launch tonight, with nobody to collect. Who's going to pay for *that*, I'd like to know?" She swallowed, and pried a Truffled Maraschino from its frilled paper cup.

"Don't go on so, Momma." Candy yawned and stared disinterestedly out the window at the reflection of the sunset on the eastern haze. "The Sheikh wants us out of the way because he's planning some kind of a delicate operation, is all. Right now, he has everything fixed fine. But if the wrong folks got to know of his business connections with us—well, it wouldn't look so good for him."

"Maybe not. But this will make Mr. Graziano mad as well."

"Look . . ." Candy sighed, a tired parent explaining the obvious to a backward child. "Nessim could buy out Mr. Graziano for ten times what he's worth and not notice the difference in the figures on his bank statement. If he has statements. He probably owns the bank."

Margie was attacking a Montelimar Hardbake. "Because

181

he has so much loot himself, he forgets other folks might want to increase their holdings on the side," she said. "Shit! They talk you into buying the goddamn box, then they fill it with nothing but hard centers!"

Nessim himself was at that moment installed in the white-hide chair behind the desk in his tower control room. Each screen on the bank of monitors behind him was illuminated; every one showed a different sector of the estate. Soon, when it was completely dark, the cameras would switch to infrared and he would swivel the chair and watch nothing but the screens. But for the moment he stared out the great panoramic window and watched the start of the manhunt he had organized.

He was pleased with the idea. A straight execution benefited nobody. What he had arranged, on the other hand, would be good for the students on gun duty: instead of the obligation to aim and miss, as they had to do during the battle-course exercises, they would have a live target to shoot at, with orders to bring it down. The hunt would inject some excitement into the theory course contrasting pursuit with escape methods. The offer of a cash prize should sharpen the appetites and stimulate what Nessim termed the "kill will" of each hunter. And in addition there was of course the matter of his own enjoyment; he had always considered himself a sporting man, an enthusiast for the chase.

There had been no ill-treatment of the prisoner. He had been neither beaten nor tortured nor even interrogated. Nessim had been warned of an attack; now he knew when it was and how it was coming. He wished Dean and his paratroops joy in it, in view of the precautions he had taken with the beacons! If, as he supposed, there was to be a land-based attack at the same time—well, he was ready for it as he had always been. There was no point questioning Mazzari about that. If he lied, it wouldn't stop Nessim's forces being prepared; if he told the truth . . . well, they were prepared anyway. He didn't even feel any hostility toward the man: rather he admired the courage and resourcefulness of an enemy willing to take such perilous risks. The little pulsator taped to the top of the thigh—that had been really ingenious!

Nessim got to his feet and approached the window. Mazzari himself appeared beyond the roofs of the outer ring of houses below, a battle-dress figure, dwarfed by distance, with his hands manacled behind his back. He ran across the rough ground toward the firing range.

Nessim clicked the button of the stopwatch on the console. Beyond the undulations of his land, the modeling of the cliff faces along the length of Cap Corse was no longer visible and the promontory was a dark silhouette against the evening sky. By the time the half hour had elapsed, it was quite dark, and a single star gleamed over the invisible cape. The stopwatch buzzer sounded. Nessim leaned over his desk and pressed the microphone switch. The perimeter guards had been detailed to stay in place but the rest of the students could go anywhere they wanted. It would be good practice for them all, Nessim thought, using infrared equipment and the Trilux night sights on their weapons. "HQ calling all units," he said into the mike. "The hunt may begin."

He swung around the white chair and settled down to watch the bank of monitor screens. Mazzari was visible as a swiftly moving white blur in the sector at the far end of the artificial street. Nessim operated a zoom control, wondering how long he would have to wait for the kill. There were already signs of movement fanning out on the screens, showing images relaying from terrain nearer the village.

There were just two factors that the fanatical head of the terrorist school had failed to take into account: first, Mazzari's phenomenal strength; second, the fact that—whatever the sensors detect—a computer-directed machine-gun battery can only fire in one direction at a time . . .

Raoul Ancarani knew these things (though it was only later that he realized there was a relationship between them), just as he knew that Jason Mettner's rented car was parked on the quayside at St. Florent, and the newspaperman himself was toiling up a rounded hill to the southwest of the port that overlooked the Foreign Legion artillery range.

Ancarani also knew that the furious major in charge of the night exercise on that range, receiving a signal on his return from Corte, warning him to be on the alert for an attempted *coup* by Corsican separatists, had shortly afterward received a second signal, contradicting the first. This latest affront to his sense of military order was in the form of a teleprinted message informing him that the separatists had already infiltrated the property of the rich Arab bordering the range. He was to await the arrival of a small group of specialists who would parachute onto the range at midnight, and then, with their aid, attack the intruders on the estate.

Utterly bewildered—for the first signal had said that the *paratroops* would be the invaders—the major had finally telephoned his GOC in Paris. But it was Friday afternoon, and like the rest of Paris, the general and his staff had left their offices in the ministry early. And of course the *commissaire* had known this very well.

In principle or in detail, he had been informed of all these events concerning Dean, Hammer, Mettner, Nessim, Mazzari, the Henschels, and the Legion throughout the day. Now, outside a hunters' lodge perched on a hill on the far side of the road from the *domaine*, he sat by his radio nursing a pair of night-vision field glasses awaiting events.

18

Marc Dean

Toward the end of the Vietnam war, the American firearms designer, Gordon B. Ingram, perfected the world's smallest, most sophisticated machine pistol. With the wire stock retracted, the weapon was less than nine inches long, weighed only three pounds eight ounces, and fired at the astonishing rate of 1,200 rounds per minute. Manufactured by the Military Armaments Corporation of Marietta, Georgia, it was known as the Ingram MAC-11. At the end of the war, the US government, aware of its potential danger in the hands of terrorists, prohibited its export. But 200 had already been jobbed off to private arms dealers after the makers halted production. Treasury Department investigators recuperated more than half of these, though 70 had been smuggled out of the country in the diplomatic bag by members of the Iraqui UN delegation. Most of these found their way into the hands of Palestinian guerrillas (Abu Daoud used one in the Munich Olympics massacre in 1972), but three wound up as study models at Mansour Nessim's "school." The score that were unaccounted for filtered into the international arms market . . . and Marc Dean contrived to obtain these for the mercs in his miniature paratroop brigade. He had chosen them not only for their accuracy and firepower but because each one was fitted with a super-efficient silencer that weighed no more than 21 ounces—and this, Dean felt, could be vital in the matter of surprise when they landed behind Nessim's lines. And perhaps decisive when it came to the discretion demanded of them!

The Dakota dropped to a thousand feet before De'Ath operated the red light on the shuddering bulkhead separating the troops from the pilot's compartment. He looked at his instruments (which were a great deal more modern than the plane) and yelled over the racket of the motors: "Beacons comin' in strong." Then, peering through the perspex side-window at the paler blur of the Gulf of St. Florent, "Good bit farther east than I'd've thought, but there you are. First stick in about thirty secs, I should say."

Dean leaned through the doorway into the cabin and shouted: "All right, you guys. Stand up; hook up; wait for the light!"

He flung open the port and the wind howled. The men stood in line along the starboard side of the cabin, grim-faced and belligerent in camouflaged battle dress, netted steel helmets, and combat boots. In addition to their MAC-11's, they carried grenades slung to their belts and extra ammunition clips. The three biggest had ropes attached to grappling hooks coiled around their waists. The red light blinked, then changed to green. Dean slapped the first three men on the shoulder and they jumped into the night.

De'Ath was maneuvering the ship skillfully, according to the beamed signals from the ground beacons. " 'Fraid I'll have to make a circuit at least once again," he told Dean when the second three-man stick had dropped. "Chap's placed them a funny way, almost a bally circle. Too close together to do 'em all on the one run, y'know."

There were four men in the third stick and the last, three in each of the others. Dean jumped last of all. Before he hooked up, Duclos, from the navigator's seat, turned around and said: "Good luck, Monsieur Dean. If you succeed—I am sure you will—you will find the balance as arranged in Fribourg, Switzerland. In which case, as I am sure you will understand, you and I will not meet again." Dean nodded. De'Ath looked over his leather-clad shoulder and permitted himself an Americanism: "Take it easy, old boy," he said. Laurence had been dispensing hot coffee and glucose tablets to the jumpers. She squatted now at the rear of the fuselage, her flowerlike face shadowed in the feeble overhead lighting. "We're at Amalfi next week," she said. "Even at this time of the year, they say the bathing is good. I thought of checking in at the Rialto."

"I'll be there," Dean said. He dropped into the dark.

The paratroopers were equipped with miniature versions of

the directional apparatus in the plane; within a few minutes each stick was grouped around its beacon . . . and each man was utterly bewildered to find that the configuration of the bare, rocky terrain around him bore, so far as he could see in the obscurity, no relation whatever to the maps he had so carefully studied. Dean caught on at once that something had gone very wrong. He recalled De'Ath's comment: the beacons were farther east then he had expected. Before he could decide what to do, he must gather his men together . . . and try to find out where the hell they were. They all had directional bleepers: he thumbed the button on his master control and waited for them to arrive.

Within ten minutes they had all appeared out of the dark. What Dean had not expected were the fifty other soldiers who came with them. They were led by a spruce little officer in the uniform of an artillery major. "We have been expecting you," he said, "but to tell you the truth, I'm damned if I know what to do. It's really too confusing."

Mystified, Dean played for time. "Perhaps you would explain?" he suggested. The major was glad to. He told the story of his conflicting orders and quoted the two signals. Then he said: "I assume, sir, as you are not French, that you come from some NATO formation? Perhaps you could tell me the name of your unit?"

"I am afraid that is classified information," Dean said gravely—thinking: Mazzari has been caught. They got Edmond and staked these damned beacons out here as a trap, tipping off these guys that we were invaders, in the hope they'd shoot us down. But somebody else got wise to the plan and faked a contradictory message. So Nessim knows we're coming, but we have a friend in camp too. Who?

"Classified," the major was saying. "I see." He pushed back his *kepi* and scratched his head. "You don't have any confirmatory note?"

"I'm afraid not. Normally, in a series of messages different in detail, the last received takes precedence over, and supercedes, the others," Dean said helpfully, realizing how much easier his task would be if he had these trained and hardened soldiers to help him.

"I don't know," the major said. "It's most irregular. And I could get no confirmation anywhere. Lefèvre, what the devil do we do?"

The pragmatic officer from Corte pushed his way through

the ring of soldiers. He said: "We have orders to operate a night exercise for infantry. Here in this range. I suggest we get on with that—perhaps in the restricted area on the far side of the high road. If we do not see these gentlemen, we—er—we cannot take action on either of the conflicting mesages, can we?"

"Lefèvre, you are a genius!" cried the major. "If you would care to withdraw your men, sir, via the Murenzana estate, there is a track leading that way behind the copse over there. That suit you?"

"It suits me down to the ground—literally and metaphorically," Dean said. He gathered his men around him and led the way across the stony plateau toward the copse.

Although Mazzari had been caught, thanks to Nessim's craving for the theatrical, he was now free again. For a man of his experience it had not been too difficult.

Once out of sight of the village, in among the trees, he lay down and drew his knees up to his chin. Then, passing his manacled hand over his hips, he "stepped through" the loop of his arms and came up with the handcuffs in front of him. His next action was to visit the motor pool beyond the artificial street; there was a toolbox in one of the trucks, and from it he took a chrome vanadium wrench. With this, the serrated surface of a granite boulder, and his own enormous strength, he was able to pry open one of the links of the chain sufficiently to pull free the connecting link. There were still steel circlets around his wrists, but they were no longer chained together.

Only then did he start to move. There were no keys in the motor-pool vehicles, and he had neither the time nor the materials to hot-wire one. But with his strength he could push. He shoved out a jeep and manhandled it along the rising trail that led to the head of the valley. There was an opportunity to coast some after that, but this was followed by a series of short, sharp hills, where the track led over undulations in the wilderness. Mazzari pushed the jeep up each of them as if it had been a lightweight bicycle, one hand on the wheel and the other on the windshield frame, never slowing his striding pace. The last section—over eroded bedrock seamed by the weather—was the most rugged, but beyond it he was in sight of the cliff edge and the sea.

He had noted the locality twice during Ramon's "ground

cover" training; the land slanting toward a gulch hollowed from the granite in past millenia when the Agriates was fertile and a stream cascaded over the cliff into the sea. Because the dried-up valley scooped out the cliff edge to within twenty or thirty feet of the water, Nessim—perhaps fearing that it was a likely place for a seaborne assault—had doubled the defenses around the depression. It was hedged about with sensors and there was a battery of 7.62 mm, computer-directed Russian PKT machine guns on each slope. The six-gun batteries were housed in curved steel shields mounted on revolving turntables that gave them a 180° traverse. The bunker protecting the electronic software linking sensors and guns to the computer complex was sunk in the rock at the head of the valley.

Such an arrangement made it murderously difficult for an individual or an infantry squad advancing up the valley from the sea. But it had not been designed to prevent anyone *leaving* the estate. There was necessarily an area of dead ground behind each battery, to allow free movement to Nessim's own guards; and there was the additional fact that, once the batteries had been engaged by someone or something in the valley, they could not at the same time fire on anyone at the other end of their traverse. Mazzari planned to use both factors.

At the head of the valley, not far behind the bunker, he hauled the jeep to a stop. Panting, he positioned it carefully, aiming it, as well as he could in the near-darkness, at the floor of the gulch. Then, checking that the shift was in neutral and the handbrake released, he shoved the little utility as hard as he was able. It rolled away, gradually gathering speed, bouncing and clattering over the rough surface. There was a shout from the two-man crew in the bunker, a sudden volley of small arms fire . . . and then the jeep was picked up by the sensors and the appalling clamor of a dozen PKT's split the night. Shadows like black ghosts performed a dervish dance as the muzzle flashes splashed flickering light over the jagged rocks of the defile.

Mazzari ran. The next group of cliff-top sensors was 200 yards away. They would pick him up—*but not while he was in the dead ground behind those covering the gulch*: there had to be a safe place for Nessim's men to maneuver and service the batteries. He waited there, listening to the streams of lead thwacking into the jeep as it careened down the gulch, shuddered, bounced from rock to rock, and finally tipped over and burst into flames when the gasoline tank ruptured. As the great fireball boiled into the sky, Mazzari hurled himself across the ten-yard strip between the dead ground and the cliff edge. The distant battery opened fire, but by that time Mazzari was in midair.

He dove forty feet into deep water and nobody saw him go.

By the time Sean Hammer's two DUKW's trundled ashore up the sandy crescent of beach named Saleccia, Mazzari was waiting for them. He had swum three miles around the jagged, 300-foot Punta di Curza, the northernmost point of the desert, and indulged in a solitary bout of gymnastics to dry his lightweight fatigues and restore the circulation after such a long immersion in very cold water.

"Sure it's the happy man I am to see you," Hammer said when Mazzari had explained his presence. "Now at least we'll have a guided bloody tour once we've blasted our way past that fuckin' ridge!"

Getting past the ridge was the trickiest part of the operation—and Dean, after a great deal of discussion, had decided that only one of the amphibians should concern itself with this; the other was to follow the track until it zigzagged down to join the road to St. Florent, near the hamlet of Salone, where Dean had played geologist. From there it was less than a quarter of a mile to the main gates at Murenzana, which a detachment of Dean's men were scheduled to have taken by then.

Knowing from Mazzari that his leader had been decoyed away from the target, Hammer nevertheless decided to go ahead as planned. Failing some sign from Dean, there was nothing much else he could do. The trail climbed obliquely toward the ridge for eight- or nine-hundred yards, and the two DUKW's, each using its full six-wheel drive, were able to make good time in the "invisible" light of their infrared headlamps. But the defenders picked them up as soon as the track turned to run parallel with the ridge. Their arrival was not unexpected; from all along the dark crest machinegun fire twinkled and spat, and the armored hulls of the amphibians rang hollowly with the impact of slugs. "It's all 7.62mm stuff," Mazzari told Hammer. "Russian RP-46's and RPK's. We should be right as rain as long as we keep the hatches closed. Where did you think of making your breakthrough?"

"A wee bit farther on. It seems there's a valley this side of a piece of high ground they call Mount Genova; if we could blast our way through there, but we'd have flat land all the way to your man's village stronghold, or so they're tellin' me."

"It's a good choice." Mazzari held up his hands, with the short lengths of chain dangling from each cuffed wrist. "A chain is as strong as its weakest link, what! These blokes are hit-and-run guerrilla types; they don't have a clue about permanent defense. They haven't tumbled to the fact that once their bally perimeter's broken, all the sensors and computer batteries in the world are just so much junk. They're fine to keep out small bands of chaps like themselves. Top hole. But get something armored and on wheels on the far side, and it's back to the jolly old blitzkrieg: tactically, Nessim's ring of electronic hardware's about as old-fashioned as the Maginot Line! There's one thing, though," Mazzari added. "The Lord High Panjandrum knows the valley's a weak point; the defenses are strengthened there by Soviet DShK 12.7's. Those are anti-aircraft machine guns, and frankly, I doubt whether these hulls could stand up to slugs of that caliber."

Hammer chuckled. "We'll be after givin' them a wee surprise!" In the rear portion of his amphibian there was a so-called recoilless rifle—a large, 106mm, six-barreled device of the kind arming the US "Ontos" tank destroyer. When they arrived at a point angled at some 45° from the valley mouth, the German merc, Kurt Schneider, who was in the driving seat, pulled the DUKW off the track and then backed up behind a rock outcrop so that the stern of the vehicle faced the ridge. Wassermann and Novotny, the two New Yorkers, increased their speed and led the men in the second amphibian on toward the road and the gates.

Hammer, Schneider, and Mazzari, with all of their squad except for the four members of the gun crew, deployed behind the granite ledge and started firing their Armalite rifles and Uzi SMG's up at the positions below the ridge. The fire from above intensified, and soon it was amplified by the deeper reports of the 12.7mm guns. As soon as the brighter flashes had betrayed their approximate positions, Hammer fired a star shell into the air—and almost immediately afterward their ears cracked to the shattering concussion of the weapon in the DUKW as the six barrels belched flame. In the livid green light of the drifting shell, they saw the grenades bursting in groups along the stony hillside as the crew reloaded and fired again and again, pulverizing machine-gun nests and shattering the concrete face of a bunker. "That should put the bloody computer out of action, all right!" Hammer crowed. "C'mon, boys, let's you an' me get on in there while there's still some light showin'!" He waited for a final salvo from the recoilless rifles and then limped out from behind the rocks and took the trail leading up to the valley mouth, firing his Uzi from the hip. There was an M-36 ring mount above the DUKW's cab, carrying a Browning .50 caliber machine gun. Mazzari leaped inside the circle and hosed lead right and left as the amphibian turned around and headed for the pass. The other mercs gave supporting fire, some from the open hatches of the vehicle, some strung out behind, half sheltered by the hull.

But the advance wasn't so easy. The trail—it was more of a sheep run than a track for vehicles—was steep, rough, and narrow. And Nessim, believing Dean safely decoyed away on the far side of the *domaine*, had concentrated almost all of his force where the expected land assault appeared to be aimed. A lucky burst from a grenade, followed by a searing blue flash that momentarily lit up the whole stark countryside, took care of the electrified fence, and the DUKW plowed over the decimated strands of wire, still grinding upward.

By the time they made the saddle, Hammer had lost three men killed, and two wounded, one seriously. But they were through, leaving God knew how many fallen guerrillas behind them . . . and, although these were not aided by sensors or computers, a determined detail of reinforcements armed with RPG-7 rocket grenade launchers still barring the way to the village. As the DUKW drew within the bazookas' 350-yard moving-target range, another star shell, a red one, blossomed in the sky a mile away to the east. Hammer gave a whoop of joy. It was the signal that Dean's paratroops had overcome resistance in Nessim's fortress HQ.

In truth it hadn't been all that difficult. The fence between the estate and the firing range wasn't electrified. Expecting no attack from that quarter, Nessim had installed no batteries and no sensors. There was therefore nothing to impede Dean's progress from the range to the village . . . and since only a skeleton guard had been left once Hammer's assault started, it was possible to bypass the electronic gadgetry at the entrances and throw up the grappling hooks unseen and unheard so that they caught behind chimneys and projections on the roofs, and the party could swarm up into the redoubt.

Once across the tiles, the paratroops dropped into the cobbled street that snaked up to the citadel, fanning out into the several lanes and alleys branching off among the old stone houses on either side. They advanced like mopping-up patrols in World War II, kicking-open doors, smashing windows, one man leaping across the threshold while his companion, flattened against a wall, gave covering fire. There were less than twenty terrorists left in the whole small village. At first the attack had an eerie, bizarre quality, the silent volleys from the mercs' machine pistols punctuated only by the sounds of splintering wood, breaking glass, and the terse commands issued by the combat leader via the walkie-talkies each man wore clipped to his webbing harness. But once Nessim, hysterical with rage in his tower control room, realized from his monitors what had happened, the resistance stiffened.

From his command position halfway up the street, Dean could see the man's figure outlined behind the glass of the panoramic window, arms waving as he shouted into his microphone beneath the bright lights. Dean gathered half a dozen of his men and tried to rush the entrance to the hilltop citadel. But electrically controlled, hydraulically operated steel gates slammed home while they were still yards away, shutting them off from the gardens, the swimming pool, the Cadillacs . . . and the stairway to the tower.

At the same time the four-man guard detail from the main gates, obeying their master's frantic summons for reinforcements, came into the warren of underground passages through the entrance Mazzari had used when first he arrived at Murenzana. In the long run this was a fatal error on Nessim's part. For the time being it swayed the odds marginally in his favor: Dean lost three men when the guards erupted from an area that was supposedly cleared, their SMG's spitting fire. For a moment the assault was sidetracked, the mercs pressing back into doorways or crouched in deep window embrasures to escape the hail of lead. But then, Dean himself, drawing on long forgotten bowling-alley experience, darted into the center of the roadway, rolled a grenade down the hill, and flung himself flat. Foolishly, the guerrillas had stayed bunched together. There was a searing orange flash, a hollow, ringing explosion. For an instant the shapes of the old houses were printed against the night; something wreathed in flame flopped horribly once, twice, and then lay still; and the paras were free to continue their advance.

But the incident revealed to Dean the existence of the underground corridors leading to the computer complexes and ultimately the tower elevator shaft. And it left the way wide open for the second DUKW . . . for the guards, called in such haste from the main gates, had omitted to reactivate sensors monitoring the driveway they themselves habitually patrolled.

Novotny was driving. Beside him, Wassermann sat with his Uzi at the ready. A third merc stood inside the ring mounting, grasping the Browning, and the seventeen remaining men sat tensed in the rear of the machine, awaiting the order to disembark and fight. But there was nobody there. The driveway beyond the gates was empty. Novotny backed up, threw the DUKW into six-wheel drive, and trod on the pedal.

The amphibian surged forward. The armored prow slammed into the massive wrought-iron barrier exactly in the center, and the gates burst open in a shower of sparks. Novotny drove on through. "My father," Wasserman commented, "God rest his soul, he tells me when I am still in high school that it is not the act of a gentleman, gate-crashing. Still, what is life without the occasional uneducated *schmuck* he should flout the social conventions, tell me that?"

"Abe," Novotny said good-humoredly, "you can go stuff yourself."

At that moment the red star shell burst into crimson life. "Instructions in this case," said Novotny, "are that we pass this village, take a left-hand fork, and go do our backup number for Hammer." He swung the wheel and accelerated along a metaled road beyond which light flickered over the treetops, and they could hear the rasp of automatic fire and the explosion of grenades.

They arrived none too soon. Nessim's RPG-7 reinforcements had crippled the first DUKW, smashing the recoilless-rifle complex into a tangle of twisted steel and blowing off the front wheels. Hammer and the remainder of his men were pinned down among a clump of boulders and almost out of ammunition.

The unexpected appearance in their rear of an extra twenty mercs turned the tables on the terrorists. The resulting battle was brief but extremely bloody. Nessim's students refused to surrender, and by the time the last shot was fired, three more mercs lay dead, and there was not a single defender left alive.

Hammer and Mazzari were directing mopping-up operations when Dean arrived in a jeep from the citadel motor pool. After his exploit with the grenade, there had been little action before he was able to fire the red shell. They rode up to the top of the tower in the elevator—but by the time they had broken down the door of the control room, it was empty. The three people staffing it, Ramon, the girl Fawzi, and Nessim himself, had escaped down an ancient stone stairway that spiraled into darkness behind a secret door concealed in the paneling beside the bank of monitor screens.

"We'll take care of them later," Dean said. "Novotny—you take Abc and half a dozen guys in that half-track over there. Make a circuit of the perimeter and flush out any guys still hiding in the pillboxes and bunkers. Use the searchlight. I guess most of them were called in here once Sean made his play, but you never . . ." He paused in mid-sentence, listening.

Over a distant rattle of small arms blanks, where the Foreign Legion units were operating their night exercise, they heard the sudden howl of a jeep motor under load. The engine note climbed the scale and then dwindled toward the northeast. "Nessim, by God!" Mazzari exclaimed. "They must have come out of that secret passage somewhere at the foot of the rock—and then beetled off to the motor pool by our instant, do-it-yourself, city street! Shouldn't we—?"

"Too late," Dean cut in. He had remembered the twin-jet Cessna and the airstrip in that corner of the property. "We wouldn't have a hope in hell. Shit—the damned brass hats get away with it again!" Minutes later they heard the plane lift off and climb away.

It was 0234 hours. By the time they had floodlit the battlefield, collected the dead, attended to the wounded, and placed explosive charges brought in Novotny's DUKW in the control room, the computer complexes, and each bunker around the perimeter, another two hours had passed. Wassermann's sweep with the half-track had produced just five prisoners; the Irishman who had sat next to Mazzari, the pale, thin, Central European instructress, and three Palestinians. "What the *hell* are we going to do with them?" Dean asked nobody in particular.

"Turn the bastards in," one of the mercs suggested.

"Who to, for God's sake? On what charges? They're on private property; officially we were never here; whatever their *intentions*, there's no proof on which any court, in any country, could act."

"Courts!" Mazzari said. "Look, cap, you got it wrong. These blokes can't be treated the way you'd treat ordinary criminals."

"Criminals, is it?" the Irishman burst out. "I mighta known it'd be some fuckin' nigger would turn out to be the Judas! Black bastards from an inferior race, with an inferior level of intelligence. I'd—"

"Shut up!" Dean shouted. "Or I'll smash your teeth in."

"Big mouth," Mazzari said. "Big man. Ring the doorbell, shoot whoever answers it, and then run away. That's your mark, isn't it? You said so yourself. One of the Provisionals, I suppose. You and the Palestinians, you're such big, strong fellows—when there's a gun in your hand and you're faced with unsuspecting, unarmed, ordinary folks. I never heard too much about your courage, though, when it was a question of equal odds. Do you know," he said, turning to Dean, "amongst all the courses they had here, the only one all the students kept missing was a course on unarmed combat! It goes to show, don't you think?"

"Yeah," Dean said. "Okay. But that doesn't solve—"

"Look," Mazzari cut in, "what we're being paid for is to beat this lot, isn't it? All right: I've been a student here; they taught me things. And one of the things they taught me was that it's useless trying to beat them playing the civilized game. Trials are a charade. 'The only way to beat us is to play by *our* rules: shoot us on the spot and the hell with a trial.' You know who told me that? Nessim himself."

"I don't know, Ed . . ." Dean looked dubious.

"I do know, cap. These people are potential murderers; they wouldn't be here if they weren't. They're here learning how to kill. Not how to kill enemies in war. Not how to kill criminals. How to kill and maim innocent people with whom, often enough, they have no connection whatever. Not killing in passion; not killing for revenge—killing simply to make a political gesture. People who deliberately chose to come here and benefit from Nessim's obscene teachings, whose aim in life is a mastery of the filthy crafts he preached—do you really think we have the right to let them loose on the world?"

"What are you suggesting?" Dean asked quietly.

"Nessim quoted me that Biblical saw," Mazzari said. "If thine eye offend thee, pluck it out. He liked the idea. But there's another one, isn't there—about an eye *for* an eye. And don't I remember something about those who live by the sword? What I'm suggesting is that you and these other blokes go and help Novotny wire up his master detonator and leave this to me."

Dean stared at him for a moment and then nodded. "Come on, you guys, there's work still to be done," he said. He turned on his heel and led the other mercs away.

They heard the shots while Novotny, the explosives expert, was explaining how he had used the complexities of Nessim's own electronics system to ensure the simultaneous destruction not only of its exits, entrances, outposts, and control room, but also of the very computers from which the system derived.

"There's auto-destruct for you!" Dean said. But as the night erupted in thunder, and all around Nessim's ill-starred domain manmade volcanoes vomited flame into the sky, he could hear, almost like an echo of Mazzari's words, the voice in his memory of Samantha: *Ordinary, decent people don't make a living out of killing other people . . . I don't want to be within a mile of your beastly, filthy, murderous trade.* Where was the difference? Despite Mazzari's impassioned eloquence, were they not simply two sides of the same coin? I'll be judge, I'll be jury, said something old fury. Did men like him, like Hammer and Mazzari, really have the right. . . . He put the thought from him. Because there was a difference; there had to be. It was the difference between principle, right or wrong, and no principle at all. The difference between order, however incomplete, and anarchy. Men like him were paid to kill for a reason—again, right or wrong. But against reasonless violence there was, alas, only one answer; violence again. If he didn't believe that, he wouldn't be here.

A tall man in a roll-neck sweater was waiting for him at the gates. It was not long before dawn. The man had a lean face with a hairline mustache. "Certain . . . remains . . . here will be attended to," he said. "It would however be extremely awkward if you were still to be on French soil in daylight. My car will convey you and Monsieur Hammer to Calvi at once. A launch is waiting at the quayside."

Dean nodded. Mazzari, Wassermann, Novotny, and the remaining mercs, together with their wounded, had been crammed into the surviving amphibian, which was already on its way back to Saleccia and the ferry cruising just outside territorial waters. "If you see that news hawk, Mettner," he said, "tell him it was two other guys."

Epilogue ═══════════

"I don't know that I understand," Jason Mettner said to Raoul Ancarani.

The policeman was straightening up from the trunk of his Peugeot, buttoning his uniform jacket. "The point, Monsieur," he began, "is that there is nothing *to* understand. Nothing at all."

"Don't give me that!" Mettner protested."I watched the goddamn battle from a hilltop, and it seemed to me—"

"Battle? Monsieur is referring perhaps to the night exercise carried out by the *Légion Etrangère?*"

"You know what I'm referring to. They went down into Murenzana, and all hell was let loose. I want to get an eyewitness—"

"It is regrettable but that is impossible. The property is private. You would not be permitted to enter."

"But, Jesus, there were explosions! They mined—"

"Certain electrical failures, I understand. Due to the wind."

"Dean promised me an exclusive!" Mettner shouted. "Or rather it was Hammer. . . . I've been sitting on the bastard story for weeks!"

"Ah, the foreign gentlemen!" Ancarani said. "Alas, they had to leave rather unexpectedly. From Calvi at dawn. If you were hoping to see them . . . it was not entirely their fault."

"Alright," said Mettner heavily, taking a notebook and pencil from his pocket, "as a pressman I have a right to ask you, for the record, what can you tell me about last night? Officially?"

"I, Monsieur? But nothing. How could I? I was off duty."

The American fumbled a cigarette from a crumpled pack. His fingers shook. "Where is this oil sheikh, Nessim?" he demanded.

"I am unable to say," Ancarani replied truthfully.

Mettner breathed hard. He seemed to be having some difficulty striking a match. The policeman flicked a lighter, held the flame toward him. "And the spiked wine and dope ladies from Albuquerque?"

"Albuquerque, New Mexico?"

Mettner compressed his lips and refused the bait. Ancarani continued: "Mme. Henschel and her daughter left Bonifacio for Sardinia and Sicily last night. It is not thought that they will be returning to Corsica."

Drawing hard on his cigarette, Mettner sent the smoke jetting into the clear morning air. "I think," he said sarcastically, "that I detect the first faint signs of a stall. C'mon, flatfoot, what about my story? What about all that stuff you gave me? The wine, women, and dope routine tied in with Nessim? How about that?"

"If he is no longer here, it can hardly be relevant."

"And those homely tips about discretion—and scorpions?"

"You will find no scorpions here at this time of the year." Ancarani opened the door of the Peugeot and slid behind the wheel. "Discretion, of course, is always an asset," he said politely. "As to a story—they tell me there is a colorful old-time air circus performing across the water in Italy. It is directed by an English *milord*. I am sure he would grant you an interview and offer photo facilities."

An hour later, in the hotel at St. Florent, Mettner savagely rolled a sheet of paper into his portable and began to tap out:

An audacious attempt to fool the American wine-buying public, and undercut both French and Californian growers, was foiled this week in Corsica when police and custom officials ordered two mysterious women off the island. Consignments of faked Champagne, it was believed, lay behind the plot . . .

200

LOOKING FORWARD

The following is the opening section
from the next novel in the exciting new
Marc Dean MERCENARY series from Signet:

READY, AIM, DIE

Communist planes had bombed the hill village that morning, but in the afternoon low clouds blew up from the west and rolled over the rim of the escarpment, so the Cuban and Libyan pilots on that part of the front were grounded. The planes were old—subsonic Mystère II jets that had been resold several times since the French first passed them off on some unsuspecting Central African republic in the late 1950's. But even if they had been flying, they would have found it hard to locate a worthwhile target, for most of the drystone buildings had collapsed. The narrow streets were choked with rubble, dust lay thickly over the neglected paddies, and the parched brown landscape beyond was deserted.

There was more dust above the winding dirt road that led down to the village from the pass—an irregular yellow haze moving slowly around the curves and then out across the plateau toward the abandoned terraces and the bomb craters. At the head of the dust column was a small Citroën Mehari utility. It bounced and lurched along the rutted tracks, slid around a final bend in a shower of loose shale, and stopped with a squeal of brakes at the edge of a dried-up riverbed. A single wooden span had carried the roadway over the gulch, but the splintered planks now lay scattered among the pebbles that hid the meager trickle of water moistening the rocks below. The shallow door of the Citroën opened. A tall, thin man uncoiled himself from the driver's seat and got out. Although the heat had now become humid and close, he wore a Western-style suit, complete with jacket and vest. He stared at the wrecked bridge for a moment and shook his head. "Jesus Christ!" he said aloud. "That's all I need!"

He turned and walked along the bare earth of the riverbank, looking for a gap where he might be able to drive across. Behind him, the motor of the Citroën, which had been running unevenly, spluttered and stopped. The thin man cursed. He had seen a place lower down where the bank was less steep and a determined driver might possibly force a passage. He hurried back to the stalled vehicle.

The corrugated bodywork beneath the tattered canvas top had once been bright orange, but now the paint was dulled, the fenders were scratched and dented, and behind the cracked glass of the headlamps the reflectors were rusted and peeling. The license plates were unreadable beneath a veneer of mud, but the rear panel bore a rectangle of faded blue on which white lettering spelled out the words "P. Ramirez, Plomberie-Zinguerie, Vientiane."

The thin man's name wasn't Ramirez, he was not by profession a plumber, and he had not come from a border town between Laos and Thailand. He was in fact American, and he had bought the Citroën for two hundred dollars, cash, from a Cambodian refugee in Luang Prabang five days previously. He was still unsure which party to the deal had cheated the other.

He lifted the canvas-and-mica dust flap above the door and eased himself into the threadbare driver's seat again. The back of his jacket was dark with sweat where he had leaned against the scruffy tergal covering. Pumping the accelerator pedal with his foot, he activated the starter. The engine wheezed, moving slowly, like a man with laryngitis clearing his throat. At the third attempt, it coughed and finally stuttered to life. He drove to the place where he figured the riverbed could be crossed, gunned the motor, banged the gearshift into second, and sent the Citroën careering down the stony bank.

They were halfway across when the front wheels hit a

patch of soft gravel. The car stopped bouncing and slewed sideways. The bald tires slipped, spun; the wheels churned up the gravel and then sank to the axle. The overheated engine stalled once more.

The American opened the door, swung his long body out, and crunched wearily around to the front of the hood. Maybe if he could locate a couple of planks and slide them beneath the wheels . . . ? But the car had sunk in so deeply that the drive shafts were resting on the stones. He swore again and shook his head—a lean-faced man with a prominent nose and lines of fatigue etched around his gray eyes. Finally he shrugged and scrambled over the trickle of muddy water to climb the far bank. There was no point wasting any more time down here; it would take a tractor or a team of oxen to drag the Citroën back onto hard ground. "I just hope," he muttered furiously, "that there's still some son of a bitch in this godforsaken hole who's willing to be bribed or blackmailed into action!"

It was only a hundred yards to the first broken houses. Between the shattered walls, the air was acrid with plaster dust, sour with the stench of death. The American took a cigarette from a crumpled pack and felt in his pockets for matches. He struck one and shielded the flame with cupped hands, gazing at the ruin of the village square as he sucked in smoke. Blast had ripped away the front of a two-story house, allowing the sagging joists to shower chairs, picture frames, smashed china, and a striped mattress into the street. Farther on, a cloud of flies buzzed over the entrails of a dog half-buried in a slant of rubble. Nothing else moved among the charred beams and fractured stonework: even the scrawny fowls that seemed to have the highest survival count in the East had vanished.

Inhaling deeply, the thin man shook out the match flame and strode on. But he saw nothing and heard nobody. Away to the north, local militia were said to be making a stand against Khmer Rouge troops advancing along a tributary of the Pa Sak River. Whether or not it was successful, the peasants in this part of the range were evidently taking no chances: the survivors of the bombardment had fled, and the only ox to be seen lay dead by an overturned cart outside a roofless Christian church.

Why should they have bombed the hell out of this isolated village anyway? the American wondered. Was some fugitive Laotian anticommunist leader supposed to be hiding there? Had they been tipped off to an illusory arms cache? Was it expected to be a stronghold of capitalist imperialism because there had been a missionary settlement there before independence and the houses were built of stone? There was no way of knowing. The nearest fighting, other than isolated patrol action, was twenty miles away. Most likely the raid was simply a mistake: the fliers had picked the wrong valley and unloaded their lethal cargo on the innocent. Local wars in southeast Asia were like that.

He pitched away the stub of his cigarette and lit another. Through a gap in the scorched and bomb-scarred wall of the church he could see the dull gleam of gold behind the altar. There were bodies in there, like bundles of old clothes among the splintered chairs. Huge splashes of red stained the whitewashed stone.

The American rounded the corner of the building and halted in mid-stride. The narrow mud-packed lane beyond was blocked by a battered Citroën Mehari utility with its hood propped open. Another body was draped over the front fender, the head and shoulders apparently resting on the motor. Apart from the fact that it had once been painted beige, the car could have been the twin of his own. "I'll be damned!" the thin man exclaimed.

A sudden spasm shook the body. It heaved backward, then straightened up and turned around to reveal itself as a very large black man of about forty, dressed in khaki shorts and an oil-smeared bush jacket. "English, by God!" he said. "Spoken with a curious accent, but the genuine native tongue nevertheless! You wouldn't happen to have a spare Citroën carburetor about you, I suppose?"

The thin man gave a snort of laughter. "Funny you should say that," he drawled. "Right now, there are precious few things I could lay my hands on . . . but as it happens, a Citroën carburetor is one of them!"

"You wouldn't be pulling my leg, would you? You wouldn't have a fellow on?" The black man's own accent was unmistakably English, of the kind little heard since the halcyon days of flanneled fools before World War II.

He was extremely tall, demonstrably muscular, and deep-voiced with a smile that revealed a flash of white teeth.

"Certainly not," the American replied. "I'm driving a buggy like this, but the bitch is bogged down in the river-bed. Immobilized. About the only thing that still works is the goddamn carburetor." He shrugged. "Seems reason-able to make one serviceable automobile out of two wrecks. Take the bastard, if you can raise the tools to get it off—on condition that you take me too, wherever you're headed."

"Done!" the black man said. "We'll shake on that, eh?" He held out a huge hand.

The American took it. "The name's Mettner," he said. "Jason Mettner of *Worldwide,* presently on Southeast Asian assignment as a war correspondent."

"A newspaperman! I might have known it! My name's Edmond Mazzari."

"Glad to know you, Ed. What are you doing in this neck of the woods? Writing up the parade too? Or are you prospecting for oil?"

"Er . . . not exactly, old lad. Matter of fact, I'm on sort of a police-job."

"A *cop?*" Mettner laughed again. "What the hell did they send you out *here* for, in heaven's name? To direct the traffic?"

Mazzari looked vague. "Not exactly," he repeated. "More of a guard duty, really. Protect Red Riding Hood against the wolf."

"*Red* Riding Hood? You don't mean . . . ? Not the Khmer—?"

"No, no. Absolutely not. Boot on the other foot, actual-ly. Figure of speech, old boy. No more than that. . . . Look, do you think we could go ahead with this carburetor show? Every single jet in this perisher is choked. You can't go a yard in this bally country at this time of year without the dust getting into everything."

"Sure. Bring the tools and I'll show you where my little darling died on me." Mettner turned to retrace his steps.

The express-train screech had hardly registered before he was blinded by an orange flash. The ground beneath their feet shook to a thunderous detonation, and a cloud of brown smoke billowed into the air on the far side of the church. Tiles and fragments of stone clattered to earth all around them.

"Jesus!" Mettner said. "That was—"

"ZIS-3 76mm cannon. Must have the glasses trained on us somewhere along the jolly old ridge." Mazzari gestured toward the distant rock crest just visible over the rooftops. "Probably think they're breaking up a secret rendezvous."

"Yeah, but why should they—?"

"Dust again, old boy. Followed you across the plain, if you came in from the east. They must have waited to see what you were going to do." The big man sniffed. "Vietcong or Malay gunners! They'd've scored a direct hit three minutes ago if it'd been a crew supplied by the johnnies who sold them the gun."

"The Soviets? You seem to know a lot about artillery for a cop."

"Professional experience, chum. Know the sound of the old 76mm. It's war-surplus stuff, designed as an antitank weapon, sold off cheap to the third-world small-timers. Very distinctive bang." Mazzari flung himself facedown on the packed earth as the whistle of another approaching shell seared the air.

Farther down the narrow street, the wall of a house leaned outward, separated into individual blocks of stone, and then crashed to the ground. The roof caved in and disappeared behind a pillar of dust. Mettner was on his hands and knees behind the Citroën. "That was too darned close for comfort, Ed," he said when the echoes of the explosion had died away. "You figure maybe those Malay gunners got spelled by their Russian friends?"

Mazzari was coughing. "Bloody dust!" he choked. "For three flaming days—" They lay flat as a third shellburst smashed a crater in the square beyond the church.

"As the song says," Mettner gasped, "let's you and I go down by the riverside. If we can wrench off that carb—"

"Don't be a bloody fool. Fatal. They'd see us and knock out the crate as soon as we got to her. There's a cellar under what's left of the old mission. I vote we nip in there and lie low until the panic's over. They don't have all that many rounds to waste, you know. If we vanished, they might think they'd got us . . . and it'll be dusk pretty soon; then we can get on with the job, and do it safely."

"Okay," Mettner agreed. "Just so long as we're not left with a carburetor but no car."

"That's a risk we'll have to take." Mazzari glanced at the Citroën. "But if they see us scooting across the square, it should draw their fire away from this corner anyway."

The newspaperman nodded and scrambled to his feet. "Let's go," he said.

Bombs dropped by the communist planes had blown out all the doors and windows of the old mission and set fire to the thatched huts surrounding it. But the main brick-and-stucco structure was still standing amid the charred timbers. There was a basement at one side with a flight of stone steps worn smooth by the passage of countless feet leading down to the cellar entrance. Before they descended, Mettner turned and looked over the savaged rooftops at the ridge. Even at this distance the twinkle of flame as the gun fired was visible against the dun cloud background. The shell burst harmlessly on a piece of waste ground. "Good-oh," Mazzari said approvingly. "That was a couple of hundred yards from the car. They must have spotted us as we took off."

The cellar was cool and damp, but even here the air was thick with dust. "I'd hoped the good brothers might have used it as a wine cellar," Mettner said with regret, "but I see we scored zero there. Boy, what I'd do for a drink!"

"My dear chap!" Mazzari produced a flat fifth of Japanese saki from the pocket of his bush shirt. "Most remiss of me. 'Fraid it may be a bit above room temperature, but you're supposed to drink the stuff warm. Do help yourself."

Mettner unscrewed the cap and swallowed a mouthful of the tepid liquor. "Hey! Not *bad*!" he said when the smooth fiery spirit had washed the dryness from his throat and spread through his veins. "Not quite as thirst-quenching as a mint julep or a stein of cold beer—but not bad!" He wiped the palm of his hand across the neck of the flask and handed it back to Mazzari. "How much longer do we have to wait for the monsoon to lay this fucking dust?" The dark, vaulted walls of the cellar trembled.

"Hundred and fifty yards, I should say," Mazzari observed. He drank. "Yes, it's good stuff, all right. I'd prefer a drop of Scotch or a Cognac, but at least it's better than that rice . . ." He paused. The next explosion had been considerably nearer. A small stream of plaster pattered down from the roof of the cellar. "Bracketing us," he said. "That one was on the other side. They're not very big shells. Ordinary HE, something like a British six-pounder, perhaps. Unpleasant enough, though, if one happens to be caught in the blast area with one's pants down."

Mettner produced some wisecrack in reply. He knew that it had pleased him at the time, but he could never remember what it was. In the same way, the only thing that he recalled of the direct hit on the mission was the brightness of the flash. It seemed to him later on, when he tried to fix the exact sequence of events in his mind, that this flash had started at maximum brilliance . . . and then slowly brightened even further, brightened until its intensity was intolerable and he passed out from the pain behind his eyes. That of course might have been an illusion produced by the concussion. What was certain was that he regained consciousness in total darkness: the slits up near the vaulting that had allowed a dim light to filter down when they came in were now blocked with rubble. Something heavy lay across his chest. His mouth and nose were full of dust again. "Mazzari?" he called faintly. "Ed? Where's that fucking *saki*?"

"Still in the flask, old lad," a voice replied from somewhere in the blackness. "Bottle's intact, thank God, but I seem . . . that is to say . . . some bugger threw me under a train or something!" A match scraped. In the circle of light cast by the wavering flame, Mettner saw slivers of wood emerging from a slope of pulverized masonry, a buckled steel filing cabinet sitting incongruously at one side of the rubble, a single star gleaming in a triangle of night sky exposed by the fallen ceiling. Mazzari was struggling to sit up. The slabs of plaster pinning him down slid to the floor. He coughed, holding the match high as he searched for his companion.

Mettner had been hurled by the explosion halfway into

a niche between two of the vaulted arches. He was lying on his back among the debris. There were no bones broken but one end of a huge timber supporting the floor above had dropped, falling across his hips and immobilizing him as effectively as a butterfly in a display case. "A fine thing," he said as Mazzari staggered across. "He knocks down half a building to avoid a short walk and a little work with a screwdriver!"

"Come out of that corner fighting, old bean, and I'll teach you about screwdrivers!" Mazzari grinned. "It wasn't me took a two-hour sleep to shake off the effects of an economy-size Indonesian shellburst." The match burned his fingers and he dropped it with a curse.

Mettner grunted and struck one of his own matches. Plaster dust still swirled in the wrecked cellar where Mazzari had walked. Somewhere overhead, a cool breeze moaned among the ruins. "Why the hell should the Khmer attack a tiny undefended village like this?" the American complained as Mazzari maneuvered himself under the beam before the match flame died. "I guess it *was* the Reds firing at us, huh? And their buddies who bombed the place this morning?"

"Absolutely." Mazzari was shifting his position in the dust. "The loyalist forces don't have any big-caliber anti-tank guns in this sector—not even outdated ZIS-3's. Most of the detachments are lucky to come up with a couple of Jap bazookas and half a dozen old Armalites stolen from stores when your lads were in Vietnam. As to the village, they say it was the birthplace of Ngon Thek."

"The ex-guerrilla chief? The guy was made Minister of Home Security when the King came to power? But he's in Bangkok, trying to drum up support from the Thais."

"They say that too. But intelligence reports in a civil war are more rumor than fact. You're a newshawk; you should know that."

"I guess they figured they might as well rub out the village anyway. That way they have a fifty-fifty chance of getting the guy. Unless they did it as a hate gesture, what the Nazis used to call a show of frightfulness." Mettner struck another match. Mazzari had managed to wedge one shoulder beneath a section of the slanting beam. He was immensely strong, but Mettner dared not think how

much the beam weighed—fortunately he was not bearing
its full weight himself—or how much rubble it was holding
up. For a few moments there was no sound in the dark
cellar but the straining of his breath. Then plaster and
small pieces of debris showered to the floor as the massive timber moved slightly. Once more Mettner struck a
match.

Through the coating of dust, the bunched muscles on
Mazzari's bare calves gleamed like oiled teak. The veins
on his neck were corded and the muscles of his great
shoulders rippled against the bush shirt as it darkened
with sweat. He inched toward the lower end of the beam
and heaved afresh, thrusting up with one shoulder as he
flexed his knees. The remainder of the rubble slid from
the beam.

"Swell! . . . That's great, man. . . . Couple more inches,
and I . . ." Mettner gasped, scraping his body along the
ground, dragging it through between timber and floor.
"And I'll make it . . . out from under . . . this goddamn
tree!" Shoes clattered on the flagstones and he finally
pulled himself free. "Thanks, Ed. Obliged . . ." he panted.
And then groaned in the blackness as the blood began
coursing back into his constricted lower limbs.

This time Mazzari struck the match. White dust covered
the American from head to foot, and his pants and jacket
were ripped at the knee and hip, but apart from severe
bruising around his middle and a crimson gash in the
brow of his clown's face, he was unhurt.

As soon as the circulation in his legs was restored,
they finished the contents of the flask. Mazzari then
helped him across the heaps of fallen masonry and began
to look for the doorway. The shell had burst somewhere
in the center of the building, destroying the upper story
and collapsing part of the ground floor into the cellar. But
the outer walls were still standing, and it was simple
enough to clear away enough of the rubble to permit them
to crawl through to the area and the undamaged stairway
leading to freedom.

The wind had blown away the clouds. Above the blasted roofs and smoldering rafters of the village, stars shone
brightly in a clear sky. They picked their way over the
wreckage and went back to the church. Mazzari's Citroën

was just as he left it. "Thank Christ!" Mettner said. "They can't see us now. Let's tread on the gas and make it down to my jalopy as quick as whenever. Once those carbs are switched, I want out of here, but fast! You don't happen to have a flashlight in there, do you?"

Mazzari laughed. "Funny you should say that," he mimicked. "Right now there are precious few things I could lay my hands on . . . but, yes, as it happens, a flashlight *is* one of them." He reached into the rear of the utility and produced a small, flat torch.

"Great," Mettner said. "Bring the tools and we're on our way."

It was an eerie task, dismantling the carburetor of the American's car in the dark, with only the thin beam of light escaping between the fingers of his hand to guide them. It was unlikely that the communist gunners on the ridge would be keeping watch at night; they might even have withdrawn altogether, finding no resistance in the village while Mettner and Mazzari were buried beneath the mission. But there was always the risk that an unguarded light could bring an artillery barrage down on them, and they thought it more prudent to mask the beam —just in case a lookout was posted on the heights.

The nuts and bolts fixing the mechanism to the inlet manifold were reluctant to move. Screwdrivers and wrenches slipped and skidded in the obscurity, and soon both men were nursing bleeding knuckles. Apart from the chink of metal on metal and the smothered curses of one man or the other, there was no sound but the rustle of wind in dried grasses and a faint chuckle of water beneath the stones forming the riverbed. Mettner finally succeeded in disconnecting the fuel feed from the float chamber. Liquid splashed to the ground, and the thin, aromatic stink of gasoline swamped the odors of defeat and corruption carried on the breeze. Soon afterward, the first of the bolts locating the backplate loosened. "Thank Christ!" Mettner said for the second time. "Five more minutes and the bastard should be off. All we have to do then is sneak back to the village and play the whole scene over."

In the narrow lane behind the church, they permitted themselves a wider beam of light. Mazzari, furthermore, had already started work on his carburetor before. Even so, it was another half-hour before they were successfully interchanged. "There you go," Mettner said, tightening the final joint in the fuel line. "I was on my way to do an eyewitnesser on the fighting in Pa Sak province. If it's not being indiscreet, what the hell kind of work brings a *policeman*—an African policeman—to this village?"

Mazzari was in the driver's seat fiddling with the controls. "Not actually a member of the constabulary," he said absently. "What I meant to convey—doing a job of poli*cing*. I say, would you mind awfully giving us a shove? there's a slope at the end of the street, and the battery's pretty wonky. I'd rather not risk exhausting it, and it'll be a while before she sucks up enough juice to fill the float chamber of the new carb. Quite apart from the noise that starter makes."

"You're not after Naon Thek?"

"God, no. Absolutely not. Nothing to do with the chap. Nothing to do with this blasted village, if it comes to that. The car just happened to die on me here. No, I told you: kind of a bodyguard job."

"Okay. A bodyguard. Whose body? Here in Muong-Thang?"

"The fellow that signs the check. Look, I really think we should push on. I'd like to be quite a few miles away by the time the sun rises. Mind your knuckles on the tailgate handle."

Mettner grinned. "I guess I know when a guy's stalling me. If it's all that secret, why not just say 'No comment'?" He moved around to the back of the Citroën. Leaned down to place his hands on the rear panel, and then suddenly straightened up. "Just a minute," he said. "Mazzari? Bodyguard? Writing out the check: paying for your 'police' work? *Mazzari!* I knew I'd heard that name before. We didn't meet, but surely you were on that terrorist job in Corsica last autumn? You're a mercenary: you work for that guy Dean. Marc Dean. Isn't that right?"

"Hole in one, old boy," the voice from the front of the car said cheerfully. "Bravo! Not to say work *for*. We're all free lances, but I've worked with the Colonel a number of times, yes."

"And you're working together here, now?"

"I'm afraid that's classified information," Mazzari said. "If you wouldn't mind giving her a bit of a heave . . ."

The car was light and the roadway relatively smooth. Even so, Mettner was drenched in sweat by the time he had pushed it the seventy or eighty yards to the top of the grade. The noise, when Mazzari let in the clutch and the motor caught, was ear-shattering after the silence of the deserted village. Since their return from the riverbed they had heard nothing but the distant hoot of a night bird and an occasional stealthy rustle as wreckage settled or rats moved among the dead.

"The headlamps are blinkered," Mazzari said. "Government orders in time of war an' all that. Should we take a chance and use 'em? Or would you rather play safe and do without? I think I could kind of feel my way by starlight—if you walked ahead with the torch."

"Take a chance," Mettner said. "I've had just about enough of this dump." He tossed the canvas hold-all he had salvaged from his own car into the back and climbed in beside the big man. Mazzari shoved the lever into first, switched on the lights, and sent the Citroën grinding down the incline.

Mettner swung around in his seat and stared anxiously out the clouded perspex panel in back of the canvas top. But no gun flashes brightened the hard line of the escarpment bulked against the starry sky; no orange shellbursts charted their progress across the darkened countryside.

The road was rutted and at times rocky, the spread of light cast by the hooded lamps limited. For a long time they could average no more than fifteen miles per hour. But at last they spiraled down a scrub-covered hillside and passed through another village. This one was more typical of Indochina: mud walls and thatched roofs around a central market. It was undamaged, but the place looked as deserted as the first. Beyond it, nevertheless, the terrain altered dramatically. Now the track wound between steep wooded hills corrugated by closely packed terraces where every available square foot of earth was cultivated. They had left the plateau and were driving down into the monsoon forest.

" 'Muong-Thang: a small buffer state between Thailand and the Khmer Republic, only recently granted autonomy,'" Mettner quoted scornfully. "'The capital, Am-Phallang, population 65,000, is the only industrial center in what is largely an agricultural region,' it says in the *Worldwide* morgue." He sighed theatrically. "And do you supose I'd be heading for that capital even for one night if it wasn't for . . . We *are* heading that way, aren't we?"

"If the route isn't cut," Mazzari said. "Since, like every other Southeast Asian country, they have Red trouble, one never knows." He negotiated a sharp curve and shifted into fourth gear for the first time in five miles. "If you're headed for Am-Phallang," he said casually, "how come you're up in this part of the country? Wouldn't it have been simpler just to fly there?"

"I was already in northern Laos," Mettner said. "Color-supplement special. Now that the war clouds have withdrawn, how do these simple, lovable people rebuild their age-old traditional life in the shadow of the Electronic Age? Then the simple, lovable people of Muong-Thang, aided by certain left-wing neighbors, decided they wanted to chuck out their king. Rebellion and civil war." He shook his head. "Folks will do anything to get on television."

"So you decided to drive down and see what's cooking?"

"That's about the size of it. Come to that, if you're headed for Am-Phallang yourself, why didn't *you* fly there?"

"Airport people too heavily into security checks. It's important that I stay . . . er . . . incognito. Doing another color piece, are you?"

"Tell you the truth," said Mettner, "we got a tipoff that there's likely to be an assassination attempt, heavily financed from outside, on his royal majesty. Send Mettner, the man on the spot."

Mazari laughed his deep, rumbling laugh. "Tell you the truth," he echoed, "on condition you promise not to use it—I'm here to squash that attempt!"

Less than a minute later—the road was arrowing through flat paddy fields that stretched away to a line of distant hills in the east—a battery of 88mm antitank guns opened fire on them.

JOIN THE MARC <u>DEAN, MERCENARY</u> READER'S PANEL AND PREVIEW NEW BOOKS

If you're a reader of <u>MARC DEAN, MERCENARY</u>, New American Library wants to bring you more of the type of books you enjoy. For this reason we're asking you to join <u>MARC DEAN, MERCENARY</u> Reader's Panel, to preview new books, so we can learn more about your reading tastes.

Please fill out and mail today. Your comments are appreciated.

1. The title of the last paperback book I bought was: _____

2. How many paperback books have you bought for yourself in the last six months?
☐ 1 to 3 ☐ 4 to 6 ☐ 10 to 20 ☐ 21 or more

3. What other paperback fiction have you read in the past six months? Please list titles: _____
_____
_____
_____

4. I usually buy my books at: (Check One or more)
☐ Book Store ☐ Newsstand ☐ Discount Store
☐ Supermarket ☐ Drug Store ☐ Department Store
☐ Other (Please specify) _____

5. I listen to radio regularly: (Check One) ☐ Yes ☐ No
My favorite station is: _____
I usually listen to radio (Circle One or more) On way to work /
During the day / Coming home from work / In the evening

6. I read magazines regularly: (Check One) ☐ Yes ☐ No
My favorite magazine is: _____

7. I read a newspaper regularly: (Check One) ☐ Yes ☐ No
My favorite newspaper is: _____
My favorite section of the newspaper is: _____

For our records, we need this information from all our Reader's Panel Members.
NAME: _____
ADDRESS: _____ ZIP _____
TELEPHONE: Area Code ( ) Number _____

8. (Check One) ☐ Male ☐ Female

9. Age (Check One) ☐ 17 and under ☐ 18 to 34
☐ 35 to 49 ☐ 50 to 64 ☐ 65 and over

10. Education (Check One)
☐ Now in high school ☐ Graduated high school
☐ Now in college ☐ Completed some college
☐ Graduated college

As our special thanks to all members of our Reader's Panel, we'll send a free gift of special interest to readers of <u>MARC DEAN, MERCENARY</u>.

Thank you. Please mail this in today.

NEW AMERICAN LIBRARY
PROMOTION DEPARTMENT
1633 BROADWAY
NEW YORK, NY 10019